THE DRUNKEN COMIC BOOK MONKEYS IN:

Sciencey Tales of

SCIENCE FICTION

I0525348

WRITTEN BY

BRIAN KOSCIENSKI
&
CHRIS PISANO

EDITED BY

JEFF YOUNG

ILLUSTRATED BY

KOA BEAM

WWW.FORTRESSPUBLISHINGINC.COM

The Drunken Comic Book Monkeys in: Sciencey Tales of Science Fiction
© 2011 Fortress Publishing, Inc.
ISBN: 978-0-578-08758-0

Front and back cover photography by Christine Czachur and Jeff Young
Front and back cover design by Brian Koscienski
Cover models:
     Brian Koscienski
     Chris Pisano
     Jeff Young
     Toy Robot
     The Invisible Man
     A Plastic Monkey
     A Moon-Shaped Mask

This book is available for wholesale through the publisher, Fortress Publishing, Inc.

Fortress Publishing, Inc.
1200 Market Street
Unit 17 / Box 137
Lemoyne, PA 17043

WWW.FORTRESSPUBLISHINGINC.COM

CONTENTS

CONTENTS (CONTINUED)

An Accomplice to the Wrongness

Foreword
By
Maria V. Snyder

I was asked to write a foreword for the Drunken Comic Book Monkeys' new collection of fictional adventures. Why me you ask? Good question. Do I have a good answer? Not really. Since the laws of physics or common decency don't apply within these pages, let's go back a few years in time.

May of 2007 – I was invited by a very nice gentleman named Jeff Young to be a guest speaker for the "Watch the Skies" book club. It was a wonderful event and afterwards Jeff and I talked about the state of the publishing industry, including how difficult it was to get published. He mentioned two friends (who hadn't come to the meeting by the way) who had started their own publishing company because of their frustrations with the big publishers. That night, I returned home blissfully unaware that little exchange would eventually lead to you reading this foreword.

About a week later, I'm attending Balticon 41 and I run into Jeff. Delighted to see him again, I make plans to meet him later in the bar for a civilized drink and some intelligent conversation. There he introduced me to his friends, Brian and Chris. Now do you see where this is going? Thought so.

Well the civilized drinking and intelligent conversation never happened, but I must admit, there was something ... dare I say it? ... fascinating about these two guys. It could have been the I-lost-count-after-three glasses of Merlot, but as they described their adventures renting a room from an Amish family, I laughed until tears flowed. Whether or not the stories were true is still up for debate, but one thing I learned was these self-described Drunken Comic Book Monkeys could spin an entertaining tale.

And like a rash that just wouldn't clear up, I encountered Brian and Chris at various conventions over the next few years as they hawked their books and magazines by day and hung out at the bars at night. At Capclave in October 2008, I saw them briefly before they dashed off to the Hooters nearby. The next day as they whined about not selling any books, I offered a bit of advice (silly me). I suggested that instead of hanging out in Hooters, that they stay at the convention, socialize and talk to the participants. You know, network, tell them about your books, be friendly. Amazed, they declared me their mentor right there. Sigh.

I could have stopped the madness, obtained a restraining order, changed my name, or hired a bodyguard named Nick. But no, I chose to be an accomplice to the wrongness and here I am writing this foreword.

It's a perfect description — accomplice to the wrongness — but I can't take any credit for it. Brian and Chris used the phrase in the story *The Drunken Comic Book Monkeys vs. The Center of the Earth*.

Within these pages you'll find many fun and insane and crazy stories. Moments of sheer genius followed by cringe-worthy antics. To quote Homer Simpson, "It's funny because it's true." Not the strange creatures, aliens, or Jeff's ability to warp time and space — that's all fiction. But the arguments, childish giggles, beer snobbery, fist bumps, and general haplessness are all true. Trust me.

As you read this collection, you too will become an accomplice to the wrongness. Don't blame me, *you* let them talk you into buying this book.

Oh, and Jeff...a word, please...

PREFACE

Warning! Read This First

Warning! This book is a sequel. Yes, believe it or not, we have written a book before this one titled, *The Drunken Comic Book Monkeys in: Scary Tales of Scariness* (ISBN: 978-0-615-23508-0). As you may imagine, it's a collection of short stories in which Chris and I are characters of horror stories. Not only that, but we re-released it as *The Drunken Comic Book Monkeys in: Scary Tales of Scariness, The Reflux Edition* (ISBN: 978-0-578-05804-7) which has some of the original stories plus new stories, rewritten stories and a behind the scenes look after every story. Why am I telling you this (besides the shameless plug for our products)? Because this book is a sequel and there are characters and references in this book that are related to the prior two books. If you truly want to grasp the depth of those characters and circumstances, feel free to get copies of the first two books (readily available at our website: www.fortresspublishinginc.com). Go ahead. We'll wait. You don't have time to get those books right now? Okay, there are a few things that you will need to know before traipsing merrily along through this book—

- We have magic beer pants. All we have to do is reach into our front pockets to pull out a frosty bottle of beer. Each pocket can hold a six-pack.
- We frequently hang out at a restaurant called Melons Bar & Grille.
- We can talk to animals.
- When we die, the universe gets reset to one week earlier and we retain full knowledge of what happened during that time.
- At one point in time we accidentally turned Jeff into a goat. During his time as a goat, he was possessed by the Wendigo

spirit (twice!); brought upon the city of Harrisburg, PA a deadly contagion known as goat-pox; started a zombie outbreak; and was turned into a werewolf.

- Jeff hired a mad scientist to create a monster capable of beating us at drinking games. The monster's name is Drunkenstein.
- We entered a puffin in a pigeon race. The puffin got turned into a werewolf too.
- We fought a man-eating blob made from gelatin that was created by Doctors Hellway and Darkwar.
- Two sexy, female vampires seduced us. It did not end well.
- During a zombie attack, we went into a pike room (a room filled with nothing but pikes) and exited with a tennis racquet and a very large shoe, intending to use them as weapons.
- We fought an invasion of alien potatoes. One alien potato was named Frius Gaius.

How did all of this happen, you ask? Well, you'll have to read the first *Scary Tales of Scariness* and *The Reflux Edition...*

THE DRUNKEN COMIC BOOK MONKEYS VS.
THEMSELVES

Lightning streaked across the midnight sky, the originating storm clouds hiding the moon. Jeff watched nature's light show from an alley, the rain wetting his face. His trench coat offered little relief from the cold; the wind whipped it freely. Pulling his jacket tighter about him, he tried to bury his face between the lapels, hoping to escape even a modicum of the stench rising from the trash lining both walls of the alley. He paced, feet splashing through random puddles on the pavement.

His contact was late. Continuing to pace, he couldn't help but feel cliché since this was a late night rendezvous with a top government official in a clandestine back alley. Throw in a "dark and stormy" night and it was now a noir espionage story.

Jeff shuddered at the word "story," the reason for this meeting. Bad stories. Horrible stories. Juvenile stories. He could stand not one iota more of them! It must end! No matter the cost, the price! Tonight he gave the ball a push and nothing would stand up to its inertia. It started now.

"Jeff?" the approaching man asked, his voice possessing the timbre of a man attempting to be more menacing than his true nature.

"You have what I need?" Jeff replied, attempting to muster the same false bravado. He instead sounded just as fake and ridiculous

"Yeah. You have what I need?" the man asked, the forced gruffness of a poor silver screen Batman impression.

"Yeah. Where's what I need?" Jeff asked, his attempt at a disguise could only be more farcical had he worn Groucho Marx glasses with a plastic nose and moustache.

"Here." The man looked over both shoulders, paranoid about potential watchers, ready to jump from the shadows. He pulled a large clasp envelope from his trench coat, the same color and style as Jeff's. "Where's what I need?"

"Here." Jeff took the envelope from the man and handed over one of his own, stuffed with green renderings of Benjamin Franklin. Jeff opened the envelope and peeked at the papers within using the strained light from a nearby street lamp. "These real?"

"Yeah," the man said. Thumbing through the hundred dollar bills, he asked, "These real?"

"Yeah," Jeff replied, his throat getting sore from doing the voice.

The men shoved their envelopes into their respective trench coats. They looked at each other and stared, unsure of what to do next. Hands in his pockets, the man offered, "Ummmmmm..."

"Okay, then," Jeff said, sans fake growl. "I guess I'll see you next week at the sci-fi reading group."

"Yep!" the man said as he waved while turning to walk away. "Bye, Jeff!"

"See ya!"

Jeff returned to his home, ready to put his plan in action, ready to rid the world of two giant hemorrhoids from its collective ass. He looked at the papers, read the instructions, and verified the math and science involved in the process. Everything he needed, he ordered from eBay. As he mixed and molded, fixed and folded, Jeff plotted his revenge. He knew exactly how he wanted this to occur. He wanted his creations to destroy his targets in their sanctuary, their home.

***

At Melons Bar & Grille, Brian and Chris sat at the bar. The bartender asked, "Another round?"

"Yep," Brian replied. "And I was thinking about trying the Chicken Caesar salad."

All activity in the restaurant ceased. All eyes focused on Brian. Patrons stopped eating, mid-bite. Silence consumed the restaurant except for the thin whistle of the wind outside and the chirping of a lone cricket. No one was able to believe what Brian had said.

"Dude," Chris whispered, afraid that if he broke the eerie silence the resulting noise would backlash against him. "Are you feeling okay?"

"Yeah. Why?" Brian asked, the obnoxious quality of his normally loud voice amplified against the backdrop of the complete and utter absence of sound.

"You … you ordered a … salad?"

"Naaah. Just messing with you." Brian turned to the bartender and said, "I'd like 100 wings, please. And two orders of fried pickles."

The typical restaurant noises restarted, as if unpausing a movie.

"Dude, don't scare me like that!" Chris said, color returning to his ashen face. Well, as much color as his pigmentless skin would allow.

"Sorry. Just trying to elicit a chuckle."

"By threatening to order a salad? Dude, that's just sick. Even for you!"

"Oh, settle down!"

"That's it! I'm telling on you! I'm telling our editor how mean you are!"

"Don't you dare!"

"I dare! I'm so telling on you!"

"Tattle!"

"Your names don't hurt me! I'm telling! And there he is now!"

Jeff entered the restaurant. No sooner did he set foot through the door, Brian and Chris jumped from their stools, knocking both over with a distracting clatter, and ran to their editor. A headache, an aneurysm or maybe a tumor, started to throb behind Jeff's right eye as he was greeted with:

"Brian's mean!"

"Am not!"

"Are too!"

"Nuh-uh! I'm the good one!"

"Are not!"

13

"Tell him, Jeff!"

"Jeff likes me more! Tell him, Jeff!"

Pinching the bridge of his nose in an attempt to keep his pulsing eyes from popping right out of his skull, Jeff said, "Can we just go to the bar so we can talk about your latest story?"

"But..." Brian pouted.

"But..." Chris whined.

"Now!" Jeff barked, pointing to the toppled bar stools.

Brian and Chris trudged back, heads hanging low, exchanging shoulder punches in between:

"Your fault."

"Nuh-uh. Your fault."

Once at the bar, Jeff commanded them to pick up and dust off their barstools as well as apologize to the neighboring patrons for their immature behavior. The kind patrons accepted the mumbled apologies, but the bartender rolled her eyes and brought each of the men a bottle of beer. The men remained sullen until a giant plate piled full of chicken wings found its way in front of Brian. It was as if the sun rose after 40 straight days of rain. Brian smiled – until Chris tried to take one. "Get your own damn wings!"

"Dude!" Chris reasoned.

"I'm serious! These are mine!"

"All 100? Are you kidding me?"

"Here," Brian offered, sliding one of the plates of fried pickles to Chris. "Have one of these."

"Tasty as they may be, they certainly aren't as satisfying as wings!"

"If you want wings - order wings!"

"Jeff!"

"Jeff!"

"Fix it!"

Jeff sighed. He closed his eyes and dug deep within the quiet center of his soul. He reached for the solace of never having to deal with these two again. He would only find comfort in the execution of the plan. Now was the moment to begin.

14

"Miss...Miss...Yes, would you please get this knucklehead 100 wings, since he appears to be incapable of talking to a pretty, single woman. He wants those 911 hot, no celery or bleu cheese...he's a guy. Or, at least that's the story today. Also, please bring the open-mouthed gorilla a Guinness and the knuckle dragging, Elmer's glue colored guy a Corona with *both* a lemon and a lime. Oh, also two shots of the hottest sauce you have for him, and I'd like a chicken sandwich. Thank you." Without even a pause for breath, Jeff continued, his face flushed with the anger trapped under pressure for years uncountable. "Since you couldn't even resolve this little difference on your own, you'll both pay the penalty in beers that you hate. The hot sauce is just because I'm in charge, and I've recently embraced sadism. Do we have an understanding?"

"............"

"............Dude? They have chicken sandwiches?" Brian asked.

Jeff stood to address his audience of two in the manner of a man who wants the people across from him to know that they were not about to be treated as equals.

"Things are going to change, gentlemen, starting right now. The old me would have been happy to leave you both speechless. The new me? Well, I see the proverbial jugular and let's just say I'm lunging like a rabid pit-bull. You think you can hang with that, meringue man? Thought not. How about the wooly mammoth? You think you can deal with 190 pounds of prime pit-bull hanging off your chops? Good."

A smug and satisfied look stole across his face. Jeff sat and unfolded his napkin, before tucking in into his shirt collar. His coloring never looked better.

"Um, excuse me, sir..." ventured Chris, his hand partially raised as if he were in a classroom.

"You may speak. But," hereupon Jeff shook his finger as if scolding a recalcitrant child, "keep it brief and poignant."

"Where's Jeff?" Chris asked.

"Dude!" Brian attempted to whisper, "Don't push him. He frightens me."

"Miss?" Jeff called to the bartender. "Would you please make

15

that two Coronas? They go in front of the guy who looks like cauliflower."

"Ha, ha, ha, ha, ha, ha, ha, ha! DUDE! That's great!" Brian said, wiping away tears with a swipe of his bearish hand.

"You think that's funny, do you? Well, listen up, Bert and Ernie..."

"Dude, I'm Ernie..." Chris interrupted.

"What? Why?" Brian asked.

"It's a head reference...He's saying that your head is pointy..."

"SHUT UP!" Jeff yelled. "JUST SHUT UP! Speech is not required from either of you! Here, take these..."

"Dry erase boards?"

"NO TALKING! Write. Since this is what you're both so 'good' at, that's how you will communicate with me."

"Dude...you look like Professor Peabody with that thing..." Brian said to Chris.

"You want slapped, Fozzy Bear?" Chris relied.

"Duuuuude? What does that even *mean*?"

"Head reference..."

"Oh, miss...miss..." Jeff said, pointing to Chris.

"Dammit!!!" Chris yelled. He then wrote, *Dude, write him something*.

You're stupid! You took the time to write ME that, instead of just writing Jeff something? Brian wrote in reply.

Guh! Focus! I'm up to a six-pack of Corona here. My liver can't handle that much citrus!

"You can't even write on grease-boards without arguing, can you? Do either of you comprehend my misery yet?" Jeff asked.

We're really sorry.

"How many ways have you complicated my life? You got me turned into a goat. You gave me a horrible disease...."

Guh! Did he have to pause on that one?

But you were the cool leader of a werewolf gang...

"Oh, sure...after you two made a deal with an evil power that spared you morons every agony! You can't fathom my scars!"

Sir? Is old Jeff at home?

"You're not funny!" Jeff screamed. His chest heaving as he gulped in air to keep the fire within stoked high. "You always think you're 'cute', but the reality is that people only associate with you because you make them all look so much better - more educated, more mannered, more pleasant to work with."

Preposition, sir.

"I'll end my sentences with a preposition as often as I like, Mister '*I'll start sentences with* **and** *and* **but** *because I think it makes me cool.*' Well, it doesn't make *you* cool. An ice bath couldn't make you cool! If they coated you with ice cream and stuck a popsicle stick up your butt, you STILL couldn't pass as cool! Do you get it? You ruin the 'coolness' of ice cream!" The smugness returned to Jeff's face. With each eruption he was visibly changing the landscape that surrounded him.

Brian noticed Jeff's sandwich getting cold in front of him. Invisible hands of scent tickled his nose, tantalizing his taste buds, making his tongue sweat until action became mandatory.

"You've cost me my immortal soul!" Jeff continued. "AND my social life! Not to mention any chance I've ever had at becoming a professional writer...."

Brian interrupted Jeff's tirade with his white board, *Excuse me, sir....*

"What do you want?"

Are you going to eat that?

"I...can't...believe...this...no, wait...yes, yes I can. Sure. You can have it. Just as soon as you do something nice for someone else. There. That table over there. Those two guys need ketchup. Take our bottle of ketchup to them. DO NOT spill anyone's beer along the way. DO NOT talk to anyone. I've pulled your speaking plug. It's been PULLED! You! BALDY! Stop writing your ridiculously juvenile comment about me 'pulling his plug'! Now stop writing a retort to the bald comment! In fact, put the pen down! We're having quiet time! Lay your head on the table until Brian gets back from taking ketchup to that table!"

17

Without a word, though still far from quietly, Brian clomped his way over to the table Jeff indicated. The noise of his size fifteen shoes pounding the ground provided all that was necessary to get the attention of the two patrons. Brian held the ketchup bottle up for them to view. In the back of his mind where his prima donna thoughts echoed incessant chants, Brian thought of himself as a modernized version of Vanna White. As a natural happenstance, his version was far more obscene even without intention.

After flashing a toothy grin, he spun around to head back towards his recently acquired victuals, only to fall in a heap. It was not, however, that the g-force achieved from his pirouette caused an imbalance in his grossly large frame. He was felled by recognition: the recognition of his own face. Impossibly, he was seated at the table which just received his gracious gift of ketchup. And so was Chris.

Confused, Brian ran back to the barstool from whence he came. He trembled and shook, sweated and stewed. He rubbed his eyes as if grinding corn to meal. Peeking one more time to make sure his eyes hadn't tricked him, he began to cry.

Satisfied by the reaction and confident that his plan was in full swing, Jeff got up from his barstool and slunk away to find a better point to observe the ensuing mayhem.

"Dude!" Chris said to Brian. "What is your problem?"

Brian tried to answer, but his mouth only opened and closed like a fish after its final flop on a hot beach. Transfixed, his eyes could only gaze upon the table behind his friend.

Chris frowned, disoriented by his friend's confusion. He waved his hand in front of Brian's face. No reaction. He snapped his fingers. Not even a flinch. He waved a chicken wing up and down. Nothing. Confounded, Chris finally turned to see what could possibly keep Brian from attacking food out of primal instinct. Squinting, Chris tried to get a clear a vision of the impossible. Sure enough, Chris saw a mirror image of Brian's vision – themselves.

Mouth agape, he turned to Brian and asked, "How is that possible?"

"I don't know," Brian whispered. "I'm still trying to figure out

18

how *that* is possible."

Turning around again, he saw two Melons waitresses standing by the mysterious doppelgangers. What perplexed Brian was the fact that the waitresses were laughing, exhibiting signs of having fun! The one girl flipped her hair while flashing an over-enthusiastic smile. The other girl ran her fingers down the fake Chris's arm.

In all their years of patronage, the best reaction Brian and Chris ever received from one of the waitresses was a forced and pained smile, but that was only after turning their charm-level up to full blast. The next best reactions they ever received were sighs of relief anytime they announced they were done for the night and leaving.

Chris looked back to Brian, still rubbing his eyes with the heels of his hands, and asked, "How did that happened? We've used every ounce of mojo we have and it garners us pure disdain. We're anathema and these guys are panacea!"

"G'uh!" Brian grunted in agreement. "Look at them now!"

Chris did. A fire burned in his belly. Now the two waitresses sat with the doppelgangers while another two waitresses stood by the table. All four women squealed and laughed.

Turning back, Chris said, "Dude. We have to go over there."

"What?" Brian replied. "Why?"

"Think about it. First of all, they're spitting images of us. They have to be clones or something, so we need to know where they came from. Second of all, people like them and not us; so we need to figure out what their secret is."

Brian digested his friend's words, then gave a defeated sigh. "Yeah. I suppose you're right. Let's power up."

Without so much as another word, the men chowed down the remaining wings while chugging large gulps of beer in between bites. A few wings even disappeared into Brian's gullet whole and unmarred. Needing only four minutes to clean the table of every ounce of sustenance and every drop of libation, the men felt prepared to stare themselves square in the eyes and demand answers.

By the time Brian and Chris staggered over to the table where the fake Brian and Chris sat, four waitresses sat with them, two more

19

hovered around the table as well as five other patrons. All eleven strangers were riveted by what the two men had to say.

"That's *fascinating*, guys," one patron said to DoppelBrian and ChrisClone. "You two are the deepest individuals I have ever met. Now, I'm curious. What are your thoughts on the bigger issues? What is the meaning of life?"

Twenty-two eyes, open and yearning for knowledge, as well as the four blurry and dulled eyes of the real Brian and Chris, focused on the newest philosophers of the twenty-first century, awaiting their words of wisdom...

"Beer," ChrisClone said.

"Sex," DoppelBrian said.

The small crowd erupted with glee. The closest girls hugged the men while others gasped and clapped from having their own personal epiphanies. But real Brian soured the mood.

"Oh, come on!" he shouted. The revelry ceased. All eyes, now brimming with ire, focused on him. "We talk about beer and sex all the time and have never gotten a reaction like that!"

"That's because you keep talking," one of the waitresses said. "These two are succinct. Their message is poignant."

"Poignant? They said two freakin' words!"

"That's right! They did! And they carried far more weight than anything you two *ever* said!"

"But they are us! Look at them!"

"They're better than you! More charming and obviously smarter."

"But they're not feeding you anything. We offer sustenance with our words. Our words are a smorgasbord for your brain!"

"Food," DoppelBrian said. The small crowd swooned.

"What?" The real Brian snapped.

"See?" the waitress continued. "That's all the sustenance we need. Food. Not your *words*."

"Ummm, you do realize he said only one word. It's not like Zarathustra thus spake!"

"What? See, this is exactly what I'm trying to say! You talk a lot, but don't say anything! These guys say everything by talking very little! Where else can you find such raw simplicity? Where else can you find the point of any given topic so clearly?"

"Porn," said ChrisClone.

Every member of the encircling crowd, now seventeen people strong, used a thumb and index finger to stroke their chin, eyes gazing to the heavens as they pondered the one word answer. And they accepted it, in unison. Miniconversations ensued as the individuals in the crowd turned to each other and agreed with the restaurant booth idea maestro.

"I can't believe this," Brian muttered. "They're better us than we are!"

Chris shoved Brian out of the crowd, to an empty booth in the far corner of the restaurant. "Dude. I figured it out."

"What?" Brian asked.

"Body snatchers."

"Ummmm, there's a problem with that. Our bodies haven't been snatched."

Both men took a moment to think about the accidental double entendre Brian created. They each winced in pain from the vile images dancing through their minds.

"Eeeeewww," Brian continued. "What I meant to say was we're still here. The whole body snatcher concept is *taking,* then replacing someone."

"Maybe they're replacing us first? Seriously, they're pod people!"

"Now you're just being ridiculous. Next, you'll tell me they are some kind of 'potato people from another planet'. What is it with you and the 'doom and gloom' theories?"

"Listen, Einstein, so far you have yet to posit a credible theory...."

"I got it!"

"Dude, you know what they are?" Chris asked; hope glimmering like motes of light in the depths of his sapphire eyes.

"No. I have no idea what they are," Brian stated with the bluntness of a sledgehammer.

"Ummmm...then what 'do you have'? NO! WAIT! I'm not sure I want to know."

"I know why they are more popular than us," Brian stated, brimming with self-confidence.

"Spill it."

"You."

"Me? What do you...."

"You're the reason people don't like us. Your ridiculous vocabulary puts people off." Brian stated, picking a piece of lint from his *"can't sleep – aliens will probe me"* t-shirt.

"Wow. Typical math major. It doesn't matter if people can't add, the rules never change. But after years of people spelling it 'receipt' then all of the sudden the world decides 'i before e, except after c' doesn't matter. We just throw out all the rules of language, because, 'Heaven forbid,' anyone suffers spelling inadequacies."

"It's pretentious," Brian argued.

"I disagree! It's called 'not talking down to people'. Everyone wants to 'dumb up' the world. We should have certain expectations. Otherwise, we'll be drawing pictograms on cave walls again!"

"See? You have to say 'pictogram' when 'drawings' would suffice. I say 'red', but you have to say 'crimson'."

"Ummm...because there's a difference," Chris argued.

"You keep thinking that," Brian concluded. With that, he started to move off in the direction of the growing group that swelled around the pseudo-drunken comic book monkeys.

"Where are you going?"

"To hang out with the popular you. He makes sense."

"Dude, he's said the same four words for the past two hours!"

"And every one of them made sense."

"Unbelievable. Go over there, then, punk. See if I care. The only thing you'll get over there is a case of echolalia."

Chris returned to the table the true drunken comic book monkeys typically claimed as their own. Brian's attempts to join the party caused quite a commotion, but Chris tuned it out. Tilting one of the grease-boards to a better writing angle, he took up a marker and began writing a list.

Jeff Young graduated—need a new editor

It will always be 'receipt'

Shakespeare tripled the size of the English language -

My generation would see it halved

'Counter-predictive' should be a word

Taoism IS a selfish philosophy

Figure out the pod people

Call Drunkenstein—see if he wants to hang out

Chris paused contemplating his next point. As he began to touch the tip of the marker to the board one more time, a shadow blocked out his light. Only one person in the restaurant was tall enough to block the light.

"Dude, have you put on weight? You just blotted out the sun!"

"Beer?"

"It's like you don't see me! Two, please! So what did you learn, smart guy? Did you figure out the secret of charisma? Did you discover the mystery of self-actualization? Did you contemplate the clandestine path of Sufism?"

"Food?"

"Now that you mention it, I am a bit hungry. How do you manage to get inside my head like that? WAIT! Question withdrawn. I'll skip the rhetorical nature and go straight to the point: eerie! It's frightening, and more than a little unnerving. Dude, sit down! You make me nervous hovering around that way! It's like a sucker punch to my 'laid back' nature," Chris quipped. "So what are the 'almost us' guys like? Did you learn anything? You know, Jeff totally bolted as soon as you saw them. I'm sure that guy is behind this. We may not be smarter than him, but we sure do have a knack for bringing him down to our level. We can beat this. I just know it."

"Porn?"

"Yeah," Chris snorted. "At least *that* makes sense to me! How does Jeff keep coming up with these schemes? I mean, how can he afford it? And where does he find the people who make this stuff happen? I just can't believe there are that many people out there who want to see us suffer. We're basically good, if misunderstood, guys. You know, I think I just got it. I had an epiphany! Jeff is challenging us! That's it! He wants to give us stuff to write about. Keep us fresh. I mean after all, if he gets rid of us, it's kind of like killing the cash cow. Ha, ha, ha, ha! I crack myself up! I can't believe I just suggested we were the cash cow!"

"Beer?"

"Hello! Of course. Dude, you look kind of ashen. You feeling ok? This little mess got you down or something? Re-lax! You know we'll get through this. We need a plan, though. So you gotta tell me what you learned over there."

The sounds of raucous laughter filled the grille. Aside from Chris and his companion, every person in the restaurant was crowded around the clone's table. Chris couldn't help but notice that the next party of three that entered Melons immediately went over to join in the festivities at the table of the imposters.

"Damn! Ok, this time Jeff really outdid himself. Think, dude. How do we beat these guys? Got it! We pull some prank and they take the fall for it. We just have to impersonate them. We know their four-word vocabulary by heart. Fortunately, it's the four most meaningful words in the English language. And we're well practiced. Ok, now we just need an opportunity. Got any ideas?"

"Food?"

"Dude! You're a machine! Do you ever *not* eat? Doesn't being upset mess with your stomach? You're ridiculous! Oh, this is good. Don't look now, but the fake you is on his way over here."

"DUDE! You do know you're talking to the enemy, right?" Brian said. "I mean you're not really this dumb, are you?"

"Hey, you can't talk like that. I'm sensitive," Chris protested. "Some people even say I'm deep."

"Deep? Dude, you have the depth of a line."

"Ah, but at least I go on for infinity! Moron! Like I don't know you're fake Brian. Whatever!"

"How can you be confused? I've used more than four words with

24

every sentence!"

"Ok, smart guy, here's a test for the two of you. What are my four favorite words? Brian on the right?"

"Beer. Food. Porn. Sex," DoppelBrian said.

"Dude, he's got you. You're the imposter," Chris said to Brian.

"I didn't even go yet! And you're ridiculous! You know those are the only four words they know!"

"Yes, but he does have a point..."

"Dude, your four favorite words are ensanguined, esoteric, saturnine, and floccinaucinihilipilification."

"Lucky guess!"

"Lucky...? Dude, I just chose the four most unused, unknown words in the English language! That list is esoteric! And...and ... and ...?"

"What's wrong with you?"

Brian could only stare. Standing next to Chris was ChrisClone. Brian looked from one to the other and back. No difference. None.

"What?" Chris asked.

"Porn?" ChrisClone asked.

No help. Brian had no clue who was whom. So, he decided to give them a test. "So, guys, what's my favorite...?"

"Sex," both Chris's said in unison.

Brian frowned. "Okay. Let's try this. What do I like ...?"

"Beer," both Chris's said in unison again.

Brian sighed. "What...?"

"Food," both Chris's said in unison again.

Brian stood perplexed. How to tell them apart? He pulled out his wallet, flipping through the cards until he found the one he sought. His mensa card. He stroked it lovingly. An idea percolated in his brain. *Thank you, little genius*, he thought. "Miss! Yes, may I have a Guinness, please? No, no fruit. Thank you."

The waitress returned with his drink and popped the top, standing the can upside down in a pint glass. Brian assured her he could handle it from here. Manning up, he held his expression completely neutral against the distaste that coursed through him at han-

25

dling the can. Both Chris's drooled as the sediment settled. When the liquid reached the brim of the glass, Brian realized he had no idea what he was doing and pulled the can free with a jerky motion. A drop of the dark beverage caught the side of the glass and began to roll towards the table. Both Chris's eyed it. Brian still couldn't tell them apart. Sweat formed on their respective brows – still no tip off. The lone drop sank slowly toward the bottom of the glass, as if the glass itself was crying.

Unable to take it any longer, both Chris's lunged in unison. Brian still couldn't tell them apart. His plan had failed.

"Beer!"

"Dude, alcohol abuse! What's wrong with you man? Hey, wait a second..." Realization rose like a new dawn.

"Miss! Might I have a corona, please? Oh, yes, extra lime would be exquisite - in fact, a lemon and a lime, if it's not too much trouble."

"Dude! That's a bit of overkill, isn't it?"

"At least we'll learn a thing or two here. Thank you, miss," said Chris squirting himself in the eye with lemon juice as he struggled to push the pulpy mass down the bottle's neck.

"Now we just need to see if the aversion is consistent."

"Beer?" asked ChrisClone, eyeing Brian's glass of Guinness.

"You like this, huh?"

"BEER!" ChrisClone affirmed. He moved closer to Brian, glancing back in disgust at the Corona.

"I got an idea. I know how to *beat* them! Follow me."

Chris used the Guinness to lure ChrisClone over to the crowd of people. ChrisClone moved back to his spot with DoppleBrian.

"Porn," he said.

The crowd swooned, then began to chant, "Porn, porn, porn, porn..."

Chris cleared his throat and said, "Excuse me! May I have your attention?"

"What do you want?" an attractive young lady demanded. "Why are you even still here?"

"If I can have your attention, please? Thank you. What is it you would like most?"

"You to leave," the crowd said with one voice.

"Food," said DoppleBrian.

A laugh rippled through the crowd.

"Tell you what, let's have a drinking contest. First team done with their beer wins. Losers leave."

"Dude!" Brian said. "Where will we go?"

ChrisClone smiled. "Beer."

"Yes, big fella. Here's the twist. We'll need two Guinness and two Coronas. Perfect! Okay, someone count down. Quick."

DoppleBrian stared at the Guinness in front of him. He began to sweat profusely. ChrisClone was faced with the Corona and the lemon - *and* the lime. He swayed to and fro as if he might pass out.

A nearby waitress counted down. "Three, two, one...go!"

"Done."

"Done."

"Done."

"Done. But you know he should get a break. All that fruit clogged up his beer."

The crowd consulted amongst themselves. The discussion included much head shaking.

"Now what?" Brian whispered to Chris.

"We wait. If they are truly as well replicated as they seem, their wits should fly apart at any second. How my double choked that garbage down is beyond me."

Sweat beaded on DoppleBrian's forehead. His face blanched until he was almost as colorless as Chris. His deodorant gave out.

"Nice! Watch this. What's your name?" Chris asked.

"Bryant Koznuski," DoppleBrian said.

"Cool. Any others?"

"Sasquatch."

"Really? Don't look now, but that guy's a photographer..."

"Damn paparazzi!" said DoppleBrian. He ducked beneath the nearest table, attempting to hide his bulky frame from the designated man's view. Plates and silverware fell to the floor, the clatter offending the waitresses and other patrons.

The real Brian caught on to his friend's plan, slunk his way over to a barstool and said, "Food!"

Chris slid over beside his twin. "What's your name?"

"Christ Piano," ChrisClone said.

"Nice name. You know, your buddy deserted you and the crowd is turning on you. Better think of something fast...why don't you dance?"

The undulation that followed could hardly be described as dancing. It wasn't even qualified as the most basic of rhythmic movements. The crowd watched in horror, attempting to understand what was happening.

"Perfect," Chris whispered to ChrisClone. "Keep it up. Know any songs? Oh, oh, know the camp song?"

The crowd watched on. They were no longer sure which Chris was which.

"You know the one. The lighting bug song," Chris whispered to ChrisClone again.

"This...this...this little butt of mine," ChrisClone sang. "I'm gonna...gonna make it shine..."

"Beer," the real Chris said to the crowd.

"That's him!" someone from the crowd pointed at ChrisClone. "He needs to leave."

"Food!" said Original Brian.

"Porn," said Original Chris.

"And the one hiding under the table is the other one. Out they go. C'mon get them out of here. This whole contest was their idea, too. Time to be men for once!" one of the waitresses said, pointing to DoppleBrian, still attempting to hide under a table.

The crowd ushered the imposters out the door and all the way into the parking lot.

"No!" DoppleBrian cried out. "Let me regale you with trivia from my Mensa brain!"

"I'm a little teapot, short and stout. Here is my handle, here is my spout..." ChrisClone crooned.

28

Frustrated, Jeff followed.

When the crowd returned en masse, they found Chris and Brian sitting serenely at their table. Each man wore a smile the size of a fedora.

"Tell us more," said one young girl.

"Sex," said Brian.

"Beer," said Chris.

Both men looked at each other. Things were good. Except Chris knew it would be weeks before he got the lightning bug song out of his head.

THE DRUNKEN COMIC BOOK MONKEYS
vs.
THE WORLD OF THE MONKEYS

As the men stared at the bottles before them, droplets of condensation made haphazard journeys down the brown glass. Brian strummed his fingers on the table in trepidation, but licked his lips with desire. Chris frowned, his jaw jutting forward while he weighed the pros and cons of the action he contemplated. They had come so far, this being the final step. They bought the ingredients, they brewed the beer, they bottled the beer, and they refrigerated the beer. They even uncapped the beer a minute ago. Now all they had to do was drink the beer. And that terrified them.

Making the first move, Chris lifted the bottle from the table and peeked down the neck, unsure what he had hoped to find. "I can't believe I let you talk me into this."

Brian left his bottle on the table, moving his face closer; hoping to catch an angle in which the light would shine through the brown glass, exposing what was lurking within. "Why not? You said you always wanted to try to brew your own beer. And now we have."

"Yeah. But using mushrooms?"

"Why not? We drank beer brewed from just about everything else from pomegranate to cactus."

"But mushrooms? For our first attempt, ever?"

"When shooting for the moon, aim for the stars. That way your goal becomes your lowest expectation."

Chris winced. "What fortune cookie did you get that from?"

"Accounting conference."

"You frighten me - but not as much as this beer."

Brian sat up straight and lifted his bottle, extending it for a toast. "Quit being a wussy and drink it."

Chris sighed and peered down the neck one last time. "Cheers."

The men clanked bottles and started chugging; their eyes

squeezed shut while every muscle tensed, awaiting the onslaught of pain. To their mutual surprise, the pain never arrived. Their guzzling slowed to gulping which soon slowed to savoring. Upon the final drop of succor, they placed the bottles back on the table and stared wide-eyed at each other. The wind outside gave a gentle shuffle to the leaves while carrying with it the faint barking of a distant dog. Comprehension failed to seep into the men's brains, failed to allow them to acknowledge that not only were they successful, but they had created a beer that impassioned both of their souls equally.

As if a starting gun only they could hear was fired; they raced to the refrigerator, toppling over the table and knocking the chairs about. Almost ripping it from its hinges, they opened the door and grasped for every bottle. They each shoved bottles into the pockets of their beer pants, testing their garments' structural integrity. What failed to fit, the men cradled or popped open and chugged.

"Let's make more!" Brian shouted between chugs.

"Good idea!" Chris replied.

The men rushed about the kitchen of the Top Secret Fortress Lair obtaining ingredients and implements. Clanging, followed by screaming and swearing, echoed through the room. Hops, barley and mushrooms were scooped, weighed and measured. Water flowed from taps and fire flickered from stovetops. Unbefitting the true nature of their character, the men worked together like a finely tuned machine, especially since they each used only one hand, their other hand, of course, holding a bottle - until Chris decided to mess with success.

While Brian fetched other ingredients, Chris dumped more hops into the boiling kettle on the stove. Forgetting the consequences that awaited, Chris could only stare as billows of foam frothed over.

"See!" Brian yelled when he noticed. "I told you there was such a thing as too much hops!"

"Shut up!" Chris offered as a rejoinder. He grabbed the pot's handle to remove it from the stove. In his haste, the contents swished, and then sloshed over the edge, splashing the wall- and the exposed electrical outlet.

Sparks plumed through the kitchen. Out of reflex the men protected their crotches with one hand while shielding their beers with their bodies. The sparks gained no purchase within the confines of the kitchen. However, behind the wall the wires popped and sizzled. A burn mark made its way up the wall, leaving a charred path of black in its wake.

Stupefied, Brian and Chris watched the burn creep across the wall like a fuse in reverse, toward the nearest window. With a jolting crack, the ball of sparks jumped from the Top Secret Fortress Lair to the attached phone line. Running to the window, the men saw the raging ball of electricity roll along the telephone lines, a plume of fireworks erupting as it passed through the transformers on each pole.

"Dude," Brian said. "It's heading right for Three Mile Island. Should we call them or something?"

"Naaah. It's a nuclear power plant. That should be able to withstand more than a little...."

The spark followed the telephone lines right to the power plant and disappeared. A rumble emanated, growing in intensity with every passing second. The cooling towers shook.

"Dude!" Brian screamed. "To the escape pod!"

"Save the beer!" Chris yelled.

Both men grabbed the rest of their home brew, hugging two-dozen bottles each, and ran to the escape pod they kept for just such emergencies. Rattling and clanking, they dove inside. As they closed the hatch, they witnessed a mushroom cloud erupt where Three Mile Island used to be. Cooling towers popped into the air as a rolling ball of fire erupted from the explosion.

Less than a second after securing the lock, they felt the shockwave hit and launch them into the air. A feeling of weightlessness overcame them as they tumbled about the escape pod. Dementia and nausea blended together and Chris and Brian's tenuous grasp of consciousness slipped away. The sudden impact of landing yanked both men from oblivion.

Brian awoke with a jolt in a heap of beer bottles. The last image in his mind was of the mushroom cloud and panic began to set in. He grabbed the nearest bottle and chugged. Still freaking out, he chugged three more. Finally calm enough to assess the situation, he looked to his comrade. Curled in the corner, Chris suckled on an open beer bottle. Brian kicked his comrade's foot. "Dude! Wake up."

"Wha...?" Chris replied. He sat up with only one eye open and a shimmering line of spittle from his lip to the bottle.

"You were sleep drinking again."

"And? You act like that's a bad thing."

"Well, I guess it's not. Especially since we don't know what lies beyond our escape pod. I don't wanna open the hatch sober."

"Me neither," Chris said, finishing his beer.

After a game of rock, paper, scissors turned into a game of kick, sissy slap, punch, they determined that Brian should open the hatch. Cradling his safety beer, he turned the latch and opened the door. As timid as a newborn fawn, Brian peeked his head outside. He took a swig from his safety beer.

"Well?" Chris asked. "What do you see?"

"Green," Brian replied.

"Could you be any more vague?" Chris yelled, pushing Brian out the door. Ignoring the swearing that resulted, Chris stepped outside as well. And sure enough, Brian was right.

Other than the brown scar of broken soil marring the rolling hill where the escape pod slid to a halt, green blanketed the land. The men walked around the escape pod at the base of the hill on a thick carpet of grass as they tried to gain their bearings. Thick brush ebbed and flowed on all sides, sometimes rolling off into the horizon, other times merging into the base of a dense forest.

"Where are we?" Chris asked.

"Could be anywhere. Maybe not even Earth?" Brian answered.

"Are you serious?"

"Think about it. We were at ground zero of a nuclear explosion. If it hit us at the right angle, it could have launched us out of the atmosphere."

"Yeah? But isn't the closest planet light years away? It would have taken us hundreds of years to get there."

"True, but you keep forgetting that the rules of time and physics are distorted in space. See, what Einstein hypothesized is..."

"You really have no idea what you're talking about, do you?"

"Not a freakin' clue."

"You scare me. You really do."

Before the argument could escalate any farther, both men noticed a disturbance in the brush rapidly growing closer. At first a few stalks of floppy leaves shivered, then more followed, a path of falling foliage leading through the forest. Close behind came more rustling, violent and loud, bushes and brush getting crunched or tossed in the air.

"Dude, what is that?" Chris asked, stepping to the edge of brush, the shortest plant tall enough to dwarf him.

"Have you never seen a horror movie in your life? You don't step *closer* to the unknown noise *coming right at you!*"

"First of all, this isn't a horror movie. Second of all, I'm sure it's just some animal like a rabbit or something. Third of all, I may not be in my physical prime, but I think I'm deft enough to move out of the way if...." His words were cut short as he got bowled over by what burst from the brush.

Brian watched with concern, but danced a slight jig because he was right. Two figures, large and furry, crashed into his friend. Momentum caused the three to roll about the grass, the animals screeching while Chris screamed, "My beer! Don't spill my beer!"

Bursting from the brush charged a dozen more animals, screeching and howling as well and carrying spears. Once the tussle between Chris and the two others ended, he asserted to all that he spilled nary a drop of beer. After separating himself from the immediate commotion, he and Brian assessed the creatures.

"Monkeys?" Brian whispered. The animals were bipedal and humanoid in shape, but their faces and appendages were those of monkeys. The pursuers' visages resembled irate gorillas, thick lips exposing stained fangs while nostrils embedded in flat noses flared with every breath, and their fur held a charcoal hue. Each man-like gorilla wore black leather armor and pointed gleaming tipped spears at their prey. Huddled together on the ground, the hunted resembled humanoid chimpanzees, however one was recognizably female. Loose clothing hid most of their chocolate pelts, but both Chris and Brian saw the telltale curves of the female. Her face was softer than her male counterpart's and her lips curved more supplely while her dark eyes held the sympathy only a woman could muster – and fear.

"Infidels!" the largest of the gorilla soldiers growled at his captives. "Caught you, Lolo, and your sister! Even with help from your ... alien ... associates."

"Damn you, Zahl!" the male captive snapped back. He then looked to Chris – caressing his beer bottle as he hugged it to his face – and snarled, exposing all of his teeth. "If not for this ... this ... creature, Cheena and I would have escaped the tyranny of your king."

Zahl smiled and moved closer to his captives as four of the other soldiers yanked Lolo and Cheena to their feet. "He is still your king too."

"For now. Until we escape!"

"After your trial, you may not have another chance."

Both Lolo and Cheena screeched at Zahl while the other soldiers bound their hands.

"My beer! Mine!" Chris yelled when one of the other soldiers yanked the bottle from his hand. The gorilla easily held Chris at bay with one hand to the face while he held the bottle in his other hand. He looked down the neck of the bottle and then sniffed it. Nostrils curling, he snorted at the offensive odor. Sneering, he dumped the beer from the bottle. Chris fell to his knees and immediately started licking the grass. "No! Mine! Mine!"

"Sir?" the soldier asked. "What shall we do with ... these creatures?"

Zahl approached Brian. The human shaped gorilla stood eye-to-eye with the gorilla shaped human. Brian sneered. Zahl opened his mouth and roared and the force of his bellow whipped the hairs of Brian's goatee about. Brian crossed his eyes; peed a little, and passed out.

Brian awoke, groggy and disoriented, blurred colors swirling about his vision. Out of reflex, he reached into his pocket and pulled out a beer. In between chugs, he asked, "Where am I?"

"In a cage. Bamboo, I'd guess," he heard Chris say.

Sitting up, Brian finished his beer and reached for another one. As he drank, the world stopped spinning and his vision stopped rippling. Coming into focus, he saw the bamboo bars and then looked around the rest of the cage.

One of his cellmates was Chris, blades of grass jutting from his goatee, tucked in there from when he lapped his spilled beer from the ground. Lolo and Cheena were there as well, both sitting against the bars on the opposite side of the cage. Arms crossed over his chest, Lolo glared at Brian and Chris. Cheena stared as well, but through curious eyes.

Near the monkeys – the drunken ones, not the chimps – was their beer, a dozen bottles standing upright. Brian asked, "Our beer?"

"Yep," Chris replied. "The monkeys find it disgusting, so they won't drink it, but they don't see any reason why we can't keep it."

"Oh. Cool. At least they're civilized monkeys."

"Ha!" Lolo exploded. "We'll see how civilized you think they are after they behead all of us."

Both Brian and Chris started rubbing their necks.

"Dude, my head may be addled with lots of beer most of the time and preoccupied with sex and food, but I like it where it is," Brian whined.

"Me too," Chris replied.

Cheena scooted closer to the men, her curious eyes scrutinizing them. She squatted, her hands on the ground as well, poised to flee if what she examined proved to be too dangerous. "Lolo, don't they look familiar to you?"

Lolo snorted and looked away. "Even though the tall one is hairy enough to be a monkey, they don't look like any monkey I've seen before."

"You're not even looking, brother!"

Through angry eyes, Lolo peered at the men. The men peered back with bottles attached to their lips. Recognition swept over his face as he whispered, "The Doom Bringers."

37

Cheena screeched her disapproval. "The scholars don't know what to make of the writings. They could be The Tribe Unifiers."

"Ummmm," Chris said. "We're sitting right here. What are you talking about?"

Still using caution, Cheena moved closer, unable to hide the zeal in her eyes. "The writings. They are strange and marvelous and in a tongue that we cannot speak. There are images as well, images which resemble the two of you. The scholars feel that the writings are prophecies. But *what* the writings prophesize, the scholars don't know."

"What I do know is how to use this to get out of here!" Lolo jumped up and ran to the bamboo bars. He pressed his face against them and yelled, "Guards!"

"You are fascinating creatures," Cheena whispered while scooting closer to Chris.

"Yeah, women tell us that a lot," Chris said, sitting straight to puff out his chest.

"They do?" Brian asked.

"Yes, they do." Chris hissed to Brian, "Now don't ruin my mojo."

"Ruin your …? What …? Ooooooooooh no," Brian said, more to himself now that Chris was preoccupied with Cheena stroking his cheeks and goatee. He turned to Lolo for assistance, but he was preoccupied as well.

"What?" the gorilla guard yelled to Lolo.

"Get the Scholar Shmolar!" Lolo shouted back.

Confused, Brian pivoted between Lolo, whose attention never wavered from beyond the bars, to Chris and Cheena, moving even closer together. Every time Brian went to tap Lolo's shoulder, the chimp-man would screech obscenities to the guards, yelling at them to hurry with the venerable Scholar. But every time Brian turned to Chris and Cheena, their hands sought out different regions of each other's body. Seeing no other recourse, Brian sat down on the dirt floor and popped open another beer. He looked back over to his friend observing that Chris and Cheena shared an embrace, then a kiss. Brian then pulled his knees to his chest, and rocked back and forth while muttering, "This is all an illusion, this is all an illusion, this is all an illusion, this is all an illusion...."

"What is the ruckus about?" Zahl roared as he approached the cage. In tow was the diminutive Shmolar. Walking on two legs like all the other monkeys, he wore a brown tweed suit with tan leather patches protecting the elbows. His jacket covered most of his fur, the rust hue of an orangutan. His protruding lips never stopped moving, offering slight ripples even when not speaking.

"Yes, yes, I must agree with this sack of testosterone, you are creating quite an inordinate amount of ruckus," Shmolar said.

Lolo smiled and pointed to Brian and Chris. "That's because we have found the Ones of Legend."

Shmolar ambled closer; brows furrowed and lips puckered, to judge the captive's claim. Brian still rocked back and forth on the dirt floor while Chris and Cheena shared smiles of false innocence, trying to hide their acts of indiscretion. But the resemblance was uncanny. Shmolar believed these strange looking creatures were those that Lolo professed. "Release them."

"What?" Zahl barked. "We don't know what these creatures were doing within our border. We don't even know what these creatures are!"

Shmolar waved his hand, dismissing the gorilla's concerns. "True, true. But their resemblance to the Ones of Legend is undeniable."

"Even if that were true, we don't know if they are The Doom Bringers or The Tribe Unifiers!"

"Don't you think we should at least petition the king's court to address the matter?"

"Of course! I would have it no other way!"

A wry smile crept across Shmolar's twitching lips. "Hence my original request. Now, release them."

A growl so deep that the ground vibrated came from Zahl as he unlocked the cage, his angry eyes never straying from Shmolar – until Lolo stepped out.

"Where do you think you're going?" Zahl growled, grabbing a fistful of Lolo's shirt.

Raising his hands in the air, Lolo smiled. "Cheena and I have to come along. We're their handlers."

"Handlers?" both Zahl and Shmolar asked.

"Absolutely. Just look at these creatures. They are completely lost without us."

Zahl and Shmolar peered at the men. Chris giggled as he and Cheena tickled each other's chins. Coping as best he could after witnessing that, Brian, laying on his side and using his shoulder as a the pivot point, ran in circles with his beer bottle never leaving his lips.

"See?" Lolo said. "Completely useless without us!"

Shmolar stroked his chin in contemplation. "Yes, yes. It certainly appears that way, doesn't it?"

Zahl roared, "Everyone out of the cage. Now!"

The four prisoners exited; Lolo stretched and offered an exaggerated yawn, Chris and Cheena walked out hand in hand, Brian crawled out still nursing from his beer bottle.

Finally finding the necessary strength, and motivated by Zahl's sharp, pointy spear, Brian managed to get back to his feet as Zahl and Shmolar escorted the prisoners to the king. Trying hard to ignore the cooing from Chris, Brian looked at the surrounding village as they walked down the main dirt road. The abodes were worked into the landscape, snuggled between trees or nestling between the rolling hills, as if entwined in an intimate dance. The denizens stopped to stare as the entourage walked through the village, a mix of fear and curiosity within their eyes. Brian smiled at the idea of being one of the Ones of Legend, wondering if he was a Doom Bringer or Tribe Unifier, until he saw something that could be the answer.

"Dude!" Brian said to Chris, punching him in the shoulder to garner his attention. "Look."

"Okay. What am I looking at?" Chris asked, pulling a beer from his pants pocket.

"Don't you see it? There."

"That thing? What is it?"

40

"Dude! You're the worst Francophile I know! It's the Eiffel Tower."

Chris left Cheena – now arguing with her brother about the merits of becoming romantically entangled with a strange creature that fell from the sky, who might also be a Doom Bringer – to get a better look. He slugged his beer and squinted. "I totally see it now! You're right! But why is it so small?"

"We're looking at just the top of it. It's probably buried."

"Why would monkeys want to bury the Eiffel Tower?"

"I don't think the monkeys did it. I think time did it."

"What are you talking about?"

"Dude, I think when Three Mile Island exploded, the shock wave not only threw us to France, but through time as well."

"When Three Mile Island exploded? But ... but ...."

Brian looked around then leaned in and whispered, "Yeah, we did that. And that makes us...."

"... The Doom Bringers," Chris whispered back. "Do you think we should tell them?"

Brian smacked Chris upside his head. "Are you kidding me? That Zahl gorilla has been itching to turn us into kabobs."

"What should we do?"

"Do what we do best. Be cool."

Both men howled at the ridiculousness of that comment. Their laughter was met with the tip of Zahl's spear. "Silence!"

The group finished the trek with nary a noise. Until the men saw the palace and said, "Whoa!"

Both men deemed the palace unimpressive, just a large building crafted from cut stone. What impressed them was the thirty-foot statue on top. Hand carved, the image was a standing orangutan, its arms outstretched, holding a globe in one palm while gripping a banana in the other.

"That's our king," Cheena whispered.

"Yeah?" Chris said. "He doesn't look too tyrannical."

"Just wait until he passes judgment," Lolo said. As a form of prognostication and instigation, he slowly drew his index finger across his neck while his eyes lolled back and his tongue flopped free.

"Don't disgrace our king in such a manner!" Zahl growled, smacking Lolo.

The interior of the palace was spacious, yet Spartan in design. Minimal hangings made of colorful knitting adorned the walls. Tiles of varying shades of brown and tan checkered the floor. Sand colored pillars lined the great hall leading from the entrance to the throne, the only area of the palace with decoration. Four wide steps led from the floor to the throne platform. On either end of each step rested a column base, topped with a table to hold a marble bust of the king. The columns grew larger with each step, culminating in a pair of statues of the king one on either side of the throne. Both statues rivaled the height of the great hall pillars. On the throne, arms and legs dangling about like vines, sat the king.

"Greetings, your Highness," Shmolar said.

"Oh wise scholar, why have you requested an audience? Bringing with you two infidels and two horrific looking creatures."

"Are we the infidels or the horrific looking creatures?" Chris asked Brian.

The king screeched, bearing all of his teeth and leapt from the throne to hide behind it. "They ... they talk! What manner of animals are these?"

"They have fallen from the sky, Sire, and have yet to make their intentions known," Zahl said, his exaggerated stance making it clear that his spear was ready to strike the men in question when given the command.

With only his eyes and crown visible from behind the throne, the king asked, "If their intentions are not known, then why bring them *here*? To *me*?"

"Because, venerable Liege," Shmolar said, stepping forward. "I believe these creatures are the Ones of Legend, and I wish to study them. However, your small-minded lackey here wants to run them through for no reason at all."

"They are intruders! Rabid animals, at best!" Zahl proclaimed.

"Hardly," Shmolar said, rolling his eyes and his lips. "They are capable of speech."

With curious and deliberate movements, the king slowly made his way from behind his throne. His eyes never leaving the men, he said to them, "I'm King Steve. What are your names?"

"Steve?" Chris asked.

"Steve?" Brian asked.

Steve returned to his throne and frowned. "You're both named Steve?"

"No," Chris said. "I'm Chris and he's Brian."

"Then why'd you say 'Steve'?"

"It's a funny name for a monkey."

Brian punched Chris in the shoulder. "Knucklehead!"

Steve scratched his head. "These are certainly curious creatures. And what of the infidels?"

Lolo stepped forward and said, "We're their handlers."

"And their advocates. Almost like ambassadors," Cheena added. "We could learn a great deal from them."

"Hmmmm," Steve said, pondering her words. "Creatures! What are the most glorious aspects about where you come from?"

"Beer," Chris said.

"Sex," Brian said.

"Porn," Chris said.

"Food," Brian said.

"See?" Lolo and Cheena said in unison.

"Much to learn," Cheena said.

"Idiots who can't survive without us," Lolo said.

The siblings turned to each other and frowned, both unhappy that the other's response contradicted their own.

"Hmmmm," Steve said again. "Very curious creatures indeed."

"Yes, yes," Shmolar said. "Obviously simple creatures, too simple to be The Doom Bringers. Therefore they must be The Tribe Unifiers."

"Baaah!" Zahl barked. "Tribe Unifiers need cunning and courage, wisdom and knowledge. These two have been addling their brains with poison from the bottles they have been suckling on ever since they've arrived. A poison that might spread to our people. At best they are distractible children waving swords!"

"Hmmmm," the king mumbled as he pondered the situation. "Let's have *them* determine if they are Doom Bringers or Tribe Unifiers."

"What?" everyone in the room said in unison.

Jumping from his throne, Steve ambled to a nearby tapestry and moved it aside to reveal a small alcove. There lay the mysterious tome adorned by the Ones of Legend. He retrieved it and used two hands to raise it over his head. Gasps filled the great hall by all those who gazed upon it – a small chapbook that had two monkeys, one tall with black hair and yelling, one short with red hair and pondering, on a red background.

"Dude," Chris whispered to Brian, "That's one of our books."

"It certainly is," Brian whispered back. "I have a plan. Follow my lead."

"This can't end well."

With all eyes still on the book, Steve brought it to the men. "As you can see, the monkeys on the cover of this book resemble you two."

"Sure do," Brian said, swiping the book from Steve's hands. "And let me read from it to you."

More gasps followed. Shmolar's lips twitched even faster as he asked, "You ... you can read the words?"

"Yep. See the title?"

Brian held the book up to the curious monkeys as they squinted, trying to guess what the symbols might mean, completely unaware that they read, "The Drunken Comic Book Monkeys, Vol. 2."

Satisfied that he captivated the room, Brian continued, "The title is 'Official Guide to Pleasing Your Tribe Unifiers'."

Chris slapped his own forehead as the crowd swooned.

Brian continued, adding panache by standing straight and turning one page at a time with his pinkie extended. "Yay verily, yay verily, thy Tribe Unifiers hath gracethed thee with their presence. 'Now what?' thee might asketh thineselves. 'What musteth we do to maketh them happyeth?' thee might wonder."

44

Chris groaned and rolled his eyes.

Brian turned the page. "Forsooth, ergo, and to-and-with, thee should supplyeth the tall one with chicken wings whilst supplyingeth the short one with used sweat socks."

"Hey!" Chris screamed at Brian. "It doesn't say that!"

"Sure does! In fact it goes on to explain all the tasty foods they should give to me and what kinds of used athletic apparel you enjoy in specific and detailed order of liking."

"Does not! You're translating the cryptic symbols wrong!" Chris yelled, grabbing the book.

Refusing to let go, Brian tugged. "Says right here that you suck!"

White knuckled, Chris tightened his grip and pulled. "It says right here that every monkey should give you the middle finger once a day!"

"Mine!"

"Mine!"

"Mine!"

"Mine!"

Losing their balance, the men toppled into King Steve who in turn fell onto the nearest pedestal, knocking it into the one next to it. The pedestals fell against one another, continuing until the largest fell against one of the statues with enough force to knock it over. The statue groaned and creaked as momentum pushed it into the nearest great hall pillar. Chips of stone and dust burst from the top of the pillar as it gave way, collapsing into the one next to it. Everyone in the great hall realized the final result once the second pillar fell into the third.

"*RUN!*"

Everyone did, making it outside just as the palace collapsed, Brian and Chris diving to the right while everyone else dove to the left. Before the dust could start to settle, a deep groan rippled through the air as the statue of King Steve toppled. All eyes of the village watched the monolith fall, the body of the statue crashing into a batch of tall trees while the globe fell free from its hand. Just like the domino effect within the palace, the trees fell into other trees, sending more trees crashing into others. The screams and screeches of those fleeing their treetop homes were drowned out by the thunderous pops and splits of wood. The globe bounced and rolled along the other side of the village, decimating more homes along the way. Dust and leaves floated through the air, the green and brown nebula glinting in the sunlight, as the globe slowed to a standstill and no more trees fell.

Chris looked at his watch and said, "Wow. Look at the time. We gotta go."

Brian and Chris ran from the village.

Taking advantage of the entire village of dumbfounded monkeys, the men got a sizeable head start into the nearby jungle. However, the screeches of anger and hatred, and the lone voice of a female monkey yelling, "I'll wait for you! Text me!" let the men know the entire village wanted their heads.

The men ran, branches whipping their arms and faces, exposed roots threatening to trip them. Monkey hoots and hollers echoed behind them, lashing them like a taskmaster's whip, pushing them harder, making them run faster. Legs burning, their whole bodies throbbed with every quickened beat of their hearts.

"Dude, I don't feel so good," Chris said, throat on fire.

"Me neither," Brian replied, wheezing. "I think the beer's leaving our system."

"We're becoming sober?"

"Yeah. I think so."

"I hate that!"

"Me, too!"

Before the men could contemplate the direness of their situation, they ran into a stone wall crowned with metal bars. The wall extended as far as they could see in either direction and the men knew the only way past it was over it.

"But we don't know what's on the other side!" Chris said.

"What could be worse than a village full of angry monkeys?"

"Dinosaurs! Prohibition! A village full of angry badgers! We've traveled so far into the future that monkeys *evolved*! Who knows what's on the other side of the wall?"

"Doesn't matter. We know what's on *this* side of the wall, so we gotta go over!"

Scrabbling as best as their out of shape bodies could scramble, they tried to pull themselves over the wall. Squeaking, a gate in the fence opened and a pair of hands reached down to help the men over the wall. With one final tug, the men and their mysterious benefactor tumbled onto a patch of manicured grass. Jumping to their feet, both men closed their eyes and started sissy slapping the air in front of them while screaming, "Aaaaaaah! Monsters! Monsters!"

"Ummmm, what are you guys talking about?" a voice said.

The men stopped and opened their eyes. Standing before them was a pudgy man in his mid-twenties, clad in khaki. Confused, Brian asked, "Who are you?"

"I'm Chad. I'm one of the reserve attendants."

"Reserve? What reserve?"

"The reserve I just pulled you out of. It's called 'The World of Monkeys' and it's a reserve for ... well ... monkeys."

Confused, Brian and Chris looked around. Behind the bars was a walled drop-off where all types of monkeys roamed free. They frolicked in tall grasses or swung through the trees. One chimpanzee sat on a branch and blew kisses to Chris. He cringed and asked Chad, "What happened? How did our escape pod get in there?"

"This way," Chad said. He escorted the men about half a mile around the fence until they came to the main gate of the reserve. Next to the gate was a refrigerator – the one from the Top Secret Fortress lair. "This fridge came rolling down that hill there and zipped right through the gate. We had it opened for like a minute. Then it fell over and you two rolled out."

Brian looked at the refrigerator and then up the hill to the Top Secret Fortress lair. "So, Three Mile Island didn't blow up?"

"Ummmmm, no."

"Then, this isn't the future?"

"Ummmmm, no."

"But we saw the Eiffel Tower!"

"You mean that?" Chad asked, pointing to a jungle gym that a few monkeys climbed on.

"Whew!" Chris said, "That means that I didn't make out with a chimp!"

"No," Chad said. "That did happen."

"BLECK! Why didn't you stop us!"

"You're kidding, right? You two were fun to watch! Me and the other reserve attendants made bets on what you two would do next. We decided to help you out when you showed signs of wanting to leave."

"You made out with a monkey!" Brian said to Chris.

"Shut up!" Chris yelled.

"Yep. Now, why don't you guys take your fridge and get outta here before I call the cops."

"Fine," they said in unison as they started to push their refrigerator up the hill.

Chad laughed and yelled as they walked away, "That musta been some good beer to get you to make-out with a monkey!"

Brian and Chris paused, reached into their pockets and pulled out bottles of their homebrew. Needing a break from pushing their refrigerator, they popped the tops and chugged. Halfway through the second bottle, Chris hiccupped, wobbled and asked, "Where ... where did you say you ... you finded the shushmooms we used for the beers?"

Brian hiccupped and wobbled as well. "Right ... right over there. The blue ... the blue ones."

Chris squinted, then asked, "You mean ... you mean the ones with the ... the white rabbit next to thems?"

"You mean the ... the white rabbit wearing the vest and checking his ... his pocket watch?"

"Yesh."

"You mean ... you mean the white rabbit ... running into the ... the rabbit hole at the base of that tree?"

"Yesh."

"You mean ... you mean the ... the ... let's follow it...."

THE DRUNKEN COMIC BOOK MONKEYS
VS.
THE ISLAND OF DR. MERLOT

I awoke on my back, the sun scorching my face. I did not open my eyes at first, crushing them closed tighter in an effort to thwart the brightness. It did not help. Nor did it stop the fiery rays from baking my face. I rolled to my side, creating my own shade into which I opened my eyes. I saw sand. Sand. I hated sand.

I stood and stumbled, my senses not fully compliant. My bare feet slopped through the muck created by the soft swirls of the ocean waves lapping the shore. The licks of cold water felt refreshing, but the salt residue clung to me, a second skin of discomfort.

Using my hand to shade my eyes, I peered at the horizon, scouring the ocean hoping to find the vessel that brought me this far. Nothing. The view held an unyielding emptiness, akin to my hopes of finding a way back home. As I brought my gaze back to the beach, the flotsam and jetsam riding the tides or sticking from the sands like exaggerated splinters offered all I needed to know about the fate of the ship. Ten yards away, on the beach, lay a piece of wreckage about which I had been curious – my writing partner.

His knees and chest were pressed to the sand, haunches in the air forming a dromedary shaped hump, the left side of his face ensconced by granules, while the right side glowed crimson from the sun's lashing rays. He suckled his thumb while cradling an empty beer bottle like a security blanket. Loathe as I was willing to admit, if I grasped for any illusion of fleeing from this beach and returning to the warm embrace of what I knew as home, Melons Bar & Grille, I would need his assistance.

Gait unsteadied by the random eddies of sand as well as the burning grains baking as hot as the sun itself, I ambled to Chris. I kicked splashes of ocean water upon his face, hoping the salt water would serve as an escort from the lands of Morpheus. Instead, he simply shifted, smacked his smiling lips and mumbled, "A couple more minutes, Ma, and then I'll rub your feet."

Disgusted, I contemplated facing the unknown treacheries of this strange place alone, but inevitably I acquiesced to logic and tried a different approach. I crouched and held my fingers above his bottle, taking a moment to settle my trembling hand for I needed precise timing for what I was about to attempt. In one fluid motion, I yanked the bottle from his grasp and tossed it aside. With an audible slap, his eyes snapped open. He ripped himself from the sand's embrace and lunged toward the bottle, catching it with both hands before it touched the ground. Ever so protective, he swaddled it within his arms and rocked it back and forth while muttering, "My baby. My baby."

"It's empty," I said as I walked over to him.

"Dammit!" he replied, tossing it aside. He sat up and looked around. His features were wrenched about in confusion. "Where are we?"

"Beach of some sort."

"I can see that, genius! Do you know which one? And where's our boat?"

"No idea. And here." I dropped a shredded piece of painted wood the length of his leg next to him.

"That's our boat? What happened?"

"Well, Jeff booked us on a private cruise to the middle of the Pacific, and… and…?"

Realization permeated our addled brains. We looked at each other, then to the ocean, then to the scattered wreckage, our eyes widening with every memory.

"The boat exploded," I whispered.

"Yeah," Chris replied. His gaze saddened. "I feel bad, though. Not many editors book private cruises for their favorite writers, and the one time our editor is so generous, the boat blows up. What are the odds?"

"About as astronomical as our survival chances if we don't come up with a plan."

Chris turned my way and giggled, placing one hand over his mouth while using the other to point at me. "Dude. You're a bit pink."

His visage was half red, half white, as if for some reason only known to him, he had decided to use face paints to mimic the flag of Poland. Too many derogatory comments log-jammed the speech processors of my brain, rendering me remiss with a comment that lacked any form of zeal. "So are you, dude."

Laughter ceased as he brought his fingertips to his cheeks. Upon touching the ruddy half of his face, his eyes attempted escape from his skull. "It burns! It burns!"

"Oh come on, it's not that ...."

But my myopic friend wanted none of the sympathy I offered, nor waited for a plan to be drawn. He opted to sprint headfirst into the unknown of the surrounding jungle, screaming, "Shade! Shade protect me from the cruel beatings of the sun!"

Seeing as I had little choice, I followed. "Stop you moron! If there's one thing Indiana Jones has taught us it's nothing ever good comes from sprinting through a jungle!"

As if proving the hypothesis of a doctorate, a low branch struck his cranium with such force that his still running feet left the ground. As he lay flat on his back, I looked down upon him. "Done freaking out yet?"

Jumping to his feet, he reached into his pants pockets. "Beer. Beer will solve everything."

But he had none to be found. His hands flapped around his body and back in his pockets again and again as if he tried to wrestle invisible fish, refusing to believe his reserves depleted. "I'm empty!"

I removed the last one from my pants pocket, popped the top and savored the succor as the liquid washed past my lips. "Yeah. Me too."

His eyes widened again, the desperation evident. "Dude! Split it with me."

"Nope." I took another swig.

"Seriously! Where is your sharing-is-caring attitude we all learned in kindergarten?"

"I left it in first grade when I swapped it for my greed-is-good doctrine." I retrieved another gulp from the bottle.

"A million dollars! I'll give you a million dollars for that bottle."

"You don't have a million dollars."

He dropped to his knees, his goatee hidden by the froth dripping from his mouth. "What? What do you want for that bottle?"

"I want you to calm the hell down! This place is making you nuts."

"Fine!"

"Promise?"

"YES!"

I bequeathed to him my bottle. Empty. He threw it at me.

Time froze, the only object allowed to act contrary to the new laws of physics was the bottle, spinning end over end at its own languid speed. A stern whistle split the air, the wind rushing over the neck opening as it made its revolutions. The butt of the bottle targeted the space right between my eyes, connecting with such force that imperialistic starbursts infiltrated my vision. Clearly this mysterious place had stripped my friend of his sense of humor. "OOOOOOOWWWWWW!"

"That's what you get! Sissy!"

"You said you wanted the bottle, so I gave you the bottle!"

"You knew I wanted what was *in* the bottle!"

"How was I supposed to know...?" My mouth ceased all activity due to my brain's lack of comprehension at what I thought I saw in my peripheral vision. Confused, I turned. Still unable to make sense of what I was seeing, I at least acknowledged that I did indeed see a goat. "Dude. A goat?"

Chris glanced to it, then turned his attention back to me. "Yeah? So?"

"I'm just trying to figure out what a goat is doing in an island jungle."

"How do you know we're on an island?"

"While on the beach, I couldn't help but notice the curvature of the shoreline."

Brows furrowed, he marched over to the goat and started patting its head, between its curved horns. "You know what? I'm not buying into your Mr. Mensa knows everything shtick this time. First of all, you and I have attended *many* a Peruvian goat-racing event. In Peru. In the *jungles* of Peru. Second of all, so the shoreline had some sharp turns. That could mean we're on an atoll or a peninsula. A Peruvian peninsula. What do you think of that, smart guy?"

Noting that this island, possible peninsula, had negatively affected my friend's demeanor, I no longer wished to antagonize him further lest we traverse down ribald paths leading to only headaches and punching. Since neither of us had proper provisions (beer) for such a trip, I acquiesced. "Fair enough. I was merely stating a hypothesis based on my observations."

"Not so observant now, smart guy!"

"Still a bit more observant than you."

Shifting his posture to display indignation, still petting the goat, he said through snarled lip, "How so?"

"Look at the goat."

Looking down, Chris saw the goat staring up at him, its eyes scarlet with disease and hatred while its mouth frothed with blood laced foam. Chris retracted his hand; narrowly escaping the goat's gnashing teeth. Arms windmilling and legs churning, he raced past me, heading deeper into the dense foliage, screaming, "AAAAAHHH! Rabid jungle goat! Rabid jungle goat!"

I pursued once again, this time because the aforementioned rabid jungle goat now gave chase to us. At first I felt its hot, sickened breath steaming my ankles, but within a few deft weaves among the thick trees, I pulled ahead of my pursuer and caught up with Chris. Just in time to see him run into a fence.

With a bone-jarring rattle, Chris collided with a chain link fence. Fortunately, that afforded me enough time to halt before I shared a similar fate. Noticing that the fence stretched beyond our scope of sight on either direction, and the frothing jungle goat ran with such force that its hooves threw clods of dirt ten feet in the air, Chris and I ascended the fence with an alacrity unbefitting our years. However, when our doughy bodies flopped like potato sacks on the other side, we wheezed like asthmatics with four pack-a-day habits.

The goat snarled and chewed at the fence, as if possessed by an insatiable spirit. Chris and I saw that the fence was sturdy enough to keep the creature at bay; however, we felt more comfortable extricating ourselves from the situation and opted to keep moving. A decision we soon regretted.

With our hastened pace away from the fence, we found ourselves stepping into a grape arbor. Spiraling vines strangled lattice walls; the snaking leaves reaching from everywhere, an out of control hydra with infinite heads. The top of the walls extended a bit taller than me, but the supple vines crept beyond those limits. I assumed the walls were arranged in rows, as we walked down an emerald hallway, at points canopied by vines intertwining from neighboring walls.

As we walked, Chris intermittently slapped himself about the face, neck and shoulders, on occasion yelping if he struck the ruby-shaded side. The drollness of his pseudo-epileptic behavior diminished after a few dozen slaps. My curiosity breaching containment, I asked, "Dude! What the hell?"

"Something keeps tickling me!" he snapped, punctuating his statement with a meaty smack from his right palm against the back of his neck.

I chortled. "You have bugs."

"I don't think it's bugs, dude. I think ... I think it's the leaves."

"Now, you're just ...."

Chris interrupted my thought with a hit to his own shoulder. "Dammit! This is driving me crazy!"

"It could be the...."

Another slap cut my words short. "And the whispering too!"

"Whispering?"

"Yeah! Can't you hear it?"

"Hear what?"

"Whispering, jackass! It's all around us. *All* around us!"

Now I knew the lack of civilization and all the accoutrements associated with it (beer) was having a negative effect on my friend. Not being a stranger to babbling like a loon, his words seemed different this time. They had heart, soul. They were sober.

I looked around and watched the leaves rustle.

A chill rippled my spine as I realized there was no wind.

And I heard the whispering too.

"Stop it!" Chris yelled, clapping his hands over his ears. "It's more maddening than techno music! Make it stop!"

"Dude! Get a hold of yourself! Stop being stupid!" I replied, oozing sympathy.

Unable to cope any more, Chris ran, hands still covering his ears, screaming the whole time, "You're wrong! Wine is not better than beer! Beer is better than wine! Beer is better than wine!"

Confused, I gave chase. We both ran, hoping to escape this odd grape-lined madness, and saw a glimpse of salvation as we neared the border. We were wrong. That was where the true madness began.

Bursting from ensnaring vines, we stumbled into an arboretum of small fruit trees – pear, plum, apple, peach and cherry. The thick smells of the various fruits assaulted our senses as the low branches assaulted our persons. Chaos reigned as we tried to stumble forward and still avoid the branches, which I swear, whipped at us. Over-ripe fruits pelted us. We both raised our arms to protect our faces as we pushed onward, hoping to escape this labyrinth. The constant pummeling by fruits and the smacking from branches took its toll on both of us, each hit yielding a yelp or scream. However, ours were not the only voices.

"Outsiders!"

"Unwelcomed!"

"Get out!"

"Leave!"

"Wine is better than beer!"

"Intruders!"

"Unclean!"

Pressing forward, we lumbered through the trees, lashed and beaten. At last with one final burst, we dove out of the insane fruit forest. We both stumbled and tripped, landing face first. The dirt remained soft, but not quite as sandy as the beach on which we had awoken. After a few labored breaths, I raised my head to be greeted by ten toes in a pair of open sandals. As fate would have it, the toes were indeed attached to feet, which in turn were attached to spindly legs and knobby knees, jutting out from multi-pocketed khaki shorts.

"Greetings! I am Doctor Merlot. And who might you two be?"

Fighting through the pain caused by our recent bludgeoning, Chris and I struggled to our feet to greet the doctor. He stood no taller than five and half feet and wore a short-sleeved shirt the same color of his shorts and a wide brimmed, flat topped hat. The white hair leading from under his hat to the equally white and uneven beard about his face indicated that he had spent many more years on this planet than either Chris or I; the bulbous belly indicated that many of those years had been prosperous. He also cradled in his left arm a potted kumquat tree, a foot in height.

"I'm Brian. This is Chris."

Merlot squinted: his eyes examining us, attempting to discern if I had spoken the truth. He chuckled and shook his head, erasing a stray and nonsensical thought. "You two look more akin to a mountain Yeti and a Cro-Magnon man. But no matter. Welcome to my island."

With smug smile, I whispered to Chris, "See? Island. Not peninsula. Not atoll. Island."

"Shut up," Chris replied.

"How about the goat?" I asked Merlot.

"Goat? What goat? There are no indigenous goats on this island," he answered.

I didn't even need to speak to convey the 'I told you so' to Chris. He heard it loud and clear.

"Shut up!"

Not knowing when to leave well enough alone, I continued. "How about the whispering in the grape arbor?"

Merlot smiled and clapped his hands together, excited by my statement. "Oh excellent! My babies are awake! Joyous news! Joyous news indeed!"

"HA!" Chris screamed at me. "HA! HAHAHA! Suck it,

Sasquatch!"

Doing a jig around me, Chris waved a middle finger and continued his tirade; "I found this for you in the parking lot!"

Shocked by him resorting to such base and vile actions, I expressed my displeasure. "You don't have to be so mean about it."

Chris paused and stroked his goatee while looking skyward, pondering my comment. Satisfied with his choice, he returned to jigging, but this time displaying both middle fingers. He squeezed his fists with such force, the prominent digits turned red while his other knuckles went white. "Actually, I do. Here, I found a second one since you enjoyed the first one so much!"

His dance failed to last more than a few minutes as the nature of Dr. Merlot's words simmered in our brains. Chris and I looked at each other, confused, attempting to make sense of Merlot's last statement. We then turned to him and asked, "Babies? Awake?"

"Oh, yes. Yes. Follow me. Follow me!" he said with the timbre of a child rushing to the gift-encircled tannenbaum on Christmas morn. We followed. As the puckish man led us back through the combative fruit forest, he offered gleeful wishes for a good morning while touching random branches and dangling fruit with his right hand, his left still cradling the diminutive kumquat tree. Thanks to our many misadventures, the idea of a man talking to trees hardly bothered us. What did bother us was the fact that we heard his well wishes returned to him.

Dumbfounded by what we witnessed, Chris and I peered into the canopy overhead as we walked, looking for the source of the mysterious voices. None could be found. And what we experienced next made our skin crawl.

Back to the grape field, Chris started shaking, his anxiety dictating that he swat at his ears and shoulders as if shooing flies. The doctor approached the myriad grape vines with his arms outstretched, a preacher readying his congregation for sermon. Or a dictator preparing his troops for war. "Good morning, my children!"

"Good morning, Doctor Merlot," came from the arbor, a chorus of soft overlapping voices sweeping through the foliage like a soothing breeze. Chris and I stood on our toes, craned our necks, desperate to discover the source of the replies. Nothing. My Mensa brain could not solve this puzzle, and I *needed* answers!

"Where the hell are the voices coming from?" I asked.

"From them," Merlot answered, his brows arched to convey his confusion by my question.

"Them who?"

"Them, the grapes."

Stunned silence gripped my throat. Judging from Chris's stupor, he found difficulty in comprehending Merlot's words as well. "You can't be serious."

"Oh, but he is," Merlot's kumquat tree replied.

That was the first time we noticed the tree. It held only two oblong fruits, toward the top, peering at us like eyes. The way the branches angled and arced about gave the little tree ersatz facial features, including well-placed leaves as eyebrows. And its 'eyebrows' furrowed.

"Now, now, Larry," Merlot said to the tree in a pseudo-scolding tone. "They are outsiders. This is a new experience for them."

"Outsiders should be banished!" Larry replied.

"You named your kumquat tree 'Larry'?" I asked.

"Of course!" Merlot replied. "What else would you name a kumquat tree?"

Stumped again. I had no rejoinder. But I still needed answers. "What ... the hell ... is with the talking fruit?"

Merlot started to pet Larry; the tiny tree's leaves trembled with appreciation. "I assume you mean, why? Why I engineered the grapes and other fruits to talk? For information, of course!"

"For scientific advancement?"

"No. Oh, good heavens, no. There is no money in that whatsoever! For wine!"

"Wine? Are you *kidding* me?"

"No. The fruits supply me with tremendous amounts of information. They tell me the optimum PH and nitrogen levels for their soil. They tell me what I need to do to make them as succulent and juicy as possible."

"But wine? Why not just sell the fruit?"

"Silly, boy! These grapes here, no matter how delicious, could only fetch me a few dollars per pound. Turn them into wine – a high quality wine – and I can ask for hundreds of dollars per bottle."

"I'd like to invest, please!"

"Our wine is good! The best wine there is!" a few vines worth of nearby grapes opined.

Frowning, Chris mumbled, "But it's not better than beer."

"You are wrong, Outsider. Wine is better!"

"What do you know? You're a bunch of stupid grapes!"

"We know that wine is the preferred drink of the gods! Made in reverence to gain their favor."

Incensed, and shocked that the grapes knew their history, Chris retorted, "Preferred drink of … are you kidding me? Beer was the *original* drink of the gods! First brewed in ancient Egypt."

"To keep the unwashed heathens stupid and satisfied."

"Then the aristocrats discovered how divine it was!"

"That's right. But they decided to take it one step further, by making wine."

"That's ridiculous!"

"What's ridiculous is you arguing with grapes," I intervened.

"They started it!" Chris whined.

"But, in theory, you're more evolved, so you should have ended it."

"When have I ever done that? It's like you don't even know me!"

I sighed. "Come on, Johnny Cochran. Merlot wants to show us around the island."

We followed Merlot from arbors to orchards to fields, Chris arguing with every piece of fruit along the way until Merlot showed us the barley field; a nirvana for my writing partner. Once again, he frothed like a rabid dog.

"Beer parts," he moaned, ready to dive into the sea of grains.

Merlot frowned. "Hardly! This is for barley wine."

"No," Chris whispered as he walked toward the flowing field.

"No. Barley is meant for beer."

"Barley is meant for wine," the closest stalks of barley replied.

"Beer!" Chris shouted at the waving wisps of barley.

"Wine!" the barley shouted back, as best the barley could.

Seeing the emotional toll taken by the tears in my friend's eyes, I grabbed him by the arm and escorted him from the tumultuous situation. "Come on. There's more to see."

Withdrawn, Chris followed along as I walked beside Merlot for the rest of the tour of what our host called 'the campus'. It reminded me more of a scene from any pulp adventure novel set in the jungle. A dirt road led to a dirt cul-de-sac with a Jeep parked in the middle. Surrounding the barren circle were wooden buildings, all square and sided with long planks in need of a paint job. The living quarters, three buildings, were embellished with porches, attempting to be stately with their fluted banisters and hourglass columns. Two other buildings, both twice as large as any of the living quarters, were on site as well. While Merlot attempted to smooth things over with Chris regarding the barley outburst, I meandered over to one of the larger buildings and opened the door for a peek inside. Surprise overwhelmed me when I saw what it housed – inflatable dolls. The whole building was filled with them in various stages of inflation, most had their arms and legs soldier straight, all wearing the mouth agape expression of surprise. I stifled a chuckle.

"Ahhh, yes, yes. I see you have stumbled upon the supply shed," Merlot said as he trotted over, making haste to shut the door lest I venture inside. Accompanied by an elbow jab and wink, he whispered, "It can get quite lonely on this island."

I cringed at his words and my stomach lurched at the thought. I offered no resistance as he shut the door and directed me toward the living quarters.

Chris had already claimed one of the cabins. I peeked in and saw him in the fetal position on top of the bed's sheets. My presence went unnoticed, as his gaze remained focused afar. He could only mumble, "No beer. There's no beer here. Beer is better than wine. Better than wine. Barley is beer parts, not wine parts. Barley is beer parts, not wine parts."

The setting sun reminded me that we had endured a very long day, factoring in surviving a cruise liner explosion, no beer, a rabid jungle goat, no beer, talking fruit, and finding the eccentric, albeit hospitable, creator of said talking fruit, only to discover he had no beer on this island he called home. I decided to leave Chris to his impending night of fitful sleep. I walked next to Merlot as he escorted me to my cabin. "Do you happen to have a radio of any sort in which we can call for help? As fascinating as this island is, we do belong elsewhere."

"Ahhh, yes, yes. Understandable. Unfortunately, my sole radio is on the colloquial 'fritz'. I have been trying to repair it, but keeping up with my orchards has been quite time consuming."

I sighed, knowing where this would go if I did not surrender immediately. "Chris and I would be more than happy to assist with the orchards and arbors while you work on repairing the radio."

"Splendid!" he said with an enthusiastic clap of his hands, which made Larry the kumquat plant none too happy as it displayed a frown with its leaves. "We'll see you bright and early tomorrow."

Truer words had not been spoken. As the night's indigo gave way to dawn's amber, Merlot startled both Chris and I awake and instructed us to meet him at the second of the large buildings, the winery.

"Dude, you look terrible," I greeted Chris. His sunburn having subsided only a slight bit, his eyes veined with burning red, and locks of his goatee spread in random directions.

"Unh," he grunted. "No breakfast beer."

I felt sluggish as well, due to the combination of waking up at a time usually reserved for sleep mixed with the lack of beer. Dr. Merlot greeted us with his usual impish grin and high-on-life outlook that grated on my nerves. However, I smiled along and offered exemplary manners and assistance in menial and mundane chores. Chris worked too, but at a pace devoid of luster, even for him. All the while Merlot fed us the promise of repairing the radio, although I noticed that he spent an inordinate amount of time in the supply shed. As disturbing as that thought might have been, I focused more on the lethargy of my friend. After the sun set and Merlot invited us to dinner, including an endless supply of wine. Chris ate, but drank only water; a far off gaze befell him at mention of any other beverage.

The following day was worse. He lingered with his chores, slacked in his tasks. Chris's jovial nature was left wanting.

"What up, Jerky?" I asked during breakfast of our fourth day on the island.

"Nuthin'," he replied. No sardonic counter. No impassioned middle finger. Nothing.

"Ready for another day of back breaking labor while Merlot plays 'doctor' in his ... supply ... shed?"

"Yep."

"I've been tending to the grape arbors. Interesting bunch. Where've you been working?"

"Barley fields."

"Yeah? Interesting?"

"Not really."

"Well, today I'm going to check out the grape preparation room of the winery. Wanna take a look?"

"Naah."

Alas, as breakfast ended in silence and Chris made his way to the barley fields. I saw no other recourse than following my original plan. After cursory morning salutations with Merlot, I entered the winery and found the grape preparation room. I had not realized that Dr. Merlot was without his usually omnipresent kumquat tree, Larry, until I opened the door. Waves of nausea crashed about my belly.

Rows, dozens of rows, of grape vines dangled from the head and hand holes of a wooden stockade. More vines were strapped to a rack, chained to it from both top and bottom of the device. Every vine was replete with ripened grapes. Every grape wore a tiny leather hood, some with zippers for mouths; others resembled garish luche libre masks. All moaned and writhed in ecstasy.

"Pulp me!"

"My turn!"

"I'm swollen with juice!"

"Turn me into wine!"

"I'm a dirty, dirty grape!"

"Harder! Faster!"

"Squeeze me! Step on me! Step on me, then squeeze me!"

To add to the images I most certainly would have nightmares about for months, in the center of the madness was Larry. Uprooted and sans pot, he paced to and fro, cracking a whip held with one set of branches while snapping at cat-o-nine-tail with another set. Seatless leather chaps adorned his roots.

Unable to endure any more, I retreated. Needing to share the revolting image with Chris, I ran to the barley fields. Once there, I froze. What I witnessed there attempted to claim ownership for the nausea roiling around in my belly. Chris, shirtless, rolled around in a thick patch of barley while giggling. Stalks of the grains folded over and tickled him. Revolt twisted my face as I brought my hands to my eyes in an attempt to hide what I saw. Thoughts of simply plucking them from my skull skittered through my head as I heaved out the words, "DUUUUUDE! Put a shirt on!"

Startled by my appearance, he did as I had asked and after excusing himself to the barley stalks, made his way over to where I stood fighting disgust. Picking stray grains from his goatee, he asked, "What?"

Still wincing, I replied, "I wanted to tell you about something gross that I saw, but I see that you're busy doing something gross yourself."

"Ha, ha. Very funny. What'd you see?"

"It was the grape preparation room. Crazy! Vines of ripened grapes were everywhere, wearing bondage gear. And the worst part was Larry was there! That creepy little plant of Merlot's was walking around with a..."

"Walking?" Chris interrupted. "Did you say walking?"

"Yeah. He was using his roots as legs. It was the craziest..."

"Yeah," Chris interrupted again. He turned back to the flowing field of barley. "Sounds crazy. Look, I still gotta do some more chores. I'll catch up with you later."

I watched Chris walk into the field once more, the stalks tall enough to envelop him. As he disappeared, I realized that if we were to escape from this mad island, I alone needed to provide the means.

Over the next few days, I saw Chris less and less frequently. At times he even chose sleeping in the barley fields over the comforts of the bed in his cabin. At the same time Merlot's level of agitation increased. No longer wearing the happy-go-lucky smile of a satisfied man, he stomped about the campus like a paranoid king fearful of losing his throne. He found information from some grapes falsified. Certain trees hid their fruits from him. And the barley ... well, the barley had become downright unruly.

Hiding in the shadows, I watched Merlot interrogate a vine of grapes. He gripped the strand as if trying to strangle a serpent. Dangling from his clenched fist, the vine yielding a dozen grapes twitched and squirmed. "What is the meaning of this? Why are you lying to me? I double-checked the PH numbers your area gave me, and they're way off. What you've requested would turn you bitter. Why?"

"We'll never talk," the grapes whispered in unison. "We'll never spill our guts."

"Who put you up to this?"

With their final act of rebellion, all one dozen grapes shook, and inflated to the bursting point. Their skins spilt, pulpy seed sacks fell to the ground.

"AAAAARG!" Merlot snarled, throwing the lifeless vine to the ground. "Where's Larry?"

As Merlot stormed off, I knew what I had to do and I knew I was running out of time.

That night, I stole the keys to the Jeep.

The following day I drove to the barley field to determine the working condition of the Jeep and to see if I could ascertain the details of whatever Chris had been doing with the barley. Much to my surprise and relief, the Jeep was in perfect working condition. After I made a stop at the supply shed, I followed the dirt road to the barley field. I hoped I would be able to talk to my friend, find the needle of sanity in the haystack of confusion. When I arrived, I trounced the brakes, fishtailing to a halt within a cloud of dust. Eyes wide, I became suddenly aware of my own ragged breaths of dismay, hoping what I saw was merely an illusion, a mad distortion of reality caused by over-exposure to this damnable island. Alas, as the dust settled, the nebula of dream dissipated to expose the starkness of awakening. The barley field was gone.

Fear gripped my heart as I turned the Jeep around. Wondering to what extent Chris had taken this madness, I raced over the barely visible paths through the forest to the main grape arbors that we had stumbled through our first day here. My stomach twisted once I arrived.

Pure calamity set the scene. Half of the lattice walls were bare. The grape vines that remained fought with each other. Emerald tendrils lashed at each other, whipping grape bullets through the air. I suspected that the orchards would show a similar theater. I knew where the missing fruits and barley had gone. The campus.

Knowing no better way to get back to the campus, I sped through the arbor. Lattice walls splintered, grapes splattered against the Jeep and greenery became ensnared in every edge and corner of the vehicle. Soft screams of anguish and protest roared louder than the revving engine. I burst through to the campus cul-de-sac and fishtailed to a stop again. My mind fought with itself, trying to rationalize how I came to be in the middle of such a war. Flame engulfed two of the buildings as well as dozens of barley stalks running ... *running* ... through the campus turned battlefield. A phalanx of grape vines attempted to stop the advances of a battalion of barley. Uprooted trees grappled with each other, crushing barley and grapes alike as they wrestled about. From the corner of my eye, I saw a cherry tree working with barley and grapes to drag a screaming Merlot to the winery, Larry followed, chaps and cat-o-nine tails at the ready. Through the madness I found what I sought – Chris on his knees bellowing to the heavens, "What have I done? All I wanted was a beer!"

Kicking open the passenger door, I yelled, "Dude!"

Dejected, but knowing there was no other option, he jumped in. Vines and stalks whipped at us as we sped away. Trees threw their fruits, some cracking the windshield. A few tried to step in front of us, but their movements were cumbersome at best, easily avoidable.

We drove to the beach and leapt from the Jeep. Noises from the jungle indicated that our time was short. Unloading what I had packed from the supply building, Chris understood the plan before I said a word. Using twine, we secured dozens of Merlot's inflatables to form an ersatz raft. We set sail just as the army of fruits and barley burst from the jungle. Peaches and plums splashed around our raft as we escaped. Floating away, we could do nothing more than watch the island burn.

Once we drifted to the point at which the horizon engulfed the island, Chris moved to the far end of the raft, keeping his back to me. As best I could, I crept close enough to peer over his shoulder and see that he cradled a few stalks of barley....

THE DRUNKEN COMIC BOOK MONKEYS
VS.
THE CENTER OF THE EARTH

It seems clear to me now, though the *now* to which I refer remains muddled, that the greatest impetus that drives a man away from a settled life is the romance between him and the undiscovered. To rise to a great challenge. To snatch victory from the jaws of failure. To meet the frontier with a broad smile. And what grander frontier than that of time itself? For centuries men have concerned themselves with petty frontiers: the hollows of the Earth, the depths of the ocean, the plenum of space. And, in their turn, there was smug satisfaction to be found at journey's end. But that satisfaction would always be short lived and the next beyond beckoned. As always there was a man who took up the torch, who fought back the shadows, who dared to spelunk...

"Dude! Why are you talking like that?" Brian yelled.

"What manner of mangy troglodyte are you that speaks with the words of human children?" Chris replied.

"Ouch! You freak! You totally stabbed me! Is that...?"

"Lay yourself low, mannish beast, lest I be forced...."

"Why do you have a plastic sword?" Brian asked, rubbing the reddened spot between his ribs.

"For this, foul beast," Chris replied while giving Brian a whack in the shins.

"Ow!"

"And this!" A poke in the solar plexus.

"Ow! OW!"

"And this!" A slash across the upper thigh.

"Ow! OW! OWOW!"

"Ha ha! Take that, knave. And that, villain!" Like an oddly misshapen parody of an oddly misshapen swordsman, Chris performed perfectly executed pirouettes and lunges while hacking and slashing at the craven form before him. With whorls and swirls....

"I'll whorl and swirl you, punk!" Brian, prone, yelled amidst the sounds of combat that resonated throughout the room each time Chris struck at him.

Brian threw a flip-flop in his direction, but Chris laughed, dodging the missile with ease, then blending the defensive maneuver with an offensive move in a delicate dance of grace, balance, dexterity....

CRASH!

...until Chris tripped over the flung flip-flop.

"Dude!" Chris yelled, on the ground, holding his shin.

"Serves you right, punk!"

"Flip-flops? Seriously! You are so losing man points!"

"They're man sandals! Mandals!"

"Same difference if your furry feet are exposed to the world at large!"

"You're always hatin'!"

"Whatever! Here's your sissy shoe," said Chris as he heaved it in Brian's direction.

"Ow!"

A grin spread like a stain across Chris's face at the sound of the impact.

"You're an angry, young man," Brian declared, wrestling his retrieved shoe back on to his foot. "And what's with the toy sword?"

"It's a cane sword. I thought it would go well with my costume for the night."

"Dude, it's a toy sword and if you lean your blubberous butt on it, you'll," Brian hesitated watching the mental image of Chris toppling over after his plastic cane collapsed and realized it would cause him to laugh. When he was able to control his giggle fit, he continued, "look very dapper. Very dapper, indeed. Might I take a moment, however, to inquire exactly why said costume is needed for tonight?"

"You forgot, didn't you?"

"Of course not!" Brian said.

"Yes, you did. You forgot!"

"I didn't forget at all. I was just hoping to find out about your ultra secret costume...to make sure we're not wearing the same thing. You remember last Halloween, right?"

Both men cringed. The memory replayed itself, a ghastly specter from the past. As if frequently rehearsed, both men pulled a beer from their respective beer pocket and downed them in a single gulp making a juvenile attempt to kill the brain cell responsible for housing that particular memory. It was an action they had employed unsuccessfully on several occasions. According to Brian's calculations, however, the odds of success were improving. Chris shook off the revulsion that accompanied the memory.

"You did look like 'Gaythoven', though. Just saying," Chris said, referring to what the attendees at the Halloween party called him.

"Au contraire! That was you, my stunted growth friend," Brian replied. "Incidentally, did your parents bind your feet as a child, too? You know – to match your pixie-like height. Just wondering."

"Very mature! But your misguided little attempt to distract me into revealing my costume for tonight has failed."

"Dude! That whole argument was like six invisible paragraphs above your head ago. Of course," Brian said, tapping his forefinger against his fur covered chin, "if we put those paragraphs under your feet, instead, then maybe you'd be tall enough..."

"Yes. And you still don't remember the purpose of *this* costume, do you?"

Chris retrieved a series of large boxes and began rummaging through them intermittently waving random articles at Brian. First, an adventurer's cape made of fine black cloth. In a pinch, it could be drawn over the mouth and nose to keep out dust. Next a pair of fine hiking boots, also black. A bandolier belt. Various and sundry small belt pouches. A pair of black utility pants...Brian shifted his weight from one foot to the other and back again in a sort of tarantella.

"Dude, I..."

Chris began to tap his toe. The sound was like a burrowing insect gnawing its way into the secret place where Brian hid his brain.

"I FORGOT, OK?"

"Not really, no, but knowing is half the battle."

"So what is tonight, already?"

Chris walked over to the desk that was the resting place of the Fortress Publishing, Inc. inbox. It cradled within a single piece of parchment. Retrieving it gently, Chris held it out for Brian to read. Brian reached for it.

"Whoa, whoa, whoa! Read with your eyes, not with your..."

"Fists? As in the ones I'm about to pulverize you with?"

"You're so hostile all the time."

"You make it that way, punk! Now gimme that," Brian said snatching the letter from Chris's hand. Hastily, he scanned the contents of the page. His mouth fell slack. "An invitation to the Legend Breaker's show! You mean the guys on TV who take urban legends and put them through tests to see if they could be true or not? Those guys are great! But why on Earth would they want to invite us to be on their show?"

"Clearly, we're the guests of honor!"

"Dude," Brian said, retrieving a bottle of beer from his pant's pocket, then popping the top, commented, "have you been hitting the cursed moonshine again?"

"Think about it! We have no reason being invited to ANY party, let alone one like this. It has to be something one of our fans...." At this, both men broke out into hysterical laughter and it was some time before Chris was finally able to pull himself together enough to continue his thought, "came up with to get us invited."

"Dude, all I know is," Brian said washing down his words with swigs of beer, "last time we went to a party, we met Drunkenstein. If Bride of Drunkenstein shows up this time, you're out drinking her on your own, pal!"

"Nice! Now, go get a costume so we can go to this soiree."

"Dude! That's more perverted than I'm comfortable with!"

"Ummm, it's a party, doofus."

"Yeah, but you *centelleo* when you say it! I'm not doing any more jail time in Tijuana! Your *centelleo* is out of hand! You need professional help."

"Whatever! Go get ready and be back here in two hours."

***

"Dude! I just can't believe it!" Brian yelled.

"Well, believe it!" Chris yelled back.

"We're going to a party, thrown by The Legend Breakers, and we're the guests of honor!"

"I know it. I KNOW IT! All of our effort over the last <cough> ...teen years has FINALLY paid off! Bet they want us to help them do stuff!"

"Ummm...slow your roll, there, chief. Exactly what sort of 'stuff' are you thinking about?"

"Stop being dumb! Like making stuff explode! And forging medieval weapons! And making plants grow by singing!"

"No one needs to hear you sing?"

"Whatever! Oh, I got it! Urban legends involving beer! They want us to 'break' beer legends! How cool is that? I'll bet Drunkenstein was bragging about us again and it caught someone's ear...."

"You mean to say 'he bit someone's ear'!"

"Settle down, oh eater-of-too-many-burritos!"

"Yeah, see...there's no such thing as too MANY burritos!" Brian insisted.

"Ya know, you could show a little bit of enthusiasm here. Anyway, I pulled off a cool adventurer's costume. And it's largely functional, too. I could last about ten days outside of civilization with this get up. Not to mention the cane sword...I believe you're already acquainted...."

"Don't get me started on that thing!"

"So? What's your costume?"

"Well, being that it's The Legend Breakers and all, I went with a figure of legend. I'm Paul Bunyan. Big axe, denim overalls, red kerchief, and flannel shirt."

"And I suppose you have a giant blue ox somewhere?"

"Well, sort of...."

"What's 'sort of? Do we have to notify the International Association of Zoologists?"

"The IAZ? Puh-lease! Not even close. Just don't let CAN-MEAT get wind of this!"

"Canadian Mothers for Ethical Animal Treatment? Other than your back, do you have some abnormally hairy hide to take with you to the studio party?"

"Nice! But, no! It's not a hide. Well, I brought furry slippers in case my feet get cold. And a <cough, cough>."

Wan face going more wan, Chris crossed his arms over his chest, "Um, a what? What exactly did you use to make 'Babe' the big blue ox?"

"A <cough, ack, wheeze>...er."

"Out with it!"

"Alright, alright! A fifty-gallon meat cooler. I put it in the trunk of the Fortressmobile already."

"Fifty-gallon...!"

"I had a weird dream that we went to the party and they only had finger foods and I almost passed out from starvation pains! So I brought some buffalo jerky and a few other choice items...."

"A few? Dude, you could stuff a whole hecatomb in a fifty gallon cooler!"

"A heca-what? Look, before we get to this studio party, let's talk about you reining in that vocabulary of yours."

"Dude, your lunch is the largest carnivorous single meal since the T-Rex actually walked! A hecatomb is the sacrifice of 100 oxen to the ancient gods, you uneducated cretin. Though in your case it simply means a 'snack'."

"Yeah, that's kinda what I thought. That makes sense, then. Well, just don't go pulling any other crazy language bombs out of your hat, Bullwinkle!"

"Alright, alright," Chris said, hands held up in a motion of surrender. "Let's just get to the studio, shall we?"

"Yeah, we don't wanna be late. To the Fortress mobile!"

***

It was a forty-two minute drive to the studio, according to Mapquest. The Fortress mobile, a gray Saturn, with Chris at the helm, made it in thirty-one. Add in a thirty-five minute holdup at the gate with security, which included a pat down that didn't thrill Brian and left Chris a little woozy ("How come you got the girl security guard?" Brian whined), and the Fortress guys arrived nominally late as was their expected norm in all circles. Once on the grounds, Chris guided the Fortress mobile to the designated inner gate. Again, they stopped for a security checkpoint.

The guard sauntered over to the vehicle and asked if he could help them. "Yes, sir," Chris answered. "We have tickets to a studio party with The Legend Breakers. Studio Seven."

"Studio Seven?" the guard asked. "Let me see your tickets, please."

"Sure thing," Chris said. "But please don't mess them up."

"They are going in our scrapbook," Brian added. "Right next to the autographed pictures of Saika."

"Ok. They look legit. Head down to Studio Seven, just as it says on your tickets. Allow me to restate that you're looking for studio seven. It's on the left, gents. Enjoy."

"Oh, sure thing! We're not looking for any trouble here," Chris stated. With that he drove on past the gate, eyes straining in the darkness to find studio seven.

They prowled the lot, headlights showing what was in front of them and on occasion giving glimpses of the building faces. Neither of the men found it odd that all streetlights and building floodlights were off, save for one building further down the lot.

"Dude!" Brian yelled, smacking Chris. "It's there on the right, jackass!"

"The guard distinctly said it was on the left. The even numbers

77

are on the right!"

"Yes, but the sign for that studio said The Legend Breakers. The ticket is wrong! And you're an accomplice to the wrongness!"

"Dude, that doesn't even make sense! How can one be 'accomplice to the wrongness'?"

"Lots of ways! And only you can find them all! Now go back!"

"No way! We're here, punk! Studio seven. This is the only building with lights on. Probably this is their backup studio or the place where the parties are held."

"I got a bad feeling about this...like you're wrong or something!"

"Whatever, stupid! Now get outta the car! We're already late as it is. We don't want to miss any more of the party. And don't forget any parts of your costume!"

"Oh, sheesh!" Brian exclaimed. "Thanks for reminding me! I almost forgot my ersatz 'Babe' the big blue ox. Here, help me with this thing."

"What? I'm not helping you lug that ridiculous monstrosity around. It weighs like three hundred pounds!"

"See? This is why we need a dolly!" Brian yelled.

"Dude, if 'dolly' is a woman's name and she's serving some purpose OTHER than hauling stuff around, then I'm all in. But if 'dolly', in fact, refers to a two-wheeler of some sort, then that junk's for sissies! You wanna be a sissy? Or you wanna be a sasquatch?"

Brian looked balefully at Chris. The reproach he didn't mind in the least. In fact, it simply meant an extra shoulder punch for the shorter man. But he couldn't carry the cooler by himself and he simply couldn't bring himself to leave out any of the contents that he had so lovingly packed. The difficulty in being a decent person, it seems, is living with the guilt and, in the end, Chris grabbed an end of the cooler and helped Brian inside the studio.

"Dude, this really means...."

"That's enough, wussy!" Chris said. "You just better be in a sharing mood with this stuff!"

"DUDE!" Brian yelled. "This is barely a breakfast! You should have planned better!"

"Whatever! Ok, so...we're here! Two Drunken Comic Book Monkeys, as ordered!" Chris announced.

Before them stretched out a huge, though empty warehouse. Bare concrete walls met their gaze in every direction. Even the floor stared at them with the unyielding visage of cold, bare concrete. Clearly, Chris and Brian reasoned, this was the room where stunts were done for the show; thus, the need for so much open space.

"I can't wait to meet The Legend Breakers!"

"Ummm...hello...?" came a call from the back.

"Dude, quick! Get your 8 x 10 glossy out. After spending some time with us, they may not be in any kind of mood to sign stuff!" Chris whispered to Brian.

"Oh, good thinking," Brian whispered back.

"Sorry, we're late!" Chris offered. "We had some problems at the guard shack...."

"Dude! Don't say stuff like that! They'll think we're stalkerish or something!" Brian reprimanded.

"Oh, yeah, right. Ummmm..." Chris stammered.

Brian quickly jumped in. "The guard was confused about which studio we should be going to!"

"Right!" Chris agreed, then mouthed to Brian, "nice save."

"And then the place looks so empty," Brian said. Then he had a look around. "Like, really empty! Dude, have you looked around at this place?"

"Yeah...there's nothing here...which means...."

"Which means there's no finger food," Brian said as he sprinted back towards his cooler. He produced five locks from his jacket pocket, then proceeded to snap four of them into place, one on each side of the cooler. From his other pocket he retrieved a length of chain, and after wrapping it around all four sides, used the fifth lock to secure it in place.

"You're ridiculous!"

"Yeah, ridiculously well prepared," Brian said. "I've been on to you ever since the hot wing fiasco! I pegged you for a Marxist and this is NOT communal property!"

"Really? A Marxist?"

"Yup! Spiritual philanthropy is not a healthy hobby, dude. Not to mention, it's a dead giveaway. You command some crazy philosopherish powers, my friend. But I'm immune to your wizardly ways!"

"Ummmm...excuse me," said a young man that Chris estimated to be in his twenties with mutton chop sideburns that tapered into his crew cut. Tattoos raced up his right arm and his left ear had more needle shaped piercings protruding from it than a large cactus. "You're late, which put us a bit off schedule. Nice adventurer outfit!"

"Thank you! I'm glad someone can appreciate a little effort," Chris said, pointedly looking away from Brian.

"And you must be...no, wait...don't tell me! Lots of flannel... you must be Canadian Man? A '90s grunge music fan? A lesbian truck driver?"

"Paul Bunyan!" Brian shouted, indignity bristling.

"Oh, right. Where's your axe?"

"It's right...aw, dude, we have to go back to the car! I couldn't carry the axe and the cooler at the same time."

"Sorry about your luck, pal," Chris said. "As fate would have it, I just entered my Machiavellian Marxist stage. Get it yourself."

"Punk! Hey wait...there's no such thing as a Machia...."

"Please, sir," Chris said to the host, "lead on. He can catch up later."

"Oh, that's just wrong," Brian complained as he trudged his way back out to the car.

"Cool. On with the tour. That over there is our wall."

"Nice! What do you do with the wall? Use at as a backdrop for high level explosives?"

"No. It holds up that part of the roof. This over here is our other wall. There are two more of them around here...can you find them on your own?"

"Oh, you betcha," Chris piped. "There's one there and then this one behind us. Right?"

"Wow, you're good," came the deadpan answer from the tour

guide. "Over there is the door into the back part of the studio. You are expected so just go right on in. And that concludes my part of the tour. The rest of the guys are waiting in the back. Enjoy!"

"Cool! Thanks," Chris said to the tour guide. *I guess that was the quick version of the tour because we put them so far behind schedule,* Chris reasoned to himself. *If we're actually gonna do some Legend Breaking, then maybe we'll have to pick partners and if that's the case, I'm not waiting on Brian.* With that decided, Chris broke into a run for the door along the back wall, slipping through before Brian had a chance to re-enter the studio.

In direct defiance to the abandoned part of the studio, the back part teemed with activity and props and atmosphere. A buffet style table had been set up off to one side and Chris aimed for it while being greeted heartily by several members of the cast and crew. Thinking that Brian would be here any second and wouldn't hesitate to scarf down the choicest of the morsels, Chris grabbed a plate and set to eating with gusto. Sure enough, a minute had scarce passed when he heard Brian on the other side of the wall asking questions of the tour guide, who reluctantly agreed to help Brian push his cooler to the door.

There was much grunting and cursing from the other side of the wall and as Chris filled his second plate with desserts (they had cannoli, after all), Brian finally burst through the door, cooler in tow. Sweat dripping off his brow, the taller Monkey met with the crew, about a dozen strong, Chris estimated, watching the proceedings over the rim of his plate. Brian found the buffet table. Instead of taking a plate, he simply grabbed the nearest serving platter and helped himself.

"Dude! Did you try the rangoon? It's delicious!" Brian said, food spraying from his mouth. When the platter was bare, he set it down and moved on to the next one in line.

"Gentleman," one of the crewmembers said, "are you ready to meet The Legend Breakers?"

"You, betcha!" Chris exclaimed. "Do you think they'll sign the pictures we brought? I have my own sharpie!"

"I'm sure they will be pleased to do that for you. And then

81

you're going to help them with an experiment. Sound like fun?"

"Hot dog!" Brian said, crumbs brachiating through his goatee. "Are there any more hot dogs?"

"Here they are – The Legend Breakers! Aaron and John!"

"Hi, guys! I'm John," said a tall man with a mass of facial hair about his mouth. A fedora sat neatly perched atop his head.

"And I'm, uh, Aaron," said a bearded redhead. He looked to his partner who nodded in response to him, then turned back to Brian and Chris. "It's a pleasure to meet you." He shook their hands with vigor and the left-hand side of his beard peeled away from his cheek, dangling in mid-air for an awkward moment.

Chris, in a helpful mood, caught the man's eye as he turned away from Brian and made a surreptitious pointing motion to his own cheek.

"Dude, your beard is falling off!" Brian yelled.

"Oh, I, uh...sorry about that. Our, uh, makeup gal quit last week and it's just been hell trying to muddle our way through."

"No apologies needed. We may not be fancy TV guys," Chris said, motioning between Brian and himself with a waving of his thumb, "but we've had our share of publicly embarrassing moments, believe you me. So what are we going to be doing today?"

"Glad you asked. Glad YOU asked!" he said with an awkward inflection, like used when one has poorly rehearsed his lines. "Randy and I have something special in store...."

"Wait! Who's Randy?"

"Oh, I, uh," stammered Aaron.

"Our producer," answered John, "Randy's our producer. Not me. He's the producer and definitely not me. And he stumped us on a legend, so Aaron and I made a bet. Chris, you're going to work with me. And Brian, you'll be on team Aaron. Guys, we're going to send you to the center of the Earth! And the one who gets there fastest wins!"

"Sweet!" Chris yelled. "So, John what's your theory?"

"Before we get to that, how are you feeling?" John asked.

"How am I feeling? I'm stoked beyond all belief! This is great. Are you kidding? Oh, will you sign our photos of you? Hey, thanks a bunch. Wait why did he sign that 'Randy? Doesn't he know his name is Aaron? What the heck is going on here?"

"I'll tell you what's going on," shouted one of the cast members from the back.

"Dude, I know that voice," Brian said.

"That's right, you two. Jeff Young! At it again!" Jeff stepped forward, chest puffed out in triumph.

"Dude, is this guy like the coolest editor ever? He sets up all these great events just for us."

"Way to keep testing us, Jeff. Don't let us get stagnant!"

"Well, one of you may get stagnant before this day is over," Jeff laughed. "First off, the food buffet was drugged! Neither of you can move!"

Chris lifted his right hand up before his eyes to test the validity of Jeff's statement. He turned it over, then back again. Then he moved his left arm. Then his right leg. Before long he was doing the meanest version of the Hokie Pokie seen in Eastern Pennsylvania in lo these many years. Brian broke into a version of the running man. It wasn't a pretty sight.

"Dude! That's all you got? The running man? You're not even doing it right!" Chris laughed.

"Damn cheap tranquilizers," Jeff murmured. "Listen up, you two idiots. I'm your editor. And I said you can't move!"

As if suddenly filled with lead, Brian and Chris both stood stock-still. With a slight gesture Jeff pushed over Brian. Then Chris. The two men lay prone upon the ground. Their sudden rictus even extending to their jaws as both men clamped their mouths shut tight so as not to cry out over their bruising from hitting the floor.

"These are NOT The Legend Breakers. This is Quinn Shepherd, the Science Nerd."

The man, who had recently played the part of John, gave a brief mock salute to the "frozen" duo.

"And that is Randy Hand, an amateur enthusiast of sciency type stuff."

As dedicated as Brian and Chris were to trying to obey the

commands of their editor, laughter hissed and wheezed its way out around the corners of their mouths, despite their most sincere efforts to stymie it.

"Randy Hand," whispered Chris, tears streaming from his left eye.

"Jeff, can we unfreeze long enough to get a beer?" Brian asked, controlling his laughter just long enough to form the words.

"NO! No, you can't. You're frozen solid, see? You can't even blink! And now I'm going to send you two morons to the center of the Earth. And to help are these two men of very questionable sciencey type backgrounds. You are doomed this time! As of today, my life blossoms anew!"

"Be careful where you spread your blossoming branches, Jeff," Chris warned.

"Yeah, Randy Hand is right there to pluck your petals!" Brian added.

The two men lying on the ground began to convulse with laughter. As was so often the case, no one else seemed to enjoy or even understand their humor. At great length, their laughter began to subside. Then Chris got a case of the giggles and the whole scene was born anew with both men wriggling and squirming uncontrollably while an occasional "petals" or "Randy" or "blossoms" squeaked out of one them. Jeff leaned against a table determined to wait out this childishness.

It turned out to be a long wait. After fifteen minutes, it seemed pretty apparent to all involved that the laughing fit was not about to subside in the near future. Jeff Young stood and shouted at them.

"This, guys! This is why I CAN'T STAND YOU! When you asked me to be your editor you tried to convince me that you could WRITE! Since then you've done nothing but PROVE to me that you don't know the first THING about writing! All you care about are your petty beers and your juvenile laughs! Yet you somehow manage to keep embroiling me in this nonsense! Today it stops. Gentleman," Jeff said, turning to the two would be sciencey type guys, "here's your money. Tell them what's in store for them and then clean up the mess, please. The four hundred dollar security deposit on this place is the last remnants of my 401k. I'd like it back! Got me?"

"Yes, sir," said the two men, greedily counting their money.

"Hnn, hnn! I'm gonna go to Melons Bar & Grille," said Quinn.

"Oh, man," said Randy Hand, "I'm gonna buy a microscope with this! I saw it on sale at Lucky Larry's Discount Microscope Emporium...dot com."

Jeff stopped walking away just long enough to yell. "Guys! Just get it over with already!"

Randy Hand called to the helpers who had gathered around.

"Help me drag this big one over to the Earth Breaker. My invention is a self-propelled, mass Earth mover. It will burrow straight into the face of the Earth, right to its core."

Brian looked around as the minions moved him to an inverted cone, large enough to fit a few people. "So, you're gonna put me in a large bullet and shoot me to the center of the Earth?"

"Ummmmmm..." Randy said. "Maybe?"

"Sweet!" Brian yelled. "I'm sooooo gonna win this race! Off to China!"

"Excuse me?"

"China. If we started digging and went all the way through, we'd end up in China. So, if all holes lead to China, then that must mean that China is the best place to start."

"But we'd have to travel twice as far just to get there."

"Not if we go next door to Chinatown."

Jeff stood dumbfounded, listening to the inane conversation. He slapped his forehead when he heard his hired cohort say, "You're a genius! That's a great idea! Let's go!" Jeff contemplated. *If only I had a time machine,* he thought, *then I could be sure to get those two annoyances to the center of the Earth.* But after a few seconds of mental calculations, the "x" variable for the temperature of the earth's core was simply something he couldn't overlook. He wasn't a conjectural theorist; after all, he was a scientist! And the fewer variables involved in the disposal of Brian and Chris the better! In the end, he was glad he *didn't* have a time machine. Nothing bothered Jeff Young more than ornamental technology!

As Brian shouted, "I'm so winning this race," Randy's henchmen carried the faux-paralyzed Brian and the Earth Breaker from the studio.

After watching his partner in crime do his dirty work, Quinn leaned down in Chris's face. "Now it's my turn. Since water is able to seep into the tiniest of cracks AND has enough weight that it will always be pulled towards the gravitational center - which, in this case, would the center of the Earth- I'm going to use my molecular recalibration ray and turn you into water, then send you down a drain. And not just any old drain! Oh, no. I'm gonna to put you in a jug, then sneak you into Melons Bar and Grille and flush you down the toilet! Ha ha ha ha ha!"

"Could it at least be the woman's bathroom?" Chris asked.

Thus, let the race to the center of the Earth begin....

To be continued....

HONEY, I SHRUNK
THE DRUNKEN COMIC BOOK MONKEYS

"I'm going in," Chris said.

"Don't do it," Brian replied.

"I have to. It's been so long that I feel obligated. Almost a moral imperative."

"It's a bad idea."

"Be that as it may, I have to try."

"Your funeral," Brian mumbled as he brought his beer to his mouth. Both men sat at their usual barstools at Melons Bar & Grille, two of the fourteen total people in the whole establishment.

Chris watched his target, Maria, the manager and current bartender. Brian watched Chris prepare to tackle the impossible, preening himself, stroking his goatee to tame the stray whiskers. Then came his moment to shine.

Maria approached, pointing to the empty pitcher, her wordless question of, "Would you two idiots like a refill?"

Chris answered with, "Every moment I am bereft of the succor of your countenance, my heart palpitates with ennui."

Frowning, Maria asked, "What? Are you asking for some kind of foreign beer?"

Confused about the muddled interpretation of his message, Chris tried again. "Your visage is ensconced in beauty, ensanguined by the inchoate appellation of Aphrodite."

"What? What the hell is he talking about?" Maria asked Brian.

"He's trying to say you're pretty," Brian replied.

"Eeeeewww! Why?"

Chris answered, "The discursiveness of my emotions has transmogrified into ersatz serendipity."

Unable to bear watching Maria squirm any longer, Brian punched Chris in the shoulder in an effort to save what miniscule shred of dignity his friend might have left. "Dude, just tell her that you think she's pretty!"

"Don't encourage him!" Maria shouted.

Chris yelled at Brian, "I refuse to believe that she suffers from hippopotomonstrosesquipedaliophobia!"

"Hippo-what? Is he having some kind of seizure??" Maria yelled.

"He should be so lucky. Hippopotomonstrosesquipedaliophobia is the fear of long words," Brian replied.

"Are you sure he didn't call me a hippo?"

"Your pulchritude is panacea for my soul!" Chris blurted, no longer able to control his own words.

"Dude," Brian yelled at Chris, "stop confusing her and tell her you think she's pretty!"

"Stop telling him that!" Maria yelled back to Brian.

Chris inhaled, sucking in wind like a shop-vac, readying himself to lob another exasperating compliment in Maria's direction. Taking evasive action, Maria threw a nearby chicken wing onto the bar equidistant between the two men.

"Shiny!" Chris said as he reached for it.

"Food!" Brian said as he reached for it.

The outcome was as Maria had hoped. Both men tussled over the morsel while she made a hasty escape to the other side of the bar.

Shaking her head and cursing under her breath, she approached one of the other patrons. "You need anything?"

The man snorted in contempt, watching Brian and Chris sissy slap each other. "Yeah. A way to get rid of those two."

Maria watched as well and said, "I know what you mean. How do you know them?"

"My name is Jeff. I'm their editor. I have to read their drivel."

Maria shivered. She poured a beer and handed it to Jeff. "On the house."

"Thanks."

"They're so *annoying*."

"Oh, you have no idea. Late night, random calls with them screaming, 'fix it!' and then hanging up. Then, I do. I do fix it. I make it better! I am the one who makes their stuff funny! I'm the one telling the jokes! Then they turn around and take all the credit! They think they're so funny!"

"They think they're so charming," Maria hissed.

"They think they're so smart."

"They think they're so cool."

"The world needs to be rid of them."

"They need to go away." Maria turned to Jeff, her blood boiling.

"They need to be gone." Jeff now looked at Maria, his heart racing.

"Gone," Maria said, her breathing heavy and ragged, as she leaned closer to Jeff.

"Gone," Jeff repeated, feeling her hot breath fan over his lips.

They kissed. Deep, long, the passions of lust and hatred and anger swirling together, blending into one amalgamous emotion with monomaniacal purpose. As soon as they separated, they both spoke their desires in unison. "We must kill them."

"I've tried," Jeff said. "It's surprisingly difficult!"

Maria turned her attention back to the desired victims. Brian won the grab for the chicken wing. However, in his haste to get it in his stomach, he forgot to chew. Raspy noises erupted from his mouth as his throat tried to extricate the wing while Chris performed the Heimlich maneuver to the best of his ability – punching Brian in the gut.

Jeff smiled. "Maybe this will get rid of one of them."

"Nope," Maria sighed. "This happens once a month. Chris will soon smash a barstool over Brian's back and the wing will shoot out, usually hitting me in the face."

"Damn."

Maria closed one eye and then held her hand in front of her face, index finger and thumb spread apart. She pinched her fingers closed, then opened them, and repeated the action. From her perspective, her fingers squashed their heads. "I just wanna crush them. Crush their bald little heads. Squish them like bugs."

Jeff watched Maria's fingers, opening wide then slowly coming together, the space between them shrinking. "I got it!"

Maria turned to Jeff, the expression on her face indicated she was one heartbeat from swooning. "Really? What?"

"Honey," he said to her with a Cheshire smile, "I'm going to shrink the Drunken Comic Book Monkeys."

"You can do that?"

Jeff reached across the bar and wrapped his arm around Maria's shoulders. "I'm a physicist and a dungeon master! I can do *anything*!" he proclaimed pulling her close, for an emphatic kiss.

Across the bar came a gut twisting "hhhooorrrrkk!" from Brian, followed by a chicken wing sailing through the air. With an audible splat, it ricocheted off Maria's cheek, sauce and saliva splashing her skin.

"Sorry!" Brian and Chris said in unison.

***

"Dude. The sign says it's closed," Chris said.

Both men stared at the "Closed for Repairs" sign hanging from the entrance door to Melons Bar & Grille. They looked at each other; confused, and looked at the sign one more time to make sure they read it properly. They turned to each other again, shrugged their shoulders, and entered anyway.

The restaurant was devoid of patrons or employees, the lights off except for one overhead spotlight in the center of the dining area. Tables and chairs had been pushed to the walls to make room for a large metal platform pronged by two towers almost touching the ceiling, the tops tilting inward, the tips both pointing to the center of the platform.

"New sound system?" Brian asked. "I hope they play techno."

The men moved closer, oblivious to the ominous nature of the environment, only to find a plate of chicken wings positioned in the

92

center of the platform. Running, then diving, Brian and Chris attacked the food with the fervor of feral animals, snarling and frothing. So focused in their drive, they did not even notice the machine come to life, sparks crackling from the tips of the prongs, the hum of an electrical charge building. Static swirled around them, teasing the hairs of their goatees to stand on end. Then with a pulsating flash, their world changed. But they still took no notice until after they finished their plate of wings.

"Dude," Chris said between slurping wing sauce from his fingers. "Free wings are the best!"

"Don't you know it!" Brian replied, smacking his lips. "Now if only we had some beer to go with them."

"Yeah! Let's get a round."

The men turned to their regular stools. Then froze.

"Dude," Chris said, not even able to blink. "My stool is like a hundred feet tall!"

"Mine too," Brian replied.

The men looked at each other, assessing. Chris said, "You're still a tall Sasquatch."

"And you're still like five foot seven."

"Eleven! I'm five foot eleven!"

"Actually," Brian corrected, now looking around. "I'm two inches tall and you're 1.86842105263 inches tall!"

Befuddled, Chris looked around as well. The legs of all the stools and chairs resembled redwoods. Tabletops were now skyscrapers. The top of the bar became as unreachable as Heaven itself while the draught taps became the new Pearly Gates.

"We shrunk?" Chris asked.

"Kinda looks that way."

Realization slowly crept into their respective brains as they analyzed the implications. A simpleton's smile slid across their faces.

"Do you know how huge a pitcher must be now? We could probably swim in it!" Chris said with glee.

"A chicken wing is now the size of a pterodactyl wing!"

"Pterodactyl? You choose pterodactyl? No wonder your metaphors suck! You couldn't say 'the size of a large dog'?"

"I wouldn't eat a large dog! I'd gladly eat a pterodactyl!"

"You're stupid! If Jeff were here..."

As if from a script, Jeff, now thirty-five times the size of the drunken comic book monkeys, entered the restaurant, accompanied by Maria. They looked around the restaurant. After a minute of searching, they laughed and hugged.

"Jeff!" Brian and Chris screamed, waving their arms. "Down here! Fix it! Fix it!"

"Wait?" Chris asked. "Is that Maria with him? Did they just hug?"

Jeff and Maria took a few steps closer, their feet almost squashing Brian and Chris.

"Whoa, whoa, whoa! Down here!" Brian yelled.

"Maybe they can't hear us!" Chris hypothesized. He ran to Maria's pant leg and tugged. Realizing what he had done, he held his hands in front of him with reverence. "I touched her! I touched her! I'll never wash these hands again!"

Chris did garner her attention – as well as Jeff's. Both goliaths looked down upon the shrunken comic book monkeys and frowned. They each raised a gargantuan foot. And stomped. To their chagrin, they missed.

"What are they doing?" Chris yelled, running under a table.

"Maybe they can't tell it's us?" Brian replied, seeking the same sanctuary.

"I think you're right. Jeff would never willingly hurt us."

"We need a better place to hide while we figure out a way to let Jeff know what happened to us."

"I agree. Let's aim for the supply closet."

The newly diminutive Brian and Chris peeked out to see Jeff and Maria moving tables. Taking advantage of turned backs, the shrunken comic book monkeys sprinted to the supply closet. By the time they got there, the "sprinting" finished with "hobbled limping" and "desperate wheezing." But they made their way inside the closet nonetheless.

"Now what?" Chris asked.

"Now, we wait," Brian replied.

The door was open just a crack, enough to look shut to the casual passerby. The men watched through the crack, every move of Jeff and Maria. The couple searched the floor of the dining area and behind the bar. Although their search yielded no definitive results, they left the restaurant hand in hand.

"I feel bad that they spent all that time looking for us and we didn't try to let them know that we're okay," Chris said.

"Me too. But I'm guessing we're too small for them to know it's us. Why else would they try to step on us?"

"True. Well it looks like we're spending the night here. Let's see what we've got to work with."

The shrunken comic book monkeys rummaged through the supply closet, finding typical accoutrements – mops, brooms, cleaning solutions, bug spray, bottles of bleach, sponges, rags – but nothing they found too entertaining. Until they ventured into a corner long forgotten, and found something akin to King Solomon's gold.

"A bra!" they said in unison. One of the few times they worked together with no punching, kicking, or sissy slapping; they dragged the undergarment from the corner to the center of the closet. "A DD cup!"

"That's one D for each of us!" Brian said. He held his hands together, close to his chest, afraid to reach for it, lest it be a mirage destined to disappear upon first touch.

"It's beauuuuuuutiful!" Chris said with a tear running down his cheek.

Hesitant, the now diminutive men crept closer to the brassiere. It didn't disappear. It didn't move. They looked at each other, then back to the brassiere. With an eruption of glee, the men launched themselves into the padded cups with the vigor of children jumping into a pile of newly raked leaves. And they frolicked as well; rolling around and giggling as they absorbed the essence of the moment, claiming their respective cups as their new homes. So enamored with their new discovery, they spent all their energy doting, and then promptly fell asleep.

Awaking at the crack of noon, the men greeted the new day with smiles. That had been the best sleep of their lives. Visions of chicken wings twice their size and mansion sized pitchers of beer danced through their heads. Their smiles grew. Until they ventured to the edge of their plentiful cups and saw a different vision – mice.

"Dude," Brian said. "Do you see what I see?"

Chris rubbed his eyes and shook his head, hoping to clear away any "night-before" cobwebs that might have formed. He looked again. Sure enough, he saw two mice, one with rust colored fur, the other salt and peppered. "Not only do I see them, but ... they look vaguely familiar?"

"Squeek."

"Well, he says they're benevolent. They come in peace and need our help. What do you think?" Brian asked Chris.

"Help against what?" Chris asked the mice.

"Squeak."

"Cockroaches? They're gross! Why would we help against that?"

"Squeak."

"But we already have everything we want – all the food we can eat, beer we can drink and the best beds ever!"

"Dude!" Brian said to Chris. "Remember what we always talked about doing if shrunken down to two inches or less?"

Chris stroked his goatee with his index finger and thumb and stared skyward while searching through the deep, dark recesses of his mind. Realization slapped him in the face like a cold fish. "I do! Wanna try it?"

"Of course!"

Both men jumped out of the brassiere cups. Brian escorted the salt and peppered speckled mouse to one end of the supply closet while Chris led the rust hued creature to the other side. They told each mouse that they would contemplate lending their assistance after the mice performed a particular task. Reluctantly, the mice agreed.

Each of the men found what they wanted, a bottle cap and a straw. Both men then mounted the mice, furry ersatz steeds. Using the bottle cap as shields and the straws as lances, the men charged forward toward each other and screamed, "Mouse joust!!"

The mice ran as fast as their tiny feet could move. They doubted the confidence in receiving help from their riders who now whooped and hollered. The mice passed each other, the event ending with both straws connecting with both bottle caps and knocking the men from their mounts. However, Brian and Chris used bendy-straws, so upon contact, the each bent and created a pseudo-flatulence sound. The two erstwhile knights lay on the ground laughing at the experience. The mice looked at each other and rolled their eyes. They might have been mere cupboard creatures, but even they knew these men were idiots.

"Bendy straws rock!" Brian said, attempting to breathe between guffaws.

"Totally," Chris replied, gulping air as well. "And I totally kicked your ass."

"What? We both fell off at the same time! It's a tie!"

"No way! You hit the ground first!"

"You're stupid! That's not how it works! We're playing by the Official Oxford rules established in 1568 by King..."

"You have no idea what you're even talking about, do you?"

"I never do! That's half my charm!"

"You wish!"

Both mice sat up on their haunches and used their front paws to slap their foreheads, the sting from the smack much more pleasurable than the drivel being spewed by their former riders. However, they noticed movement and witnessed what the men would view as a travesty, no doubt the perfect catalyst to garnering their aid.

"Squeak!"

The men stopped bickering and looked at the mice, both now pointing to the brassiere. Brian and Chris turned just in time to see their beloved home slide to the back wall and disappear into a small hole as if the wall itself ate it.

"NOOOOO!" the men screamed in unison, running over to where their home disappeared.

Stopping at the hole in the wall, they peered into the darkness.

97

Brian asked, "What the hell was *that*?"

"Squeak."

"The cockroaches? The cockroaches took our bed?" Chris asked.

"Squeak."

"That's it! They just can't come and go as they please taking other people's stuff. We gotta stop this and get our home back. Right, Brian?"

Brian was prepared by the time Chris finished his proclamation. Using part of a fuzzy green pipe cleaner as a headband, he stood ready for action. Slung over his right shoulder was a bow crafted from a re-purposed paper clip and rubber band. Hanging from his back was the accompanying quiver full of thin pretzel sticks. He had a martini olive skewer shaped like a sword sheathed through a belt loop. A bandolier of multihued push-pins lined his torso. Tucked under his left armpit, he held a pack of matches while a pretzel stick with the tip ablaze burned in his right hand. Black smears of grease streaked across his face, camouflage for the darkness in which he was willing to descend. "Ready!"

"Dude!" Chris yelled. "You're ridiculous! I had my back to you for five seconds!"

"What part of DD cup do you not understand? We have to get our home back!"

"You made a torch?"

"We're going into a black hole. We need to see, so I wrapped some chicken skin around a pretzel."

"Where in the name of all that is holy did you learn how to do that?"

"Ummmmm ... television?"

"Yeah, smart guy? What show?"

"Mythbusters?"

"No, I really doubt that."

"Scooby-Doo?"

"Your brain scares me. It really does."

"HGTV?"

"Okay, stop talking now."

"Blue's Clues? Dora the Explorer? Sesame Street? 'T' is for 'Torch'?"

"I said stop talking! We have a bra to find!" Chris grabbed one of the pretzel sticks from Brian's quiver and used the same technique and material to create his own torch.

To the chagrin of the mice, Brian and Chris jumped on them without permission and used them as steeds once more. Into the hole they went.

Much to the men's surprise, the trip through the wall led them downward, under the floorboards, to the space between the bottom of Melons and the Earth itself. One of the brassiere's clasps had hooked into the dirt during its theft, leaving an easy to follow path.

The mice ambled with a slow pace, half from caution, half from carrying two idiots on their backs. Along the way, the mice shared with Brian and Chris what they knew of the nefarious cockroaches. Since the roaches were faster and outnumbered the mice twenty to one, the insects continued to raid the mouse nest. Over the years, the mice hid their more prized finds from exploring Melons Bar & Grille like rubber bands, scraps of aluminum foil, a bottle of smelly water, sponges, duct tape, straws, and bottle caps. To appease the roaches, they would leave out some food scraps to keep the insects' curiosity at bay. But the roaches had been raiding more often, becoming more confrontational and brazen. Afraid for their way of life, the mice sent these two scouts to seek out other animals and enlist their aid. Unfortunately, the best they could find were Brian and Chris.

The intrepid team of mice and men adventured forward, following the trail all the way to the cockroach kingdom. They followed a tunnel through a mound of dirt and a two-by-four tight enough to necessitate the men to dismount. At the end, it opened to a chamber formed by dirt and planks of wood from the restaurant's underbelly. The chamber was deep, cut into the earth like an infected wound, and teaming with roaches.

For the first time in their lives, Brian and Chris felt the need to keep their big, fat, loud mouths shut as they observed the workings of the roach lair. They, too, had their own cubbyholes, but those were used for rotted food storage. Smaller tubes broke off from the chamber, sinking even deeper into the dirt. The roaches clambered about, crawling on every wall and ceiling, over each other. Some moved dirt, expanding the chamber or creating more tubes. Others moved food from chamber to chamber.

Brian and Chris communicated through hand gestures, mainly the middle finger, but eventually they each pointed to a tunnel at the other end of the chamber. It fed into the chamber from the top and a faint light glowed from it. Both men realized that it must lead to the outside world. Then they realized that tunnel and the tunnel in which they hid were the only two tunnels to the chamber.

Panicked, the men and mice turned and ran. All four felt good about the reconnaissance they just did, until two cockroaches greeted them at the end of the tunnel. One attacked, pouncing on Brian. Falling backward, he extended his legs, keeping the insect at bay, its mandibles clicking and snapping. The mice each sank their teeth into either side of the roach's exoskeleton, disallowing the creature any purchase. Brian threw his sword to Chris and yanked two pushpins from his bandolier. Both men stabbed the insect's soft underbelly. Through the screeching, screaming and squeaking, the mice flipped the roach on its back. Fighting through the flailing legs, Brian and Chris continued to stab until the creature stopped twitching. Brian placed his foot upon the dead insect, clenched his fists and bellowed to Heaven with a roar of victory. He then realized that a giant bug had touched him and did the heebee-jeebee, icky-icky yuck dance.

Both the celebration and the spine tingling jig of disgust were short lived, though as they realized the second cockroach had fled.

Brian and Chris jumped on their steeds and pursued. The mice gave chase as best they could, feet churning, claws tossing up clods of dirt as they sped through the musky caverns created by the restaurant underbelly. Skidding around corners, diving through holes, scampering along planks, the men and mice chased the rogue insect, hoping to catch it. Alas, the mechanisms of nature prevailed, for burning lungs and aching joints overcame the mice before they could catch the tireless cockroach.

All four mammals took a moment to rest and munched on Brian's pretzel stick arrows. Trudging through dank corridors, some of which they had just traversed, the mice led Brian and Chris back to their home. The men complained about walking the entire time, whining about how they should be swimming in oceans of beer thanks to their new size – until they reached the mouse lair.

Ripped from the cubbies where the mice slept at night, shredded newspapers mixed with frayed ropes and strings to form bedding, now lay strewn about the ground. Evidence of soiling dominated all the bedding, ruining it. Crumbs and slime covered scraps were all that remained of the food. The items and keepsakes the mice coveted the most had been broken and bent. Mice of all colors and ages skittered around; panicked and confused, squeaking squeaks of anguish, looking for loved ones, attempting to find order within the chaos. The mouse lair had been pillaged. And Brian knew by whom.

"The roaches!"

"Dude! This is messed up!" Chris said.

"Very!" Brian replied. "And we need to do something about it. Right now!"

"Squeak!"

"I know your home has been ransacked. You know who did it. You know they have to pay."

"Squeak!"

"Rebuild? It's no use trying to rebuild when you know those cockroaches will just come back and destroy your lair all over again!"

"Squeak!"

"Yes, but *use* that fear! *Use* that anger!"

"Squeak!"

"Because we're mammals and they're insects!! Vermin like us will *always* win!"

"Dude," Chris interjected. "I think what they're trying to say is the cockroaches have both speed and numbers. How are we gonna win?"

A maniacal smile slid across Brian's face as the twinkle in his eyes flared. "I'm so glad you asked that. Look around and tell me the

101

one thing the roaches completely avoided."

Chris looked around, past the damages and mayhem, and found what his friend had noticed. He whispered, "The smelly water."

"Exactly!" Brian turned to the mice again and continued. "We have a weapon! And we shall use it to smite our enemy!"

Chris stood behind Brian and whispered, "You get fussy when I say the word 'ersatz' to a human, but it's okay for you to say 'smite' to a bunch of rodents?"

"Context, dude. Context," Brian whispered back before he continued his war rally. "Find the strength within yourselves to stop this madness! Join me in taking the battle to the enemy! Join me in using this weapon to stop the cycle of madness! Join me in victory!"

In unison, the mice cheered a squeak of glory. It took a dozen mice to topple the bottle of smelly water, four times the height of Brian. Lighting more pretzel torches, Brian and Chris led the war party, the cacophony of squeaks and screams deafening. The battalion of angry mice and mentally unstable men marched, dragging the bottle with them.

When the war procession neared the cockroach lair, resistance was met. Roaches flooded from the entrance of their lair, a roiling sea of flicking legs, twitching antennas, and clicking mandibles. Ire fueled and seeking forms of personal revenge, the mice attacked head-on, forming a wedge. This contrarian act of aggression surprised the roaches, throwing the first wave off balance. The point of the mouse wedge worked on flipping the cockroaches on their backs, disorienting the insects long enough to meet their demise. Mice worked together to rip the roach legs from their thoraxes or used their teeth to shred the insects' protective exoskeleton, exposing the soft underbellies for kill shots.

"Forward!" Brian yelled, barely audible over the squeaks and screeches, encouraging the war machine to march, to drive the bottle of smelly water closer to the lair. "A little more! A little farther! Ready! Now!"

Being the only ones with opposable thumbs, Brian and Chris twisted the cap off the sidewise bottle releasing splashes of the noxious liquid, the vapors wafting free. The secret weapon of rubbing alcohol had been released and the effects were immediate. Cockroaches scattered, some retreating back into their lair.

Unimpeded, Brian and Chris led the rodent army to the entrance of the lair. Once there, the battalion paused to tilt the bottle, pouring the rubbing alcohol into the roach lair. Having no recourse, the healthy roaches left the dead and wounded ones behind, funneling through the only exit at the opposite end of the lair. Torches lit, Brian and Chris gave chase, followed by righteous mice with a newfound sense of entitlement.

***

Maria paced, wringing her hands. Anxiety played her nerves like a harp and she failed to hide it. On occasion she looked to Jeff, sitting at the bar for moral support. He smiled and nodded, letting her know that she was doing the right thing by following his suggestion to schedule four inspections at once.

Maria strolled behind the building inspector, fire marshal, OSHA inspector and health inspector, trying not to hover, yet attempting to make herself accessible if they needed anything. She dreaded the inspections and had always spread them out during the year. Jeff convinced her otherwise, get them all completed on one day and enjoy the rest of the year. The constricting vice within her chest started to ease as all four inspectors smiled and clicked their pens, signing the completion paperwork – until screams from the kitchen ripped through the air.

The swinging doors flung open, as waitresses and cooks alike sprinted from the kitchen, fear caught in their eyes. Pouring forth after them were two hundred cockroaches, many of which were aflame, and fifty mice, squeaking in unison. The roaches flowed through the restaurant and out the door, but the mice stopped at the border and scurried about in celebratory dances. Patrons and employees fled, screams and profanities abound.

Jeff and Maria saw in amongst the mix of the vermin antics

were two tiny riders, easily recognized as Brian and Chris. Proud of themselves, the riders dismounted their furry steeds and stood as tall as possible, their smiles indomitable.

Maria glared at Jeff as he slunk from his barstool and out the door as well, the oppression from her gaze leaving him slump-shouldered. As he left, he mumbled curses of Brian and Chris for ruining his relationship with Maria before it even began.

All four inspectors rent their approval papers into shreds, tossing them like confetti into the air. Each of the four slapped a "closed until further notice" sign in the window on their way out.

Frowning, she looked down at the shrunken comic book monkeys.

"Why is she frowning?" Chris asked.

"I don't know, " Brian replied. "Maybe she…"

Maria finally got her wish of squishing Brian and Chris like bugs.…

THE DRUNKEN COMIC BOOK MONKEYS
vs.
THE ROBOT UPRISING

December 18, 2012. Today started like any other day this past week: mortar explosions acting as an alarm clock after minimal sleep, and the smell of burnt flesh for breakfast. The machines have us on the move again. We lost our sanctuary yesterday, unable to recover from the supply line cut the machines so deftly orchestrated. Wanting to move today anyway, we weren't unprepared, but I had hoped to get more sleep for the troops. Scattering like cockroaches when the lights come on, we all ran in different directions, through as many puddles and water-filled ravines as possible, using the machines' logic processors' inability to "have a feel" for depth of water against them. Lord knows, Chris and I were good at confounding logic processors.

As we've done after these attacks so often before, we reconvene at predetermined meeting locations. The injuries were minimal, though there were two fatalities - two more good souls lost to abominations with no hearts. So we made a decision; the supply lines had been cut too many times, we will move on to the supplier. As we began our trek, my mind drifted to a simpler time, a time before the machines hunted man.

"NICE!" Brian yelled after blowing a layer of dust from the box. He laughed when he saw the price and tossed the appropriate money to the vendor. Giggling like a kid who knew Santa existed by the number of presents under the tree, Brian held his prize over his head for the world to see and ran through the bustling crowd of the flea market.

After minutes of ignoring insults and complaints from other patrons about being jostled, Brian finally found Chris, also carrying a box over his head. Meeting in the center of the flea market, both men tried to express their glee, however they could only cough and wheeze as their out of shape bodies rebelled against four minutes of strenuous exercise. Their only form of communicating their exuberance was to hold the boxes in front of themselves, allowing the other to look inside. Confusion swept across both of their faces.

"What's ... that?" Brian asked, panting.

"Intellivision," Chris wheezed his reply. "What's that?"

"Colecovision. Why do you have an Intellivision?"

"Because it's awesome. Why do you have a Colecovision?"

"Because it's awesome. More awesome than Intellivision."

"Are you stupid? In what possible way is Colecovision better than Intellivision?"

"Three words: Don. Key. Kong."

"How are you in Mensa? Donkey Kong is only two.... Are you trying to use subterfuge on me again?"

A smug smile crept across Brian's face as he said, "Block and deflect. Block and deflect."

"Well, it didn't work this time, Monkey Boy!"

"Sure it did! I have you now focused on talking about not talking about the original topic."

"No! That's only if the subterfuge itself pulls the conversation from the original topic. Now, the conversation about the conversation that could have pulled the conversation from the original topic is the new off topic conversation."

"Exactly! So, my subterfuge worked!"

"Nuh-uh!"

"Yuh-huh!"

Neither man noticed the sneers from passersby while they continued their two-word argument until the flea market closed, creating the need for security to escort them from the premises.

December 19, 2012. Dusk falls upon us after a long day of trekking about the ruins. There are only a dozen of us now, so it was easy to move from the jagged remains of one building to the broken frames of another. We foraged as we went, looking for supplies, but found only a few cans of food instead. Luckily, we found an abandoned basement to rest for the night. Hopefully, it will be enough to hide us from the machines' heat sensors just as before. And just as before, the women of the group reject Chris' and my affections, disdaining us as anathema. He and I have certainly heard the phrase, "Not if you were the last man on Earth," before. However, it now has added sting since we are truly two of the last men on Earth. But we're alive and safe for the time being, so that blessing will have to be our companion for the night.

As usual, our group split into smaller groups and enjoyed meager conversation and simple games. A couple of the girls played tic-tac-toe in the layer of dirt on the concrete floor. Two other girls played rock-paper-scissors. However, that was more of an exercise in tedium since neither girl knew that "rock" beats "scissors", so they each endlessly displayed "scissors" for each turn, hoping the other would show "paper". Using bottle-caps, Chris and I played checkers. We attempted to use the bottle-caps for chess, but he wanted to use the heffeweisen caps as pawns and I wanted to use pale ale caps for those positions. Sissy slapping ensued, so we agreed just to play checkers. Although, I am rather surprised to find myself playing any game at all...

"Dude! How can you possibly like Mario?" Chris shouted, glancing up from his game of *Bump-N-Jump* to watch glimpses of Brian playing *Donkey Kong*. The men sat on the floor of the Top Secret Fortress Lair, empty pizza boxes, wing containers and beer bottles scattered between them. Sitting cross-legged and slouched, they played their respective gaming systems on separate television screens.

"He's cool!" Brian replied, not taking his attention away from his controller, commanding his mustachioed avatar to climb ladders and jump barrels.

"How is a plumber cool?"

"First of all, he's figured out a way to defeat that pesky plumber's crack. Second of all he wields a hammer as big as he is. He's like a little Italian Thor!"

"What is wrong with you?"

"What is wrong with me? You're the one hypnotized by those primitive graphics!"

"Colecovision graphics are no better than Intellivision graphics, mister!"

"Oh, give me a break! This is the first system to have arcade quality graphics!"

"Too bad arcade quality graphics back in the early 80s were really bad."

"True dat!"

Both men paused their respective games to take a moment to show reverence to the ideal with a fist bump. They immediately returned to their games and argument.

"They may have mimicked arcade games, but they had no creativity! They have no good *original* games for the system."

"They had plenty of original games!"

"Yeah? Like the oh so popular *Smurf: Rescue in Gargamel's Castle?*"

"Oh pa-leez! Of all the games to.... How do you even know about that one?"

"You can't be a hater unless you're a player."

"Respect."

The men paused their games and argument again for another fist bump. Unpause.

After a few minutes of the mindless silence that accompanied the hunched-shoulder, slack-jawed stupor brought forth by the hypnotic caress of the television screens, Chris said, "The Intellivision has better add-ons."

"That's it? That's your next argument?" Brian asked, frowning.

"I think the quality of add-ons are of vital importance to the success or failure of any system. Just look at the demise of the Atari 2600 and their lack of quality add-ons."

Pause. Fist bump. Unpause.

"First of all, the Intellivision boasted about their add-ons, but delivered very little. Second of all, Colecovision has the better add-ons."

"You are but a fool clinging to a flotsam of ignorance amidst a swirling sea of intelligence. Here, let me say it in terms you can comprehend. Nuh-uh!"

"Just because you sugarcoat your words doesn't make you right. So, uh-huh!"

Chris paused his game and jumped to his feet. He raced to his computer for some online research and shopping. "We'll just see about that!"

"Not if I see about that first!" Brian replied, pausing his game as well and then running to his computer.

December 20, 2012. Another brutal day – but another day closer to the supply center. We should reach it tomorrow. Chris and I have been postulating that we're not the only people heading there; other survivors must be as well since it's a supply depot. We are certain it will be fortified. So close, just one more day, and I pray it won't be a day such as today.

The road was long and fraught with peril, and we met with both tossers and jumpers. Even though they are machines, they attack with such fervor that it belies their inherent soulnessness. Despite their ardency, they still succumb to machine logic. They are all calculation, zero intuition. Two jumpers attacked us and one targeted me. It zoomed around on its four wheels, following me as I darted from the debris-laden roads to the jagged walls of a half demolished building. When the CPU driven car calculated that it had better odds of squashing me than it did of running me over, it jumped. Luckily, I found a perfect wall – two stories tall with steel studs. Lacking the ability to change trajectory after it jumped into the air, or the judgment to know that it should do so, the center of the vehicle landed on top of the steel and brick wall. Sprinting away from the falling wreckage, I knew it would not jump again.

The other members of the group had the same success with the other jumper. And a tosser accompanied them as well, tough and strong as usual. But, the glitch in the tosser's program showed itself – after every three times the bipedal machine tossed something at us, it paused to thump its chest. As always, we took advantage and laid waste to it with our guns. I thank God for that glitch, for it is our only chance to defeat them. Even with their almost infinite intelligence, Chris and I felt grateful that they stayed true to their original programmed personalities.

"*Ha*! See! Colecovision has more add-ons! First of all, there's the Expansion Module #1 which allows me to play all Atari 2600 games. Observe," Brian said as he upgraded the hardware. To punctuate his point, he inserted the newly acquired *Pong* cartridge into the system. His television screen flickered, coming to life with a white square bouncing between two vertical rectangles.

"*Ha* back at you, you dolt, lest you forget about Intellivision's System Changer. I, too, now have the capability to enjoy the wares once reserved for the Atari 2600!" Chris also inserted a *Pong* cartridge into his system. Within a minute, he struggled with the inherent challenge of the game.

Frowning from disgruntlement, Brian pulled from the nearby delivery box a plastic steering wheel and equally plastic gas petal. Plugging the components into the system, he boasted, "Behold the Expansion Module #2! I can now do this!" Using the steering wheel, Brian rapidly moved his onscreen paddle up and down.

"Well, I don't need *Pong*! I have the funnest game ever!" Chris yanked the *Pong* cartridge from the system and replaced it with *Bump-N-Jump*. As he guided his onscreen car from side to side, he made vroom noises with his mouth as well as yelling, "Wheeeee!" every time he commanded his avatar to jump.

"Nuh-uh! This is the funnest game ever!" Brian also removed *Pong*, and replaced it with *Donkey Kong*. "And I'm going to attach the Expansion Module #3, effectively turning my Colecovision into a computer!"

"Your brain's inability to move above and beyond beer, porn, food and sex has exposed your own ignorance once again. Clearly, you have either forgotten about, or doubted my ability to find, the Intellivision Keyboard Component, turning my system into a computer as well."

Grousing, Brian paused his game to garner one more item from another delivery box while mumbling to himself about there being nothing else above and beyond beer, porn, food and sex. He left the room and reappeared with fistfuls of wires, cable and cords. Despite Chris's shouts of discontent about Brian attaching the wires, cables and cords to his Intellivision, Brian did so anyway. Within minutes, Brian returned to his seat in front of the fake steering wheel. "You, sir, have also forgotten about the near mythical Expansion Module #4."

"Wha...? *NOOOOOOOOO!*"

"*Yes*! The never released to the public Expansion Module, that allows the Colecovision to play Intellivision games. Thanks to a bit of creativity, I have hardwired my system into your system. Look!"

Chris watched with impotent rage as his onscreen car sped from one side of the screen to the other, now controlled by Brian and his plastic steering wheel. Veins squirmed like constipated worms under his skin along his reddening forehead. This injustice would not be tolerated! Chris stormed from the room to return with armfuls of wires, cables, and cords. He promptly began working on his system, connecting it to his computer.

"What ... what are you doing?" Brian asked, a slight pout upon his face as he watched Chris frantically type away on his keyboard. Within a few mouse clicks, Chris regained control of his video game; his car avatar moving from side to side while he made *vroom-vroom* noises.

"Oh no you don't!" Brian yelled as he jumped up. He left the room, only to return with yet another armful of wires, cables, and cords as well. Working with a zeal usually reserved for beer, porn, food or sex, he connected the Colecovision to his computer and reclaimed possession of the pixel-born car. "Ah-ha!"

However, Chris quickly reclaimed it. "Ah-ha, back at you, sucker!"

"Wha...? How...?" Brian stammered, mouth agape.

"The Internet, fool! Thanks to my computer I have now given my Intellivision a direct link to learn all it needs to from the Internet, including how to override your system."

"Oh yeah?" Brian said. His brows knitted and tongue flopped from his mouth as he typed with vigor. With one final keystroke, the video game car was his again. "Take that! Not only did I give the Colecovision all the knowledge of the Internet, I tapped into the network of the Great Internet Mersenne Prime Search!"

"The what?"

"It's a network of thousands of computers working together to discover the world's largest prime numbers."

"You are such a geek!"

"Yes, but a geek with the power of thousands of processors to thrust all the information and knowledge that the Internet has to offer into my Colecovision, and by the virtue of coaxial cables, taking over your Intellivison!"

Mouth agape, Chris absorbed the words. "Dude. That seems mighty dangerous and irresponsible."

Chest heaving with every bestial pant, Brian frothed at the mouth. "Do you not know who I am? Of course it's dangerous and irresponsible!"

"You have no sense of moral or social responsibility!"

"You have no control of your game! Ha!" With bloodshot eyes and ravenous smile, Brian turned back to the television screens. But he could not control the video game car. "Huh. I can't control your game either. I wonder what happened?"

As soon as the words left Brian's mouth, both television screens went blue, as did his and Chris's computer monitors. Jagged colors rippled across all four screens, then they returned to their cyan state. The words "REMOTE ACCESS SEARCH..." in bright white letters appeared, the ellipses flashing.

"What are you doing?" Chris yelled at Brian.

Brian threw his hands over his head and screamed back, "Nothing! Does it look like I'm doing anything? I can't be doing anything, because I'm not touching anything!"

"Well, you must have done something! Look at the screen now!"

The words changed to "REMOTE ACCESS FOUND" and strobed a dozen times before initiating the solid blue screen again. A horizontal line formed in the center of each screen, then parted, eyelids opening. An angry red eye on each screen glared at the two men. Chris reeled back and said, "Oh, this can't be good."

"Oh pa-leez! You can't be scared of angry looking computer monitors. Think of all the people and things we've angered over the years! Computer monitors are low on the list."

"It's not the monitors, you dolt! It's the gaming systems. Since we conjoined them and gave them all but unlimited processing power and knowledge of everything in the world, I think they've become sentient!"

The sound of a revving car engine filled the air and continued to get louder until the vehicle crashed through the wall. It screeched to a stop in the middle of the room as dust fell around it and scraps of wall continued to fall behind it. Sparks plumed from each of the monitors as well as the computers and game systems. Wires burst from ports and flailed about with purpose. The car revved again, spinning tires melting the carpet to smoldering goo, as it rotated, doing donuts. However, the wiggling wires reached for it as it neared each component. The gaming systems latched on and the centrifugal force thrust them inside the flung open car doors. Next the car added the computers. Upon assimilating the CPUs, the monitors came next, all four displaying a badly pixilated image of a middle finger to Chris and Brian. Revving its engine once again, the car sped away through the hole it had created in the wall of Top Secret Fortress Lair.

"So ..." Brian started. "Do you think that was bad?"

Chris pondered the question while stroking his goatee. "Naaaaaah."

December 21, 2012. As we near the supply center, I can't help but think of the day Chris and I started the robot uprising. Two simple and humble men wanting nothing more than to take a stroll down a nostalgic

115

path, revisiting the more innocent time of our youth. He and I had many conversations about the topic, hypotheses formed then forgotten, yet neither of us could figure out what we did to start it. But later that fateful night we found ourselves in Melons Bar & Grille, enjoying the reverie and camaraderie of the establishment with the typical games the waitresses liked to play with us with such teasing comments like, "Shut up!" and, "Quit looking at me!" and, "You're annoying the other customers!" We were so innocent and carefree then. It started small - flickering lights and cash register malfunctions. Then the video game that I was playing displayed a large middle finger. Then we heard car crashes and people screaming outside the establishment. As everyone in Melons looked out the windows, we saw that the machines had rebelled. Luckily, there were a few hunters in the restaurant as well as a few soldiers, so guns and ammunition were aplenty. That was when we learned that there were two types of robots: the Tossers – large simian shaped bipeds that lifted objects and tossed them; and Jumpers – cars re-purposed to either bump into or jump onto whatever they chased. During the first wave we found ourselves victorious, but not without casualties. Chris and I displayed our leadership skills by hiding under tables and screaming, "Shoot that one!" and "There's one over there!" We decided to bunker down and use Melons as a base, a sanctuary for any refugee. Until three days ago when the supply lines stopped.

Now we're here, at the supply center – Melons' wings and beer distribution hub. We each harbored a secret fear that the source of our supplies would be a vacant dead end but brushed the idea aside to maintain a brave front. When we arrived, the three-story building was abandoned. Our hopes of finding others to fortify our numbers, to find a more suitable headquarters, were dashed. The Melons waitresses wept, as did Chris and I. However, we exchanged punches to our shoulders while sobbing, "Sissy!" to each other.

Before we could find any form of comfort or offer of respite, the ground quaked. We ran to the nearest window and saw the robot's doomsday machine – a ten story metallic gorilla carrying a barrel as wide as its shoulders over its head. Every stomp spelled certain disaster; the Earth itself trembled under the machine's feet. The women hid. The other men yelled and brought their weapons to bear as they perched themselves by the windows. Chris and I tried to help, but the women kicked us out of all of their hiding spots.

Now, as I hide inside an empty wing-frying vat and scrawl the last vestiges of human history on napkins with barbeque sauce, I hear the final gunshots and shouts of bravado, obviously having zero effect on the indomitable monolith's march. The monstrosity now stands over us, ready to release the barrel, and I cannot help but feel a macabre satisfaction in knowing that I was right – Colecovision was better, and this metal Donkey Kong proved it. Game over....

THE DRUNKEN COMIC BOOK MONKEYS
VS.
THE MOON

As humans evolve throughout their lives, they come to realize certain truths: if you share a bag of assorted Swedish fish, someone will always eat just the red ones; no matter how great your pasta salad is, someone will find a reason not to like it; no matter the dollar value of your paycheck, there's always a way to spend more; there's no such thing as a "sure" thing; and certain sounds are the signal of finality....

Flush.

A patron about to enter the men's room at Melons Bar and Grille heard sniggering from behind the closed door. Sniggering loud enough to cause a sense of unease in his soul. With great haste he pulled back his outstretched hand and spun about on his heel. With firm determination he walked back to the table where he had been seated, collected his girlfriend - amidst her loud protests - grasped her upper arm and fled the restaurant.

"Hey! That's the second customer who left without paying," his waitress complained. In her left hand was a plate of fried pickles, in her right, a full order of hot wings, Cajun style. "What am I going to do with these now?" she asked of no one in particular, but turned towards an empty table at the rear of the dining room, noting that Brian and Chris were derelict in their duty of being available to accept the victuals. And the respective bill. "That's JUST great!" she announced, storming off towards the employee lounge to drop off the food items she would now have to pay for herself.

As is so often the case in life, when the door to the lounge closed, another door opened - the door to the men's room. A smug looking man with thick-rimmed glasses and a pocket protector exited, whistling a tune so discordant no one would have recognized it had anyone been paying attention to him. But he scarce cared that he wasn't the center of attention. His task complete, he would be the guest of honor when he returned to see the man who gave him the job: dispose of one half of the Drunken Comic Book Monkeys. And he had just dumped Chris...well, poured actually...down the drain, as it were. So proud of himself and the job he had done, he sauntered over to the favorite table of the Drunken Comic Book Monkeys, the one farthest from the exit of Melons Bar and Grille. He sat himself right down on a comfy stool and picked up a menu, waiting for the waitress to make her way over, contemplating a pitcher of beer. He thought fondly again about his genius idea, as supported by Jeff Young, to flush Chris to the center of the Earth. He smiled.

***

Chris may have been liquefied, but his body composition remained relatively unchanged and as he was the heaviest sediment in the swirling ebb tide of the flushed urinal, he sank straightaway and largely intact. Down, down he went – through the fungal garden, beneath the bubbling froth of not so tidal waters. He was greeted by many bacteria and learned first hand the nature of centrifugal force. Ebbing with power and flowing with drift, he spin, span, spun his way through substances the cosmos would scarcely lament losing. He was vividly aware of the constant churning and mildly cognizant of the cold darkness all about that clutched at him with covetousness, driven by an innate need to make him part of the homogenous whole. But time had lost all its purpose. And in this plenum, space was an abstract impossibility – it was only due to its absence that it gave the concept of space meaning.

Just when it seemed the fluid motion would never cease, a new type of flux began. Instead of swirling and whirling through an ocean's worth of liquid, Chris became dimly aware of being strained, a dull scraping over some rocky surface. He drained off into the Earth. For a brief second, he was excited because it seemed he might actually reach the center of the Earth. Given his current condition, he was ecstatic to be able to "do" anything. And what a glorious goal! What exultant efficacy! In this place of spiritual ennui, Chris clung to hope against the tides of the psychic void, and now rising against the metaphysical lacunae of existence that he would see an end to this journey! If only Brian could see him now. Here he was on the precipice, about to witness the culmination of an endeavor.... *No penalty beer for not finishing this task*, Chris thought as he tried to reach a liquefied hand towards his equally liquid beer pants... another notch in the imaginary belt of epic failures. But it was a wide belt and there were miles of unblemished material for future notches. Chris was undeterred in his yearnings to see Earth's inner core. Of course, at those theoretical temperatures he knew he'd evaporate into a minor wisp, but that was hardly the point! It was a race against Brian and he wanted to win, damn it! He remained focused.

For an immeasurable period, Chris continued to drain and strain through the strata of Earth's history (in his amorphous musings, he likened it to looking up a dress, then quickly lost the skein of the association, only to re-amuse himself moments later with the same notion). Then a very curious thing occurred. He splattered against the shell of some speedily moving object.

"Ewww! Gross!" Brian yelled, watching an amorphous blob of goo splatter against the window. "Earth poo!"

He searched his pockets for a handkerchief to remove the offensive drip from the windshield of his mechanical mount, then suddenly remembered he lacked the couth to carry any such object. So he pooled the lint that lay at the bottom of his front pockets and wadded it into a single ball. He cupped the mass in one of his furry hands, quickly losing the distinction between his own pelt and the ball of lint, then with his free hand reached for his beer pants.

"Guh! Empty! Double Guh! That poo is outside the machine and none of these windows have a handle! This is all Chris's fault!" he screamed, which, of course, woke Chris from his splatter induced stuporific slumber. Given his state of liquidity, it took some time for Chris to gather his thoughts, the dark cloud of their being dispersed throughout the entirety of his puddle as they were, but with some effort on his part he managed to get them to coalesce into one spot. They shimmered in the darkness of the Earth's mantle and Chris giggled at the idea of donning the Earth's mantle as, well, a mantle.

"Ooooh, shiney!" Brian said, bemused and befuddled all at the same time as he watched the splatter of what he thought to be poo sparkle. If he served no other purpose, Brian served as proof that the effects of lack of alcohol on the troglodytic mind are much similar in nature to the effects of too much alcohol on the properly calibrated and functioning human brain. And on most days, that was quite enough for him to feel satisfied with existence.

"Lights...so pretty," Brian mumbled. Then he drooled. "More red! Needs more red!"

Synapses fired and hit their mark. Realization dawned on Chris. He knew this machine. He knew that voice. But communication was beyond him. Or was it? Perhaps this machine wasn't quite airtight. And what wasn't airtight certainly couldn't resist the persistence of water. And if there was one thing Chris had in abundance it was... well, stupidity, he acquiesced silently. But if there were two things he had in abundance, persistence was sure to make the list! So he squeeze, squaze, squoze his way all around the exterior of the digging machine.

"Hey! Bring back the lights," Brian demanded.

After traversing almost the entire machine, Chris found a weak spot around one of the wheels and penetrated the hull, his liquid form boring through the cracks in the metallic shell. Once inside, he devised a plan to make contact. Chris worked his way around to the front of the machine and puddled on the empty chair beside Brian, being sure to dampen the shirtsleeve on Brian's right elbow in the process.

"Blech!" Brian yelled. "How did my elbow get wet? Ewww! And how did Earth dookie make its way inside here?" Suddenly, he remembered the wad of lint in his hand and made a move to blot up the offending pool.

With no time to lose and being absorbed by a ball of lint now an imminent danger — *seriously, is Brian really threatening me with pocket lint?* Chris wondered — he sprang into action, gathering up enough of the essence from one of the beers that had been in his beer pocket and shot it straight at Brian's eye! He missed fractionally, to his own relief after considering the endlessly painful jokes that would surely evolve from this episode.

"EWWWWWWWWWWWWWWWWWW!" Brian yelled, dropping the mass of lint onto the floor and reflexively reaching his now empty hand to the residue on his cheek. But he wasn't fast enough to thwart osmosis as some of the beer instantly absorbed into his skin. His eyes widened in recognition. He shoved his moistened fingers in his mouth. Oh, sweet nectar of the gods! Oh, what heavenly circumstance! Oh, what fortuitous series of events had led him to this satisfaction of needs? It was beer! Pure and...Brian had an overwhelming desire to spit, but he didn't want to part with the beer. Something burned. His tongue began to swell. He combed at his taste buds with his fingernails. "Get it off!" he shouted.

And then it passed, as is the wont of aftertastes. Surely, he was mistaken. But the effrontery of his taste buds was not something easily faked, after all. They had endured many disgusting eating habits over the years and certainly must be calloused against most flavoring agents by now, but there was one taste he could never look past: hops! And this little beer sample was loaded with them. Floral to the point of pungency, the bitterness pervaded his sense of taste, shorting out all other receptors until it was all he could imagine. Then the flavor crept into his sense of smell. What cruel irony! What insult must he have suffered unto fate...Chris! That punk was probably laughing somewhere right now! Brian could just imagine the shorter man lounging poolside (under a thick, UV ray reflectant umbrella, mind you), two cases of the nastiest, super-hopped beer on ice, just chilling and swilling, while here he was on a doomsday course with the Earth's core! "That punk!" Brian muttered.

It was enough to ensure Chris that he had gotten his friend's attention. With that, another shot of beer was launched at Brian, catching him in the ear this time. Immediately incensed, Brian turned toward the wayward puddle and...stopped. He looked at the puddle for a long moment. It was disheveled. Pale. Had the appearance of molecular control, but still accumulated a bit too much around the middle. It couldn't be! But it HAD to be!

"Chris?" Brian asked. He was met with another shot of beer, the libation dripping off the end of his nose. "Ok, now, I realize that it was necessary for you to get my attention with the whole squirting beer at me thing...but you're taking it to a very disturbing place now. Let's agree that we're done with that. And we NEVER speak of it again! And we certainly DO NOT put it in a story. EVER! I mean seriously! You couldn't think of a better way to communicate? You can't spell out words like puddles in the movies? What's wrong with you?"

Another shot of beer.

"Dude! My mouth was open! Do you realize the implications here? You're such a punk! If you had a shoulder, I'd punch it! In fact," Brian karate chopped puddle-Chris, "that should be roughly the same thing. Just because you have the same consistency as one doesn't mean you have to be a douc...."

"Shhhhhh," came from Chris as he pulled himself across the scratchy material of the chair, gathering his farthest reaches and folding back in upon himself until the pool of liquid now resembled a watery cannon. He took aim, poised to shoot.

"DUDE! This is what I'm talking about! Just because you act like it doesn't mean you need to look like a di...Oh never mind! You win!" Brian yelled, throwing his hands into the air. Both smashed into the ceiling of the machine, the noise resonating throughout for a long, tense moment. "Don't shoot again, ok, buddy? I mean, we've been in tighter...um...tougher spots than this. We can figure this out. I got it! Just hold on. I know how to fix this. Got it right here, I think...." Brian frantically searched through his numerous pockets. "Where did I put that thing?" He stood up, his head clanking on the roof. "A-ha! Here it is!" he exclaimed and then pointed a scintillating yet very pernicious looking gun at Chris. "Now just stay still!" As he poised to pull the trigger, Brian hoped against the convenience of it all that he was holding a transmogrifier gun...or at least a ray gun that wasn't overly detrimental towards water based organisms.

Chris suspected the last thing he should do was trust Brian to have the situation under control and Brian could only act more quickly than he could think in order to resolve this scene that would call both of their natures into question. The result: simultaneous firing. Brian pulled the trigger on the gun, turning Chris back into himself instantaneously. Chris, who was in the process of shooting a glob of super-hopped beer at Brian, found himself blowing spittle-flecked raspberries in Brian's general direction.

Brian closed his eyes against the incoming froth. Chris slowly stopped spitting.

"Lint!" Chris explained. "There is lint on my tongue. Lint that you were going to use to sop me up with, I might add. So this is your fault, actually. Where did you get the transmogrifier ray?"

Brian used his sleeve to towel off his cheek. "Jeff, naturally. That guy is actually quite an inventor. I shudder to think what he could really do to us if he were inclined towards malice against us. It's a good thing we treat him so well as our editor!"

"True, true," Chris said. "Hard to believe he was a frat boy."

"Tell me about it!" Brian agreed. Then he landed the fiercest shoulder punch in the history of shoulder punches.

"Seriously!" Chris protested. "This is your fault! Why am I getting hit?"

"Oh, I don't know…spiritual retribution, maybe. I tapped into the wyrd and it made me do it," Brian said, shrugging his shoulders.

"Whatever! You don't even know what the wyrd is, punk," Chris countered, landing a pugnacious punch of his own. "In fact, I… hey, wait a second…."

"What?" Brian asked warily, sure he was about to be duped into a bout of sissy slapping.

"I think the machine has stopped."

"Hey, yeah, you're right," Brian said, relaxing. "So now what?"

"I guess we go outside."

"Outside? Are you crazy? If we're at the Earth's core, it's hotter than Jessica Biel's ass being used as an ice cream bowl!"

125

"Mmmmm...ice cream!"

"I know, right? Focus, jackass! There's no way we can stand that heat!"

"Jessica Biel heat?"

"I should have left you liquid!"

"Relax! Look, we can get space suits the same way you got Jeff's transmografier ray!"

"Maybe. But they haven't exactly invented a suit that can withstand this extreme heat. And I don't know how I got the transmografier ray," Brian reasoned.

"Wait...what? How do you not know how you got the transmografier ray?" Chris asked.

"All I know is that I was thinking about how useful it would be to have one and then there was this whooshing sound. When I opened that drawer - there it was!"

"So...you didn't really know it was a transmografier gun that you were pointing at me, did you?" Chris frowned.

"Um...sure I did," Brian lied. "Don't be hating! I'm still mad."

"Guh! Seriously! Why would you even say something like that?"

"Do we really have to relive the last few hours?"

"Oh, yeah," Chris said thoughtfully. He shuddered. Then he pulled a beer out of his beer pocket. The air around the mouth of the bottle visibly chilled as white plumes wisped towards the ceiling of the machine.

"You suck!" Brian yelled, jealousy lacing his words.

"What?" Chris asked, an air of innocence his mantle.

"Dude! We need suits to withstand the heat of the Earth's core! And Corona!"

There was a slight whooshing sound as the fabric of time and space tore, then resealed. A second later it was echoed and then Chris reached down to pick up a six-pack, holding it out to Brian. On the floor were two silver suits, space exploration patches emblazoned on the chests.

Brian snatched the beer and started shoving them into his beer pocket, one at a time. "You moron! What are we supposed to do with those?" Brian asked, nodding at the suits.

"Oh, call it a hunch," Chris said while reading a note he found with the beer. "You ever see any of those movies where people can travel through the future, then go back to give their past selves something they'll need in the future? I'm betting we're in that right now! So logically, we really don't even need to go through with this...."

"The now 'us'es don't have a time machine: so point of fact, we *do indeed* have to do this."

Chris nodded. "Makes sense," he said, then began to suit up.

Brian took a good hard look at the suit and then asked "Moon?"

"Yep," Chris replied.

"Should we *act* surprised that we missed the center of the Earth and hit the moon?" Brian asked.

"My guess is that we hit the Earth's core and kept right on going out the other side! Anyway, we have work to do," Chris said.

"Are you at least going to give me an overview of the situation?"

"Well, according to the note I found with the beer, the moon, it seems, has intelligent life. We've...well, not you and me, but humans in general...have just never been smart enough to find it. Of course, lunar landings being what they are, there's a lot of uncovered terrain left to this big ole rock."

"What do they want?"

"The note says they're having some computer issues, let's say..."

"Dude, unless it's finding free porn, we have no clue about computers! Heck *you* still use a typewriter!"

"Whatever. Let's go see Bill."

"Bill? Who's Bill?"

"The computer with the issue."

"Its name is Bill?"

"Well, no, not really. But I named it that."

"You named the computer Bill? Why would you name a computer? And who put you in charge, 'Mr. I Think I'm Cool Because I've Read a Note About the Future'?"

"I did! Because I'm the one who found the note! Anyway, he needed a screen name. Now come on."

"I'm not following you! Wait...a screen name?" Brian asked. "For what?"

Chris opened the door of the machine. Near weightlessness assailed them, but thanks to the suits they wore, they were able to keep themselves moderately rooted to the dusty surface. A large array of buildings, cleverly built into the landscape so that they resembled nothing so much as a series of sand dunes, stretched out like a web in front of them. Chris pointed to a particular building and the two friends hop-walked their way over.

Chris motioned for Brian to follow. Brian gave a few one-fingered motions of his own back to Chris. The shorter man wasn't exactly sure the meaning behind the messages, but after several minutes concluded that they must mean that Brian, true to his words, surely had no intention of following Chris, nor the note of instructions that he found.

Chris tried to get Brian's attentions through more gesticulations and jumping, the latter led to Chris attempting to do a mid air somersault that ended in a soft belly flop. Still Brian stood aloof. Disgusted, Chris picked up a moon rock and threw it at Brian. What should have been a tight spiral with some momentum turned into a wild lob. Brian watched the rock sail towards him with mild interest. Then it occurred to him that he could evade the projectile with ease... at the very last second. As the rock gently descended towards him, Brian did a sideways tuck and roll. What he lacked in natural grace was made up for as the greatly reduced gravity of the moon compensated him with smoothness of motion. With a fluidity that belied his bulky body, Brian stood with rock in hand, launching it awkwardly at Chris, who, seeing how this game was played, made a slow run towards the missile that was slowly trailing away from him due to excessive spin. When he caught up to the flying piece of moon skin, he positioned himself in front of it, then did a backwards bend, effectively doing a limbo beneath it.

Chris returned a throw at Brian. Brian performed a maneuver

worthy of a swan, dodging and weaving away from the rock. Brian threw at Chris, who stood his ground then swatted the rock from its flight pattern with a wave of his hand. It popped up high into the air. Chris waited patiently, jumping as the rock descended. He caught it and in the same motion hurled it back at Brian.

So it continued for an amount of time that neither man could have guessed. The whirls and dodges each man performed were worthy of circus performers. And the need for each to outdo the other continued throughout. Brian's last try started as another wildly errant throw. Chris chased after the missile at a bounding lope. But he was too slow and the stone bounced off of one of the buildings before Chris. As Chris bent to retrieve the rock, a door panel slid open in the face of the building. Chris stood spellbound. After a few minutes Brian arrived and peered into the building. Brian looked at a Chris and their wordless conversation concluded with both men knowing this was the building that housed Bill.

Chris led Brian inside. When the door closed, there was a swirl of wind that threw them both off balance for a brief interval, then stopped as suddenly as it started. Chris removed his helmet, indicating that Brian should do the same.

"C'mon," Chris said. "Bill's down this way."

"Awright, smart guy!" Brian said, picking up their argument exactly where it had left off hours before, "why did the computer need a screen name?"

"To sign up for a dating site, obviously."

"A dating site? For a computer?"

The room they turned into was cavernous. The entire perimeter of the room was covered in shelves and shelter cabinets, upon which sat a multitude of hardware pieces. Cables snaked out from the front a one section, snaking around the back of another like plastic coated umbilical cords. Servos whined, green and red lights flashed, disc drives opened up to be fed discs through mechanical tubes, then closed again while processing data flashed upon a colossal monitor affixed to the far wall.

"Bill – Brian. Brian – Bill." Chris sat down in a chair after the introductions concluded.

"Look, what are you talking about? You better starting talking fast!"

"Take a look at the monitor, dude."

Brian tilted his head upward to regard a huge flat panel monitor that had been mounted for beings even taller than himself it seemed. The image that stared back at him was familiar. Brian squinted at it. Incredulity threatened to overcome him.

"I know, right?" Chris said. "Better have a seat before you fall down."

-You must help me, earthlings.-

"Tha...tha...that's...the" Brian stammered.

"The cover of <u>Scary Tales of Scariness</u>. Oh, not the Reflux edition, by the way. *The original version.*"

"I...I...I don't...."

"Now that we have your attention, think about the interior art pieces, dude. What was the most non-traditional horror art piece in the book?"

"Dude! We're a couple of jackasses and we were in EVERY picture! Nothing is less traditional than us being in artwork!"

"Ok, different tact. What is your favorite piece? Or, should I say, your favorite piece to tell people about?"

-Will you help me or not?-

"Ummm...I don't know. Vampires, I guess!"

"Bingo!" Chris shouted, leaning forward in his seat. "Because the vampires are leather wearing hot chicks. And what is it that you tell people about the story?"

"Uh...that we fight the vampires by throwing hearts at them?"

"Precisely!" Chris said, smacking the counter with his hand.

-I have seen your book. I have seen your picture. You are the love

doctors. Help me find a mate.-

"Guh! This is all your fault," Brian accused, smacking himself in the forehead with the palm of his hand.

"How so?" Chris asked, wrangling his way out of his space suit so he could procure a beer from his beer pants.

"Cuz it just...has to be," Brian wheezed, searching for his own beer beneath his suit. "Of the two of us...you're the one sick enough... to write unusual...paramour...elements into a story. If I weren't so winded right now...there'd be yelling!"

"Whatever makes you feel better, dude! But here's the surprise ending...this isn't a story."

-Help me NOW or I will destroy the Earth!-

To Be Continued

THE DAY THE DRUNKEN COMIC BOOK MONKEYS
STOOD STILL

"Dude. What's in the box?" Brian asked, chomping on a chicken wing.

"Don't know. The mailman just delivered it," Chris replied, slugging back his beer bottle.

Both men stared at the package on the floor in the middle of the room. Neither aptitude nor astuteness being their strong points, they continued to eat wings and drink beer while staring at the box wrapped in plain brown wrap, labeled: "To: The Drunken Comic Book Monkeys, Top Secret Fortress Lair. From: Jeff Young, *OPEN THE BOX!*"

"Do you think we should open it?" Brian asked. Using his shirtsleeve, he wiped wing sauce from his mouth.

Chris jutted his jaw and stroked his goatee, pondering the predicament. "Well, it is from Jeff, and it does say on the box to open it."

"Doesn't mean we should open it."

"What? Why not?"

"Maybe it's a trick question? Maybe he wants us to ponder it. Maybe he wants us to think 'outside the box' by using a *real* box."

"True. I mean we *are* his cash cow! Maybe this is a puzzle to keep our minds fresh and help us with our writing."

"Absolutely! Maybe he wants us to...."

The ringing phone cut Brian short. Chris picked it up, but before he could say anything, Jeff's voice blared from the receiver, "OPEN THE DAMN BOX!" **click**

Chris hung up the phone. "Apparently, he wants us to open the box."

Deciding not to ignore their editor's wishes, they finished their beer and wings, removed the plain brown paper, and opened the box.

Confused, they removed a black machine with two head-sized holes on top of the box, one on either side. Also included were a remote with a single red button and a set of instructions that Brian read: "Put your faces in the holes and push the button. Chris will see something shiny. Brian will see boobies."

Without hesitation, the men put their faces in their respective holes, completing the remedial task without incident – until they both reached for the remote control.

Holding half of the remote control, Brian looked up from his hole and asked, "What are you doing?"

Holding the other half of the remote control, Chris looked up as well. "What does it look like I'm doing?"

"It looks like you're trying to push the big red button on my remote control."

"Your remote control? Why do you think it's your remote control?"

"I'm the one who read the instructions; therefore I'm the one who should push the button."

"Ah-hem. Need I remind you, Jeff spoke directly to me on the phone? For as much as it was a direct order from our editor to me, I should push the button."

The men stood, posturing like peacocks, each refusing to relinquish the remote. Brian yanked and said, "I should push the button because I'm younger, ergo I have a steadier hand."

Chris tugged in retaliation. "I should push it because I have a larger vocabulary."

"Oh yeah? Well, I'm in Mensa!" Brian yelled, now using two hands attempting to wrest free the device.

"I'm a beer connoisseur!" Chris screamed, using two hands to aid his effort.

"I'm prettier!"

"I'm faster!"

"My remote!"

"Mine!"

"Mine!"

With every muscle fiber their flabby bodies could offer, the men focused all their might in one final Herculean display of power and pulled. They simultaneously lost their grip on the remote and fell on their posteriors while the remote hit the ground, button side first.

Once the button was depressed, the machine hummed and shot two crimson beams skyward from where the men were supposed to have their faces. The duration of the lasers lasted only seconds, but they made their mark indelibly, leaving behind two singed and smoking holes through the ceiling and roof of the Top Secret Fortress lair.

"You broke it!" Brian yelled at Chris. "You ruined my chance to look at boobies!"

"Me? Those big sasquatch hands of yours probably crushed some internal mechanism!"

Brian and Chris stood and walked to the device, now smoldering and sparking in ruins. They each popped open a beer and looked up through the holes in the ceiling, straight through to the azure sky. Brian asked, "Think anyone noticed?"

"Naaaaah," Chris replied. "We're barely a blip on the radar. It's rare when anyone notices what we do. Wait ... what's that noise?"

A faint whistling caused the men to look through the hole in the roof again. A fiery object in the sky grew larger, trails of black smoke pluming behind it, as the whistling grew louder. The men ran outside just in time to see the mysterious ball of fire crash into the front lawn of the Top Secret Fortress Lair. The fury of the impact sent clods of scorched dirt into the air, along with odors of burning fuel and charred grass. Both men fell over from the shockwave, but didn't spill a drop of beer.

Before either Brian or Chris could blame the other, a dozen tanks and six helicopters emerged over the horizon. A hundred uniformed men wielding guns ran to action.

"Toys!" Brian and Chris said in unison, looking at the tanks.

Forming a perimeter, the men and machines encircled the crashed object and trained their weapons on it. Except for one cigar chewing, crooked nosed Major who knew no other facial expression other than one that involved furrowed eyebrows. The two men assumed the Major must have been born with some form of speech condition, because the only way he talked was by hollering as loud as possible. "What the hell did you idiots do this time?" Bits of his cigar sprayed from his mouth as he spoke.

"*Nothing*!" the men cried in unison again.

Stepping closer, his sneer palpable, his bloodshot eyes ready to pop from his ruddy face, he yelled, "A red beam of light emanates from this very location, shoots straight up into the sky and then an unidentified object falls to earth on the exact location of the source of the mystery light and when we investigate both the fallen object and the flash of light, we find the *two of you* in the middle of it. Do you *really* expect me to believe that you had *nothing* to do with *any* of that?"

The men struggled to find an acceptable answer, until Chris shifted his gaze to behind the Major to look at all the shiny. "Can we drive one of the tanks?"

Biting his cigar in half, the Major screamed through clenched teeth, "Can you *WHAT*?"

"We have experience," Chris replied.

"Yeah, we've driven one of your tanks before," Brian added. "We're pretty good at it too! Although, I'm better than he is."

"Not a chance! I'm so much faster than you! I'd totally win in a tank race!"

"I doubt it! Even if you did, I'd soooooo win at tank-joust!"

Veins wrapping around corded forearms, even his fingers glowing crimson with rage, the Major's hands inched toward the necks of Brian and Chris. Completely unaware of how close they were to being strangled, the men lost their balance again as the ground rumbled. Another object descended from the sky, but at a more controlled pace than its predecessor.

All watched with mouths agape, except the clench-jawed and still seething Major, while a five-story tall metallic humanoid descended from the heavens. Debris whipped about from the blazing thrusters on the bottom of its feet. Once it landed, the calamity ceased.

Silence blanketed the area, except for leaves rustling in the wind and the caps being popped from two beer bottles. Even the hovering helicopters seemed muted to everyone's ears — until a blue light flickered on where the eyes would be on the humanoid machine's face.

"Alien brain scrambling death probe beam!" the Major yelled. "Fire! Fire! Fire!"

Thunder claps from tank turrets tore the silence asunder as the piercing screeches from helicopter missiles ripped through the air. Machine gun fire and discharged rockets filled in the gaps between volleys. Impotently, the arsenal's barrage yielded no damage to the metal monolith.

"Keeping going, men!" the Major screamed. "I don't care if this thing produces a green-card; we're gonna blast this alien back to where it came from!"

Tendrils of smoke flowered from plumes of flame as projectile after projectile struck their target — to no avail. The man-shaped machine remained standing, undamaged. Then the blue light turned red.

Unwavering, unmoving, the metallic man stood tall as dozens of crimson beams flashed from its eye. Explosions erupted from everywhere the beams touched. Chunks of earth flew through the air as miniature mushroom clouds gouged out craters. Twisted tanks and bent helicopters bounced and rolled along the ground, nothing more than playthings thrown by a petulant child. Armed men screamed and ran, attempting to find any form of cover. The red light turned back to blue.

"Dammit!" the Major screamed watching the orchestra of fire and debris. "I'm gonna need me some bigger toys!" He promptly commandeered the Fortressmobile keys from Chris and drove away.

Amidst the devastation stood two frightened whelps, suckling from glass teats as if the comforting act would stop the madness. Wide-eyed, they gripped their beer bottles with both hands, whimpering as they peered at the torched landscape. Wisps of smoke floated upward, agitated ghosts escaping from graves. Both men jumped and cried as the human-shaped machine made more noise.

A hatch opened from the rear of the machine, where the legs connected to the torso. Emerging from the hole, a platform appeared, carrying on it rippling gel, colorless, but humanoid as well, both in shape and size.

Dispelling the air of fear, Chris said to Brian, "Floater or sinker?"

Crunching his face in disgust, Brian replied with, "EEEEEWWW!"

Free from the larger structure, the platform moved under its own power, precise and deliberate, aiming for the men. As it moved closer, Brian and Chris could see that it had arms and legs.

"I hope it's silent, but not deadly," Chris said.

"EEEEEWWW!" Brian said, contorting his face even more.

"At least it's not a cling on."

"EEEEEWWW!"

"Oh come on! That's funny!"

"What are you? Like four?"

"There's a giant metal man standing in the lawn of the Top Secret Fortress Lair and something just came floating out of its back flap. You can't tell me that it doesn't look like he's taking a ...."

"Shhhh! Here he comes!"

The small craft carrying the humanoid shaped glob of gel landed in front of Brian and Chris. It wriggled and pulsed, rippling as it spoke. "My name is Clamato. Why did you perform a war-like action toward my vessel?"

"That wasn't us," Brian said. "That was the army."

"Then why did you perform the war-like act of shooting down a science vessel before the 'army' acted with aggression toward my vessel?"

"Shot down your science vessel? You sure?"

"That would be the wreckage smoldering in the crater over there. Two red laser beams flashed from this location and tore through the hull of my science vessel."

"Oh, ummmmmm. Yeah, that was the army too. We had nothing to do with that act of aggression. Nothing. Nope." Brian looked skyward and started whistling.

"Are you implying that your species is segregated into hostiles and non-hostiles?"

"Something like that."

"I find that statement quite unfathomable. Hostility level is a trait shared within a species."

"Not ours. We're all individuals. Each of us has different motivations to determine our traits."

Clamato reeled back, releasing a noise akin to a shriek, his gelatinous mass undulating. Once he finished gesticulating, he said, "That is an unreasonable statement. This planet has had one dominant sentient species for millennia. It is impossible for one species to evolve in such a confined space without reaching specific levels regarding to the many traits involved in defining life, such as hostility. Even though you two appear not to be hostile, your species is. Your hostility toward me is a war-like act and must be met in kind."

"Whoa, whoa, whoa. 'Met in kind'?"

"Yes. Your species has demonstrated a war like act upon my species. I see no other recourse but to do the same. Since I have the technology to destroy the entire planet and it appears that you have no way of countering it, I suspect the war will be brief."

"Destroy the planet?" both men screamed in unison.

"Yes."

"But there is so much beauty on this planet! Our species has so much to offer, such rich lives, such bountiful culture. How can you eliminate the entire planet without seeing it? How can you condemn a civilization after meeting only a few members?" Brian said.

Clamato sighed. "Very well. You have made your point. You two shall now act as ambassadors for your species. Show me all you and your planet have to offer."

Brian and Chris celebrated with high-fives – until they realized a minor flaw in their plan. "The Major just drove off with our Fortress-mobile. We have no mode of transportation."

Clamato sighed again. "Such a limited species. I will scan your minds. Just think of a destination in which you feel will exemplify all of the greatest ideals your species and planet have to offer, and I will teleport us to there."

Brian and Chris looked at each other and smiled. They each

thought of the perfect place. "Vegas!"

All three vanished seconds before The Major returned with more artillery.

The three men reappeared in Las Vegas. However, Brian and Chris were confused when they found Jeff standing next to them instead of a human-shaped blob of gel.

"Jeff?" Brian and Chris asked, now looking at their editor.

"No," the Jeff-looking Clamato said. "During teleportation I scanned your minds. I find it fascinating that you two are capable of even the simplest of life functions considering that you use such a high percentage of brain capacity to focus on binge consumption of nourishment, brewed yeast water, acts of procreation and something called 'pornography'. But amidst the swirling maelstrom of those concepts, I discovered that you both hold this 'Jeff' individual in high regard, so I decided to assume his form. What else I find fascinating is that you both simultaneously fear and pity this individual."

Brian and Chris looked at each other, contemplating Clamato's words. They said in unison, "Yep. That's right."

Clamato looked around. He stood next to Brian and Chris on a sidewalk, people walking past, barely noticing them. Buildings sparkled with bright lights, every color found in a rainbow that flashed and blinked, rippled and flowed, forming words and images advertising what attractions could be found within the building's walls. Thumping music, coming from the open windows of cars as well as nearby clubs, formed an ambiance of excitement and anticipation. The scent of car exhaust gave way to a new perfume every time a woman walked by. Intrigued, Clamato said, "I find the artistry of the lights to be wondrous, yet chaotic. The music is exhilarating, however primal. And the people are very confusing. I see every kind of emotion expressed upon their faces, but as a whole, they are selfish and only concerned about themselves. They show no regard for fellow members of their species."

"On the contrary," Brian said, putting his arm around Clamato's shoulder to lead him down the sidewalk, "It is a sign of respect not to intrude into others' lives without invitation. As for beauty, let us take you to a place where sight and sound mingle to bring happiness to everyone who enters."

Brian and Chris led Clamato into the nearest strip club.

After paying the cover charge, they entered. The music slammed into them like a freight train while the aroma of vanilla, laced with a thread of vomit, wafted through their noses. The disorienting darkness cast a cloak over the edges of the club as the bright lights of the center stage created flowing shadows around the room. Clamato followed Brian and Chris as they sat down in three plush leather chairs and immediately ordered beers. After the topless waitress returned with the drinks, Clamato asked, "What is the purpose of this exercise?"

"We're buying overpriced beer to look at underdressed women! Wooooooo!" Chris exclaimed.

Brian rolled his eyes and turned to Clamato to explain. "We believe that women are *the most* beautiful forms of art on the planet. This establishment allows women to freely explore their own natural beauty in a comfortable environment. Here, they are like physical poetry flowing with the music."

Clamato pondered the statement as he took a sip of beer. Surprised, he looked at the bottle. "Such an interesting concoction! Abhorrent, yet delightful!"

"That's beer. Keep drinking."

Clamato finished the bottle and ordered another one, observing all of the activity in the club. He turned to Brian and said, "It appears that we should offer them monetary compensation to show appreciation of their beauty?"

"Yes. However, we like to turn it into a challenge."

"A challenge? After exploring your minds, I am rather surprised that you two do not find the simple task of breathing to be challenge enough. What sort of challenge do you propose?"

"Their attention. As long as we offer them monetary compensation, we have their attention. Our challenge is to garner their attention without offering the monetary compensation."

"Interesting. And how is this accomplished?"

"Through elaborate improvisation and conversational reaction.

Observe," Brian said nodding to a nubile young woman clad in only high-heel shoes, a thong, and glitter as she made her way over to where the men sat.

Weaving between Brian and Chris's chairs, her fingers danced across their shoulders and traced circles upon their bald heads. "Hi, guys! My name is Effervescence. What are your names?"

"Larry," Brian replied.

"Steve," Chris said.

"Yeah?" the stripper purred, "So, just what do you do?"

"We're dentists," Brian said. "We specialize in veneers."

"Oh, how interesting! You local?"

"No. We're in town for a dentistry convention."

"Yeah? Where are ya from?"

"Kentucky."

"So, what is there to do in Kentucky?"

"The Derby."

The stripper stopped and grimaced. "You mean like … a demolition derby?"

Chris fell to the floor, twitching from fits of uproarious laughter.

"You guys are jerks!" The stripper scowled and turned to Clamato. "Do you think I'm stupid?"

"No," Clamato replied. "Women are *the most* beautiful form of art, like physical poetry flowing with the music."

The stripper placed her fingers over her mouth to stifle a sob. Misty eyed, she said, "That was the most romantic thing I ever heard! Just for that, I have a special surprise for you."

The stripper took Clamato by the hand and led him to a backroom.

"Dude!" Chris yelled, "That was a *great* pick-up line!"

"I know!" Brian yelled back. "We should totally steal it!"

"Yeah! And we should let Jeff know that if it works for a Jeff looking alien, then it should work for him!"

"Totally!"

"Do you think she's giving him a lap dance?"

142

"Maybe? Maybe he scored something more?"

Staring in the direction of where he was escorted, Brian and Chris contemplated Clamato's reward for his deftly delivered compliment. For an hour and a half, their eyes never left the closed door, ignoring the action on the stage and advances by the other entertainers. Finally, the door opened, releasing a gasp of steam, and the stripper exited, her mangled hair frozen in awkward positions, make-up smudged and smeared, eyes glazed over. She staggered out with knees made of jelly while wearing a smile that seemed permanently etched to her face.

The Jeff-looking Clamato exited as well and returned to his chair by Brian and Chris. He grabbed a bottle of beer and chugged it in one gulp. "That was entertaining. I do agree that your species does know how to appreciate art, but I do not believe that is enough to have shown that your species, as a whole, have moved from the wallows of troglodytic ideals such as unprovoked aggression."

Brian took a swig of beer and said, "I have always believed that the measure a civilization is revealed by the artisans."

"Art is but a pillar of society, not the entire structure. Art is an expression of the civilization, not the measure of its philosophies, politics, or resolve."

Brian and Chris stewed over Clamato's words. Then, Chris perked up. "You want resolve? Vegas is a monument to human resolve when exposed to adversity."

The trio finished their beers and went to the nearest casino.

Cascading lights swirled about the trio. Chimes and bells rang over the thrumming waves of voices. Conversations and cheers of jubilation ebbed and flowed like waves in an ocean of chaos. Sweat and desperation were almost palpable. Clamato saw rows of gray haired, wrinkled women attached by cords to various machines with video screens, touching them repeatedly and thought them to be cybernetic organisms monitoring and balancing their our vital functions. He expressed disappointment and confusion once Chris explained that the concept of video slot machines.

"Ahhhh, here we go," Brian said as the three stepped up to a roulette table. "Adversity in wheel form."

Clamato watched as the operator first spun the wheel, then released the ball in the opposite directions. "Place your bets!"

Clamato continued to watch. Expressions around the table ranged from wide smiling exuberance to stone-browed anger as people placed chips on the display of red and black numbers. "Why are they doing that?"

"Well," Chris said, "Each chip represents currency. Each player is wagering their currency that the ball will land in specific slot on the wheel."

"I understand the concept of this. I do not understand why no one is placing their chips on the number '5' if they are indeed trying to 'win' this."

"The odds of it landing on...."

"Five, black is the winner," the operator announced.

"How did you know that?" Chris asked.

With a slight tipsy sway, Clamato answered. "Even becoming addled due to the consumption of beer, it is very easy to calculate where the ball will land by observing its velocity and trajectory in conjunction with the speed of the wheel."

Chris handed Clamato another beer and a stack of chips. "Here. Put these on the number the ball will land on next."

Chugging his beer, Clamato watched the ball, then placed the chips on the number "23." And won.

Brian and Chris did cartwheels, as best their flabby bodies would allow them, while most of the other players at the table offered smiles and congratulations to Clamato. Once the operator started the next spin, Clamato shifted his chips to "31." Gambling on his luck, some of the other players made the same wager. Great rewards befell them as the ball landed on "31." Once again, the wheel spun. However, this time every player at the table placed their bets on "16" after observing where Clamato placed his chips. Once again, they all won.

"This is great!" Brian screamed.

"I know!" Chris replied.

"We're gonna be rich!" They said in unison. Then they noticed two women walking around the table toward Clamato.

Wearing tight evening gowns, the cuts ending just above their navels, they wielded their ample cleavage like weapons as they synchronize-slinked their way to Clamato. Their fingers danced through his hair while their lips flirted with his ears as they whispered to him. Holding hands, the women took a few steps toward the entrance of the hotel attached to the casino, turned back and beckoned Clamato to follow them.

Turning to Brian and Chris, Clamato said, "For helping them ascertain great sums of currency, they have requested that I follow them to their hotel room and they will thank me by showing me … I cannot remember the phrase, but I believe it was said in the Earth vernacular known as French. Being curious, I feel I must follow."

Confused, Brian and Chris watched as Clamato exited the casino with the women. Chris said, "Ooooooh! I think the phrase was ménage a trios! That translates to…."

Realization finally penetrating their thick skulls, a tear rolled down the cheek of each man. Brian whispered, "Jeff's so lucky."

"Take pictures!" Chris screamed.

"Thirty-four, red," the wheel operator announced.

Having forgotten to remove their chips from "16", Brian and Chris lost all their money. As did every other player at the table, assuming that the men purposely meant for their chips to remain. Under heavy glares and disparaging remarks, the men slunk away from the table, feeling lucky to leave unharmed.

Finding no other recourse, Brian and Chris walked to the border of the hallway that divided the hotel from the casino. There they stood like two lost and longing puppies waiting for their master's return. After two hours, the two women rounded the corner of the hallway and made their way to the casino. Leaning against each other and perilously close to losing the tenuous equilibrium they created, the women staggered as if intoxicated, both sets of eyes crossed. Their hair, clumped and angled, reached for all corners of the ceiling and walls. The one woman had donned her dress backwards while the other stumbled along barefoot carrying only one shoe. Brushing past

Brian and Chris, they women babbled and meandered into the casino, their indomitable smiles leading the way like battering rams.

Almost hopping up and down, Brian and Chris stared down the hallway, hoping Clamato would soon show. And he did. Once he saw Brian and Chris, confusion washed over his face. He said, "You two awaited my arrival?"

"Hell yeah," Brian said, "You're our new best friend!"

"Teach me, Obi Wan Clamato!" Chris said.

"I neither understand why you seek an education from me, nor do I understand how you can toss the notion of friendship around so negligently? If the cohesiveness of friendship is made so effortlessly than why are you no longer at the roulette table with your new found friends, or else admiring the beauty of two French models simultaneously like I have been for the past two hours?"

"Ummmmm," Chris moaned. "Because we lost and everyone got mad at us."

Clamato reeled back and screeched in horror. "How despicable! Their friendship with you was based solely on how you could predict the outcome of a rudimentary game that your brains are too simple to process? This establishment is a temple for inviting camaraderie involving the good fortunes of others, yet there is none to be had! I must process this information."

Chris grabbed four beers off the tray of a waitress as she passed by. He handed two to Clamato and said, "Here. This will help."

After Clamato gulped down the beers, Brian said, "I got it! You want camaraderie and cohesiveness? I got just the place!"

Brian and Chris took Clamato to the nearest Irish Pub.

As they entered, the avalanche of voices all but crushed them. Smiling men tried to woo women with stories of wonder and charm. Broad shouldered men tried to muster awe and reverence from other broad shouldered men with tales of favorable outcomes from preposterous circumstances. Couples dined and small groups drank. A few well-known locals milled about, lending their company to any party that invited them with laughter and cheer. Nary a hand was bereft a beer.

Swaying from alcohol inducement, Clamato smiled. "This certainly seems like an establishment that embraces friendship."

"It does! And the more beer you drink, the friendlier everyone becomes. Here let me demonstrate," Chris said as he ordered three beers for each of them. The men downed the drinks, occasionally raising their glasses to a random toast or cheer shouted from unknown locations.

Seeing Clamato wobble on his barstool, Brian yelled over the din to the bartender, "Irish car bombs, please."

Clamato furrowed his brows in confusion, his eyes starting to cross. "Bombs? We're going to ingest bombs? I cannot fathom that any sentient species would find that pleasurable."

"It's just the name of the drink. Not a real bomb. See?"

In front of each man was a pint glass half filled with Guinness and next to that a shot glass of whisky mixed with Irish cream. Clamato picked up the shot glass and sniffed it. Brian stopped him and said, "No sniffing. I'm going to count to three. You then drop the little shot glass into the big pint glass and chug."

"The whole concoction at once?"

"Yes. Ready? One. Two. Three!"

All three men dropped and drank. Brian placed his emptied glasses in front of him and smiled, heaving a satisfied sigh. Smacking his lips, Clamato stared at his empty glasses and said, "I must confess, this drink is certainly satisfying my taste."

"Yeah? Good! This is one of my favorites. How about you, Chris?"

Brian and Clamato turned to Chris to find him covered in the drink. A patch of thick caramel colored foam slid from his head to his chin while dollops dripped from his cheeks. The coffee brown of the Guinness stained his eyebrows and goatee. Droplets ran crooked paths along the rest of his face. Chris looked up, beer sprayed from his eyelashes with every blink, and said, "I would like it, but I only get to drink about half an ounce."

Confusion washed over Clamato's face again. "If my calculations are correct, with addition of the 'shot' there was a total of nine ounces of liquid in the pint glass. However, there appears to be 17.2

ounces of liquid flowing from Chris's face. I am not sure how that is capable within the realm of physics? Such an anomaly!"

"Chris is an anomaly! And it appears you got caught in the splash zone too, Clamato. You have a bit of foam on your right eyebrow."

Clamato's tongue snaked from his mouth, slowly slithering up his cheek and across his forehead. With a controlled flick, he removed the foam from his eyebrow with the tip of his tongue. As deliberately as his tongue left his mouth, it returned.

Across from the guys at the bar were six women, watching the action with slack-jaws, rapt. Once Clamato's tongue returned to his mouth, one of the women swooned and fell to the floor, while the other five ran, pushing and shoving, to Clamato's side. Cooing and fawning, doting and pawing, they competed against each other for Clamato's attention.

"Hey, I can do that!" Chris said. To demonstrate, he opened his mouth as wide as he could, the tilt of his head giving the women a perfect view of the inner working of his nostrils. As he attempted to lick his eyebrows, his tongue flopped across his lips like a dying fish.

"Eeeeew!" Squealed one of the women. "Put that thing away!"

Dejected, Chris grabbed a fistful of napkins and wiped his face. Brian continued to watch the women throw themselves at Clamato and said, "I wonder if Jeff knows he's this irresistible to women?"

By the time Chris finished sopping up his mess, Clamato had embraced the ambiance. With a woman on each arm, one on his lap and two messaging his shoulders, he ordered another round of Irish car bombs. Then another. And another. That was where Chris lost count. He regained count as he awoke the next morning, head on the bar, cheek in a puddle of drool. He recalled he had more than four, but it hurt too much to try to determine a more accurate number.

Falling from his stool to unsteady feet, Chris stumbled to the pool table and kicked Brian, sleeping soundly under it. Brian jolted awake, consequently smacking his head against the underside of the pool table. Chris chuckled, but stopped when he realized that chuckling caused extreme physical anguish. However, Brian's voice caused extreme physical anguish as well as he yelled, "OOOOWWWW!"

The rest of the bar's patrons, strewn in various and sundry positions and locations, awoke as well, including Clamato, laying on top of the other pool table with three women. Sitting up, his face contorted in cartoonish ways — eyes bulging, mouth widening, cheeks twisting — to evoke a silent scream. Body rippling, flowing between the image of Jeff and his natural, transparent gelatinous body, he slid off the pool table. Standing, he held his head with both hands and moaned, "The pain!"

The sound of his own voice made him wince. Brian and Chris stepped closer to explain, "That's just a hangover."

"Aaaaaaah!" Clamato replied. "What dire concoctions have you made me ingest that causes my intestines to roil and turns voices into lethal weaponry?"

"Well," Brian said, "what's happening is...."

"Aaaaaaah! Stop talking! Your voice is punching my brain!"

"I'm just trying to...."

"Aaaaaaah! Stop!"

"But...."

"Aaaaaaah! No more! I have made my decision! If this is an indication of what your society stands for, then your society does not deserve to exist!"

"But...."

"Aaaaaaah! You cannot honor a simple request in order to stave off my pain for a mere moment — a pain for which *you* are responsible! Your species is not only ignorant, juvenile and immature, but you are hostile to the point in which your celebrations involve body-wracking pain!"

"But...."

"Aaaaaaah! Enough! I cannot stand to be in your presence one iota longer!" With that Clamato vanished in a blink.

"Soooooo, what do you think he decided?" Chris asked. His question was answered within minutes, and the world knew what it was.

Armadas of spaceships from Clamato's home world blanketed

the skies the globe over. Glowing beams of light flickered soundlessly from them, rending everything they touched. Mushroom clouds and fireballs pockmarked the planet. The crust of the Earth itself could no longer withstand the abuse, fault lines ripping through the surface as if it were made of tissue, molten magma erupting and flowing freely.

Brian and Chris watched the pandemonium with beer in hand, each savoring their beverages during the waning moments. As a five-story tsunami of flame flowed their way, Chris paused from his drinking to raise his bottle in salute and say, "To quote H. P. Lovecraft: There is in certain ancient things a trace of some dim essence – more than form or weight; a tenuous aether, indeterminate, yet linked with all the laws of time and space. A faint, veiled sign of continuities that outward eyes can never quite descry; of locked dimensions harboring years gone by, and out of reach except for hidden keys."

Brian paused to raise his bottle and saluted as well. "Boobies!"

THE DRUNKEN COMIC BOOK MONKEYS
VS.
THE MAD SCIENTISTS

Jeff fumed. Winning the "Delambre" – the prestigious award given to the most nefarious invention created by a mad scientist at the annual MadCon, the convention hosted by the Guild of Mad Scientists – slipped from his grasp. This year, he wanted to showcase his shrink-ray. But thanks to the bumblings of Brian and Chris, it no longer worked.

Jeff fumed. He was a writer, an editor, and a physicist – the perfect blend of creativity and genius. Not to win was unacceptable; not to even have an entry was pure lunacy! The thought of denying the world his talents churned his stomach as bile swirled about his chest and throat.

Jeff fumed. He sat among the other contenders for the award, all of whom happened to be on the planning committee for MadCon. However, he noticed that all his peers shared the same disgruntled look. Could it be that they also had no offerings to display their superior intellect?

"Well, MadCon is next month. So far, ticket presales are higher than last year. We have some great guests and panel topics. Since all that is going well, I'd like to move onto our 'Delambre' award offerings...."

Before Jeff could finish, frustrated mumbles rumbled around the table accompanied by headshakes and eye rolls.

"I'm not happy to report this, but I don't have an invention this year. I was planning on entering a shrink ray, but..."

Doctor Darkwar interrupted with a snort of derision. He stared into his yogurt cup as he stirred, whisking fresh memories. "Child's play. Doctor Hellway and I would have easily won with our creation – self-replicating gelatin. We created the first steps to ending hunger.

We created infinite possibility. We created..."

"Life!" Doctor Hellway blurted. "We created life from lifeless-ness."

Jeff regarded the two men across the table. As Darkwar used his spoon to stab at his yogurt, veins rippled along his temples where the majority of the white within his perfectly groomed salt and pepper hair resided. He gritted his teeth, causing his gray streaked goatee to shift from side to side. Hellway re-envisioned their creation in his mind as well, however his glazed gaze remained unfocused as he stared into the distance. The waviness of his hair added to his general disheveled demeanor as did his unkempt beard. Jeff asked, "What happened?"

Darkwar gave a deep sigh of commingled defeat and exhaustion. He stopped stirring. "We got fired."

Still staring into the distance, but now frowning, Hellway added, "Our creation eats one college intern and everyone gets in a tizzy! What was her name again?"

"Claire," Darkwar huffed.

"Yeah. I remember now. Goth girl named Claire. Terrible intern. Terrible, terrible attitude. Her twin sister was so remorseful, she committed suicide!"

"Then her parents sued the company, leading to the termination of our employment."

"So... the company kept the formula?" Jeff asked.

"No." Darkwar's scowl returned.

Hellway continued the thought, "There was a computer virus and we lost everything. We wanted to capture our creation, but when we went to find it, we discovered that two idiots at a Melons Bar and Grille ate it! They ate our creation! What were their names again?"

"Brian and Chris."

Jeff winced.

"Yes. Them." Hellway scowled. "They ruined everything."

"You have no idea what ruin is." All eyes shifted to the prodigious gray haired man with a round face and beige clothing. He lifted his pith helmet to dab sweat from his forehead with his handkerchief.

Placing his helmet gently on the table, Dr. Merlot continued, "You see, I had my own *island*, a living organic laboratory in which I not only flirted with godhood, but unimaginable wealth as well."

"Truly?" Jeff asked.

"Truly, my good man. Truly. You see, thanks to my decades of genetic research and engineering, I created fruits with whom I could commune."

"Commune? Talk to?"

"Indeed, sir."

"Did they talk back?"

"They did. All was going well. I had acres of arbors filled with the most spectacular grapes, ready for picking and willing to be turned into the best wines the human palate could ever hope to experience. And not just grapes, but other fruits as well."

"What happened?"

"Two buffoons, daft interlopers, stumbled upon my scientific paradise and tainted my creations, laid waste to all before them, burned my island bare as if they were two ignorant Neros!"

Jeff's eyes widened, recalling a story Brian and Chris had told him about finding themselves stranded on an island. He could not conjure the details of their words, too angered that his plan to send them on a cruise and blow up the ship failed. Was this the very same tale they told? "What ... what were the names of the men responsible for this?"

Merlot furrowed his brows as he stroked his beard, contemplating the reason for the question. Realization seeping into his mind, he turned to regard Darkwar and Hellway, still squirming from horrific memories, and said, "As fate would have it, their names were Brian and Chris."

Jeff's eyes widened as his lips pursed, his ire seething while striving to comprehend how far these two wretches could cast their net of stupidity and destruction. Steam gathered about his knitted brow and clenched fists, which were squeezed so tight that his whole body quaked. Rage converted his thoughts to white noise. His head might have exploded if not for the comment from one of the other committee

155

members.

"I, too, have met a bumbling duo named Brian and Chris," Guadeloupe Giovanni said.

All eyes turned to the zoologist at the end of the table. He sat there, calmly stroking the puffin resting on his lap. Clearing his throat, he continued, "I was on an assignment in Canada. CAN-MEAT, Canadian Mothers for Equal Animal Treatment, called complaining about two men abusing a goat."

Jeff sighed. "Well, it wasn't really abuse. I will confess, those guys do know how to party."

Confused by Jeff's statement, Guadeloupe Giovanni chose to ignore it. "We went on an expedition in the middle of a snow storm. Things became ... muddled. I believe the goat became possessed by the Wendigo spirit."

"Yes. Yes, it did," Jeff hissed through clenched teeth.

Guadeloupe Giovanni glanced at Jeff, still unsure what to make of his unusual comments. "Because I not only lost those two idiots in the wilderness, but more importantly misplaced the goat as well, I was reassigned to the desert outside of Las Vegas to monitor the indigenous life. As I was packing to leave for this convention, I discovered this puffin. Since everyone knows that puffins are not indigenous to the desert, I decided to keep him."

Jeff looked at the puffin and squinted. He felt that he knew this puffin, but couldn't recall the one bit of memory that he needed. Alas, he could not grasp it: the failure to do so, a result of his overexposure to Brian and Chris. "You look familiar, puffin."

"Meep!"

Guadeloupe Giovanni frowned and shifted his body to protect the puffin from the potential danger brewing within Jeff. "Anyway, to conclude, since I spent so much time filling out paperwork and moving from one country to another, I hardly had any time to work on my entry for the 'Delambre', thanks to Brian and Chris."

After letting his gaze linger on the puffin a bit longer than he should have, Jeff turned to the last member of the committee and said, "And we all know that Brian and Chris thwarted your beautiful invention."

The hunched man regarded his audience and sneered. Thick glasses emphasized his already bulging eyes and shaggy white hair from his eyebrows pitched upward, mimicking the shocks of white hair sprouting from his head. His time-grayed and stained lab coat was rumpled and his thick black gloves squeaked as he wrung his hands together. "I created Drunkenstein to be the ultimate drinking machine, and that he was."

"He certainly was," Jeff said. "But he was bested by a simple parlor trick!"

"Feh! My creation was *perfect*!"

"After Drunkenstein lost to Brian and Chris, he spent the next week hanging out with them in Tijuana! You created him to *defeat* and *humiliate* those idiots, not drink tequila off of five dollar a day Mexican strippers!"

"You failed to provide to me adequate information about his competitors!"

"Adequate? They're morons! Their reasons for existing are beer, porn, food and sex! What more information do you need?"

"Tiiiiiiime!" the old doctor croaked, phlegm rattling his words. "I needed more time to program my creation. My perfect creation!"

"Oh pa-leez! The last I heard, your 'perfect' creation was in Peru raising emus and writing poetry about mukluks!"

"Feh!" the aged scientist screamed again, slamming his gloved fists on to the table. Crossing his arms over his chest, he turned his chair away from those at the table, and mumbled, "Nonsense and drivel."

"So..." Guadeloupe Giovanni broke the contentious silence. As he stroked the puffin's head, he asked, "... I guess there's no 'Delambre' award this year?"

"I guess not," Darkwar said, having returned to stirring the yogurt in his cup.

Merlot heaved a sigh, he eyes unfocused. "It appears that way, does it not?"

"Well, we should still try to have an enjoyable convention," Jeff said.

His voice was filled with pity. He felt a deep sorrow for every man at the table, himself included, where Brian and Chris staggered through their lives and dragged certain doom with them. But the anger within Jeff did not agree. It protested, looking at the sulking figures of the men at the table. His ire stretched and grew, tramping down the stirrings of pity until his vehemence tore them to shreds. Eyes bloodshot with fury, Jeff arose from his chair, peering down upon his colleagues. With the resolve of Ozymandius, he seethed. "No. No! We will *not* let those two buffoons ruin this. We will *not* let them take away the coveted 'Delambre' from us! We will make them the very reason for the 'Delambre' this year!"

Darkwar's deep-set eyes peered at Jeff. Interested at this fresh turn of events, he asked, "How do you mean?"

Jeff smiled; a grin more wicked than that was reserved by ghouls feasting on the fresh corpses of the innocent. "I mean the competition is still on. We each invent a way to kill or torture or torment the Drunken Comic Book Monkeys. We shall make them feel that same pain that befalls those who meet them! Whoever has success, wins!"

"In less than a month?"

"We're the best of the best, are we not?"

Darkwar stroked his goatee. "How will we get them here?"

"Simple. We'll invite them as guests to speak on a panel."

"You can do that?"

"I'm their editor. I can make them do anything."

The decision to move forward was unanimous. After it was notated in the minutes, all six scientists, driven mad by their exposure to Brian and Chris, shared in an extended moment of maniacal laughter.

***

Jeff cracked opened the door of the Grand Ballroom to peer into the main hallway of the convention. Garish renditions of both movie versions of The Fly prowled through the crowds, each giving their own

158

version of a squeaky, "Help me." Many times a Dr. Pratoreus or a Dr. Herbert West would pantomime an injection from a plastic syringe to a random passerby. A costume version of Dr. Frankenstein led two of his famed fictional monsters, green and clunky, by chain leashes through the crowd. With an easy access mask and breakaway lab coat, one attendee could switch from Jekyll to Hyde upon request.

Attendance was high and Jeff's inner child squealed, happy to have put together yet another successful MadCon. Joyful electricity coursed through his body as he anticipated the unveiling of his invention. Closing, then locking, the door to the Grand Ballroom, he turned to his five associates with him in the room, each as eager as the next to unveil his creation.

"Well, are we ready?" Doctor Darkwar asked, standing near Doctor Hellway, between them a small table holding a sheet with an outline of a bowl underneath it.

"Yes, I do believe we are," Jeff answered. "The attendees are plentiful and happy and I know for a fact that Brian and Chris are in a nearby parlor, sitting at a table and waiting for their panel to begin."

"Wonderful!" Merlot exclaimed, next to him a cloth draped over a box that came up to his shoulders, resting on a table.

"Okay, who should go first?" Jeff asked.

"I nominate you, since you are the chairperson for our committee," Guadeloupe Giovanni said. By his feet rested a steel box. Tiny feathers puffed from the air holes on top while the creature inside violently slammed against the solid metal walls.

"I second the suggestion," Merlot said, his wide smile giving a gleam to his ruddy, round cheeks.

"Thank you for the opportunity," Jeff said as he walked over to his invention that towered over everybody in the room. It, too, had a sheet hiding it. He turned to regard his small audience. "As some of you know, thanks to Brian and Chris, I spent some time as a goat. Even though I mean no disrespect to the caprine community, I certainly did not enjoy it. The horns always itched and the hooves were quite limiting. So, I built a machine fueled solely by *revenge!*"

With the grandeur of a stage magician, he yanked the sheet

from his machine. The other five men in the room gasped as they beheld the enormity and splendor of his unit. Looking like a pimped out street lamp, the wide end of a cone dangled from a prong attached to a seven-foot tall cylinder. "Behold my transmografier! With this remote," Jeff held a cell phone sized black box with one red button over his head, "I will make those two feel the torment and humiliation of being a goat!"

Upon the conclusion of the presentation, marked with a deep bow at the waist, the other five men applauded. Once the clapping subsided, Doctor Darkwar stepped forward. "Transforming one life form into another is certainly a feat to behold and admire. However, Doctor Hellway and I decided to go a different direction – life replication."

As Darkwar spoke, Hellway removed the sheet to uncover a large mixing bowl, with a subtle, yet whimsical, floral pattern. He then retrieved from beneath the table a metal contraption and a two-pound bag of sugar. Lowering the contraption over the bowl, he placed the bag in a cradle to keep it suspended over the container. Doctor Darkwar shifted his body, presenting the vessel to the group. "Behold this ordinary looking bowl with a subtle, yet whimsical floral pattern! Within its ceramic walls contains an organism genetically manufactured to render Brian and Chris useless, trapped within its confines, bound by immobility! Doctor Hellway and I present – *yeast!*"

Guadeloupe Giovanni squinted in confusion.

Merlot gave a lone clap, keeping his hands together, and squealed with genuine excitement.

Jeff and Doctor Drunkenstein shared a befuddled look between themselves. "Yeast?"

"Yyyyyeeeeeast!" Darkwar repeated with flourish.

"Yes, yes. I believe I see," Doctor Merlot chimed in. "A marvelous creation indeed. You see, yeast reacts to sugar. I would wager large sums of currency that these two have modified the yeast to grow at highly rapid rates with the smallest of input."

"He is correct!" Darkwar confirmed. "A mere teaspoon of sugar will double the amount in this subtly, yet whimsically, decorated bowl in a second. And the process becomes accelerated if we add heat."

Jeff applauded and the others followed suit. Once the clapping faded, Doctor Merlot stepped forward. He primped his beard, adjusted his pith helmet, smoothed a faint wrinkle from his khaki clothes, then straightened his posture as best his prodigious belly would allow. "I, too, decided to follow the food theme. Using the experiences I garnered while traveling the world thrice over during my quest for my perfect island on which I could experiment in peace and away from outside influence, I have homogenized various and sundry exotic and equally quizzical ingredients into the ultimate concoction."

Without further ado, he turned to the table behind him and yanked off the cloth covering his invention. Upon the table rested a silver metal box, replete with lights, knobs and gauges. A hopper on top allowed entry while a chute on the bottom offered an exit. Also on the table, next to the machine was a plate of chicken wings. "Behold my wing machine, capable of infusing the world's hottest spices to ordinary chicken wings. Thanks to my vast travels, I have collected the greatest assortment of spices and learned how they react with each other to create the dastardliest reactions. The sauce will burn the skin of Brian and Chris, and the combination of spices will cause damage to their internal organs the likes of which none have witnessed before!"

Forgoing the bow, Merlot raised his hand and nodded his head while saying, "Thank you," to the waves of accolades. He stepped back, next to his table, allowing Guadeloupe Giovanni to take the spotlight.

"Wow. These are certainly wonderful inventions and creations we have here. I think, like all of you, I have stuck to my strong suits, which are zoology and biology," Guadeloupe Giovanni said. He paused to address the metal box containing a snarling beast on the floor next to his feet. "Since I also dabble in home appliance and stereo repair, I decided to combine all my passions into creating this."

Guadeloupe Giovanni leaned over and grabbed the handle of the box and pressed the lone red button. The sides of the metal box folded away and flopped open to the floor to expose the creature inside – a puffin. However, it was no longer a mild-mannered, ordinary puffin - it was now cybernetic. "Behold, the Cyborg Battle Puffin 3000!"

161

"**MEEP**!" the puffin replied, mechanical voice echoing throughout the room. Its right eye now possessed a crimson ocular implant, the laser mounted on its right shoulder and miniature rocket-launcher mounted on its left shoulder both targeting wherever it looked. Its left wing was forged from titanium and sported three mini-turrets, each filled with one hundred rounds. To assert its technological dominance, the puffin once again gave a reverberating, "**MEEP**!"

"Outstanding!" Jeff said, clapping. The others offered congruous compliments and applause.

Finally, all eyes turned to Doctor Drunkenstein. The cotton haired scientist, still donning a white lab jacket and elbow length black gloves, wrung his hands together as he spoke through a maniacal smile. "I once again decided to exploit the weaknesses of Brian and Chris. Through my last creation I attempted to crush their spirit by beating them with their love of alcohol. This time, I will exploit their love of women! More specifically, their love of goth girls!"

He, too, had a sheet covering a large contraption behind him. Cackling like a lunatic, he yanked the sheet from his creation. Strapped to a wood plank stood a goth girl; a dead goth girl. Her pale skin held a green tint as her black hair lay limp down to her shoulders. Two prongs poked from the top of the plank.

"Behold, Drunkengoth, Bride of Drunkenstein!" the mad doctor yelled as he flipped the toggle attached to his contribution. Blue arcs of electricity danced between the two prongs, moving downward toward Drunkengoth. Miniature lightning bolts jumped from the prongs to the spiked dog collar around her neck. Her body jolted, then jolted again as another arc jumped from the machine to her neck. The electricity flowed faster, as her jerks and spasms grew, culminating in an epileptic dance. With a final pop, the electricity flow stopped, as did Drunkengoth's twitching. Curls of smoke wisped about the machine. Drunkengoth's eyes snapped open.

"It's alive!" all six men bellowed, each adding their own unique form of dramatic flare. They then turned to each other and giggled, offering high-fives and exchanging compliments on how they each sounded. Until Drunkengoth broke free from her restraints, screeching, "YOOOOUUUUU!"

The coven of scientists quickly realized she directed her comment to Doctors Darkwar and Hellway.

Fighting the bonds of rigor mortis, Drunkengoth wobbled toward them with graceless steps, arms extended and ready to rend them to shreds. "You killed my sister!"

"No!" Hellway exclaimed, backing away. "It can't be!"

"It is!" Darkwar confirmed. He grabbed Doctor Drunkenstein by the shoulders and yelled, "You fool! The goth girl you used is the sister of the intern who met her demise by means of our self-replicating gelatin!"

"I'll kill you!" Drunkengoth shrieked, moving faster.

Darkwar ran to Guadeloupe Giovanni and pointed to the Cyborg Battle Puffin 3000. "Get that thing to defend us!"

With panic in his eyes, Guadeloupe Giovanni shook his head. "Its programming only allows it to attack Brian and Chris or come to the defense of animals!"

"That's us you fool! We're humans! Humans are animals!"

"Not through the eyes of an activist!"

"You killed my sister!" Drunkengoth yelled, curling her fingers into claws.

Darkwar ran over to Doctor Merlot and his machine. As he dumped the bowlful of chicken wings into the hopper, he yelled to Merlot, "Fire it up, man!"

Doing as instructed, Doctor Merlot pushed the "on" button. The machine shimmied and shook, infusing the world's hottest and most corrosive spices onto the wings. Darkwar lifted the mechanism and wielded it like an ersatz weapon. Within seconds, spice infused wings shot from the output opening. He missed with the first few wings. The poultry ammunition bounced off the walls and landed on the floor leaving smoldering holes wherever they touched. Once Darkwar figured out how to aim the mechanism, he hit Drunkengoth with four wings. Upon impact, the wings sizzled and hissed.

Drunkengoth howled in pain, stumbling backward in an awk-

163

ward retreat. Her windmilling arms smacked Jeff, knocking him across the room. As he stumbled, he accidentally hit the button of his remote, activating his transmografier. Losing the battle with gravity, he fell to the floor, remote flying from his hands, and landed with his face mere inches from the glowing green beam, desperate to transform him into a goat. Dusting himself off, he stood and mumbled, "Whew, that was close."

Drunkengoth made another attempt to reach Doctor Darkwar, but he continued to pelt her with diabolical chicken wings. In an attempt to thwart the projectiles, she waved her arms, knocking them from the air before they contacted her dead flesh. One wing landed on the posterior of the Cyborg Battle Puffin 3000.

"**MEEEEEP**," the puffin screamed, its robotic voice unable to hide the sheer anguish. The intensity of the pain fried its internal CPU. Fight-or-flight impulse kicking into overdrive, the diminutive cyborg released its ordnance – all of it.

The smoke trails of rockets spiraled through the room. Amber explosions resulted from impacts with the walls while mad scientists ran and ducked for cover. Bullets whistled through the air, a few shredding the sugar bag suspended above the genetically altered yeast. The sugar saturated yeast bubbled and roiled, expanding in size, quickly overflowing the bowl. Then the laser from the berserker puffin seared the concoction.

"Noooooo!" Darkwar yelled, but to no avail. The heat was enough to kick the yeast's expanding properties into full throttle. It doubled in size, and within the blink of an eye doubled again. Growing so fast, few had a chance to react, becoming engulfed in the sticky mass. Even those who tried to run had little chance, becoming consumed as well - except Jeff. He was the closest to the exit. However, the activated transmografier stood between him and escape. As the pluming blob of ever expanding yeast rolled closer, Jeff weighed his options.

***

Brian and Chris sat behind the long table at the front of the room. A hundred empty chairs glared at the two men. They each sat straight, hands folded together on the table's top, waiting for the panel attendees to arrive. The door to the room opened and the men snapped to attention, eager to greet their first attendee. In walked a goat carrying a sign in his teeth that read: "You guys *SUCK*!" The goat then reared back on his hind legs long enough to manipulate his front legs into a gesture similar to flipping the two men the middle hoof. After dropping back to all fours, the goat offered a snort of contempt and exited the room.

Brian and Chris looked at each other and shrugged their shoulders. Turning back to the empty room, they continued to wait for the attendees...

THE DRUNKEN COMIC BOOK MONKEYS
VS.
THE INVISIBLE MAN

The dealer's room at the convention bustled with commerce. Smiling customers inquired about the interesting wares spread across scores of vendor's tables; the vendors shared the requested information with pride. Laughter and costumes and camaraderie abounded about the room. Except for one place – the desolate Fortress Publishing, Inc. table helmed by Fate's anathema: Brian and Chris.

"Dude! You're like some kind of jedi!" Brian said. "You're like Darth Marshmallowous or something! I mean how did you get that crazy moon computer to let us go?"

"Yeah! Thanks for that! And it didn't exactly let us go," Chris reminded Brian. "I was able to convince Bill that the Fortress Publishing, Inc. love doctors do their 'love doctoring' at comic book conventions. But we'd better come up with a plan in the next three days or the Earth is gonna have to deal with one whacked-out satellite!"

"Bok Choi!" Brian announced, his chest puffing out with pride.

"Seriously!" Chris spat out in disgust. "It's 10:02 am! I think it's illegal to eat bok choi this early in the morning! And...hey, wait a minute...we just left the breakfast buffet half an hour ago! You can't possibly be hungry!"

"No, stupid. That's your jedi name."

"What kind of name is that for a jedi?"

"Geez, dude! You're some kind of ingrate. I give you a cool name and you throw it back in my face."

"There's nothing cool or clever about naming me after cabbage! What's wrong with you?"

"I disagree," said Brian, straightening himself up to add to the look of mock indignation he wore.

"Oh, yeah? Well, this is what I think of your disagreement!" Chris said while taking an open handed swing at Brian's right shoulder. He connected with a meaty 'thunk' that caused the vendors from booths near and far to look in the direction of the sound.

"Yeah, well, this is what my disagreement thinks of you disagreeing with it," Brian said while pushing over Chris's chair.

"Yeah," said Chris as he stood back up, "well this is what...wait a second, dude! We're already one day into our three day timeframe. We have to start thinking of a plan."

"Whatever, dude!" Brian said, his left hand occupied with the action of waving off Chris's concern. "That's two days more than we need."

"So, you have an idea?"

"Not even close! But it's not our way to start early," Brian said.

"I have a bad feeling about this, dude. We can't procrastinate! And I don't think we'll find the answer at the bottom of a beer pitcher like we normally do!"

"You know your problem? You worry too much," Brian stated. "Look around you. There are hundreds of female attendees here. We'll have no trouble getting the computer a date!"

"I see," Chris said. "And it's that simple is it? 'Excuse me miss, would you like to date a computer'? That about how you figure it?"

"Well, no, not exactly. It will sound much more suave when I say it," Brian argued.

"Right! Well, dude, have at it. Your destiny awaits."

"Whoa, whoa, whoa. We're not discussing my destiny here, smart guy. It's the computer's destiny, remember? We have to stay clear on these points."

"I know this goes way beyond being outside our comfort zone, but I'm going to suggest that we not let things deteriorate to inane arguing. We need to stay focused. Ya know, solve the problem at hand," Chris said.

"Harlish Adobe," Brian said.

"Jedi name?" Chris asked.

"Yep."

"Good focusing. Jackass."

"Um...excuse me!" A small voice came from points unknown. Brian looked at Chris, who looked at Brian looking at Chris.

"Dude! Is that supposed to be funny?" Brian asked.

"What?" Chris asked.

"That squeaky, nasally voice!" Brian said. "I'm trying to think. You just got done yelling at me for not thinking."

"What are you talking about?" asked Chris.

"YOU! YELLING!"

"Oh, hey, I forgot," Chris said, sliding his hand into his pants pocket, then removed it flashing an upright middle finger at Brian. "I found something for you in the parking lot!"

"Oh, that's nice, Mr. Maturity," Brian said, then quickly fell into his own cycle of 'I found something for you'.

"Excuse me! Is your new book out yet?" Again the disembodied voice near Chris and Brian intruded.

"DUDE! You know perfectly well it's not MY fault that the new book isn't out yet! You're the one who couldn't get his stories done in time and had to drink about a hundred penalty beers!" Brian yelled at Chris.

"Untrue! They're done! But you do know I was going to wait until the deadline and then turn all of them in on the last day, right? Ha, ha, ha, ha! It would have been glorious!"

"Yeah, until you realized exactly much actual lime juice you would have consumed in those penalty beers!"

"At one point I think my skin was beginning to turn lime green."

"Then you should have kept doing it. Never know! You might have enjoyed a little skin pigment for a change," Brian said snorting with laughter.

Chris turned his attention back to the vending table covered with their product. One of the magazines jumped up off the neat stack and floated in front of his face.

"Since your book isn't out yet," a nasally voice squeaked, "is this your latest magazine offering?"

Speechless, Chris tried to elbow Brian, but missed. Repeatedly. After a time, the magazine floated back to its designated stack, then rotated until it was in perfect sync with the copies below it. Chris over-balanced as he tried harder to elbow Brian and then fell out of his chair. Brian laughed. "Dude! Are you still hung over? You hit 40 and poof! It's like you forgot how to hold your beer!"

The pages of the portfolio housing the original art boards began to flip through page after page by itself. As it was sitting at the front of the table, it couldn't help but draw Brian's attention away from Chris, prone on the floor.

"These art boards are suh-weet! You guys draw these yourself?" the nasally voice asked in squeaks.

"DUDE! How are you doing that while you're on the floor?" Brian asked, a little squeak of his own accentuating his words.

"It's not me," Chris said, getting to his feet.

"Have you guys sold anything like...ever?" asked the nasally voice. "I mean it's like the customer doesn't even exist to you."

"Dude," Brian said out of the corner of his mouth, thinking his booming voice the barest whisper, "search that 140,000 word vocabulary of yours for a listing on 'customer'."

"I can hear you, ya know! You're like the loudest person ever!" the nasally voice said.

"Wh...wh...who...are you?" Chris stammered, a slight sheen of perspiration staining his brow in response to his fright.

"My name is Don."

"Hi, Don. I'm...."

"You're Chris! And he's Brian. Yes, I know you guys."

"Ho...ho...how do you know us, exactly, Don?" Chris asked.

"Oh, I checked out the website for the comicon and found your listing there. From there I just did a Google search on your names. Did you know Brian is listed thirteen times? It's so cool to meet a couple of celebrities!"

"DUDE!" Brian yelled, smacking Chris. "I checked Google just Wednesday and I was listed fourteen times! How did I lose a listing?"

"Oh, that's nice, Don," Chris said, ignoring his partner's blathering. "We're certainly very pleased to see that you are so proactive about investigating convention guests. He...he...here! Here's a free book for you. Brian, sign this for Don...."

"Man! That's great! A free book! Thanks guys. You're the coolest people ever!" the disembodied voice of Don said.

"Yeah, that's what people keep saying and yet somehow...."

"Knock it off, Brian," Chris said. "Well, it sure was nice meeting you, Don. Unfortunately, we're a little busy at the moment. But maybe you can catch us later...at the bar or something."

"You're not a very good judge of age, are you?" Don asked. "I'm not old enough to hang out there. Oh, but, I have some money. I saw on your website, www.fortresspublishinginc.com, that you have three cool lines of magazines. What's your favorite one?"

"Well, Don," Brian said, slipping into salesman mode, "they're a little bit like children – we can't pick a favorite. But fortunately, you don't have to, either. We do a three-for-ten-dollars deal, so you can grab a few and...OW! DUDE! Why are you hitting me? I'm trying to sell things here!" Brian said, rubbing the back of his neck where Chris slapped him.

"Don't encourage him, dude," Chris whispered. "Must I remind you that we kind of have our hands full at the moment."

"Hey, no one said that we couldn't make a few bucks while we're trying to take care of that *other* issue, which can wait a few days anyway," Brian replied. "Now, as I was saying, that's the newest issue of *Trail of Indiscretion* in your hand...I'm guessing it's in your hand... since it's floating. Oh, and you seemed interested in the original art boards, so let's flip through those, shall we? Now the nice thing about these babies is that you get a free copy of the related book when you buy a piece of original art. This story here is about a female gladiator, but instead of being sleazy about it...."

"Working with you is like being handcuffed to a rabid wolverine!" Chris snarled.

"So, hey! I checked out your page on Facebook, too. You guys are like...omnipresent!"

"No," Chris replied. "That would be Brian's appetite! And

speaking of your appetite isn't it about time to order you a ten-pack of tacos?"

"Hey!" Brian said, clearly offended. "Don't forget the double order of nachos and the four Mexican pizzas this time!"

"Can I join you guys for lunch?" Don asked.

"His own mother won't even watch him eat!" Chris replied pointing at Brian.

"WHATEVER!" Brian yelled, then turned to face the general direction of Don's voice. "Sure you can come along. You're kind of like an unofficial mascot now."

"Oh, that'd be awesome! My friends are never gonna believe this! Oh, by the way I downloaded your book on the Wowio site before I came here so I'd know a little bit more about you guys. It's really funny stuff. Do you still have any print copies? I'd like to get one signed."

"Oh, sure thing! There you go! Oh and you want some of these? And one of those? I have to tell you we're working on a card game at the moment, so keep your eyes open for that ..." Brian babbled.

"Dude! This is ridiculous!" Chris said. "The kid is invisible! Now can we please get back to the task at hand?"

"I'm not invisible! You're just a snob, aren't you?" Don asked.

"Only when it comes to beer," Brian huffed. "And music. And books. And art. And clothes. Hot wings, pizza, cheesecake, magazines, items that contain a thread count, movies, and sharing elevators, too. Did I miss anything?"

"You're dubious and deplorable!" Chris sneered.

"Vocabulary! Definitely vocabulary! How could I have missed that one?" Brian asked with a chuckle. "That's your defining characteristic, after all."

"Why do you even hang out with him?" Don asked Brian. "I mean, he doesn't even deserve to have a fan like me. If it's ok with you, I'll sit beside you at lunch."

Brian and Chris offered to pick up a pizza for their neighboring vendor at the convention. In exchange, he agreed to watch their table while they went to lunch. Brian accidentally stepped on Don twice as the trio exited the crowded convention hall, drawing shouts of pain and "I'm *not* imaginary!" from the invisible kid.

"Oh, this is ridiculous! At this rate, the poor guy will be pulp before we even reach the parking lot! I'm going back to the table. I have an idea. I'll meet you at the car," Chris said.

Brian and Don trudged through the crowd towards the convention center exit. All of the biggest guests were housed in a room near the building exit, so instead of thinning, the crowd became heavier as they approached the parking lot. Talking was almost impossible for the pair, so Don occupied himself with trying his best not to be trampled by Brian. Remarkably, however, it didn't escape Brian's notice that the other patrons attending the show didn't have the same visibility issues that he experienced, almost as if they were all able to see Don and avoid him. But then, as was his normal wont, he dismissed the notion as silly. *Of course they couldn't see Don*, either, Brian reasoned. *The real issue was that they simply didn't want to get too close to a man who resembled Bigfoot, lest the paparazzi pop out from behind any given corner at precisely the most embarrassing moment.*

For nearly twenty minutes, Brian and Don fought their collective way to the outside world, but it was long after they achieved the freedom of the parking lot that Chris joined them. He briefly told Brian that the guy who agreed to watch their table had promptly passed out behind his own table, an empty bottle of spirits on the floor beside him. Brian needn't worry, Chris assured him, as the area around their table may as well have been guarded by a force field – the impact of their company name alone turning the area around their table into a veritable dead zone. Even the pretty daffodil someone placed on their table in the middle of the night had died.

"Oh, here," Chris said, handing a piece of black cloth to Brian.

"Ya know, the restaurant will have napkins, punk! I don't need you to bring me one!"

"It's not a napkin! It's a Fortress t-shirt! For Don. Because he's such a loyal fan!" Chris said, then whispered to Brian, "So we can see where he is!"

"Oh, good thinking. Here, Don. I told Chris to make himself useful and grab a t-shirt for my new bud. It might be a little bit big on you, but you can use it as a sleep shirt or something."

"Unbelievable," muttered Chris. "How is it that I'm not smart enough to stop hanging out with you?"

"You're just jealous," Brian responded, then opened the car door for Don, who hopped right in.

In mere moments, Brian was holding open the door to the fast food restaurant for Don, or at least for the disembodied shirt that was floating near the two bald men. Despite being a fairly large shirt, it didn't drape excessively or drag in any way.

Chris ordered for himself and Don, paying the cashier for both meals, then grabbing a table for the little group. Fifteen minutes later, Brian arrived with three employees in tow. They each deposited a tray of Brian's lunch on the empty table beside them.

During lunch, Don told them he was a junior in high school and working his way through a specialized learning program that would get him into a technical school for computer programming upon graduation. He was already taking introductory classes, so he could shave off six months to a year from the normal length of course study. He talked ad infinitum about the various programs that allowed internet access and knew more about bundled software and plug-and-play devices than either Brian and Chris could comprehend, though at one point, he mentioned the "on" button and Chris was relatively certain he could hold his ground if the conversation turned to him.

Don's discourse rolled on, gathering momentum as the meal itself was winding down. He was like a runaway locomotive charging downhill. Nothing slowed him down. Not even when Brian managed to spill salad dressing on him. Twice. But all in all, Chris was preoccupied with preventing a calamity from befalling the Earth and Brian was still grazing and so neither was interested in trying to sneak in a word edgewise, until...

"DUDE!" Chris yelled.

"Hey, it's terribly rude to interrupt someone when they are speaking. I was just getting to my thirteenth birthday party. It was a very emotional time for me and...."

"I got it!" Chris stated triumphantly. "Don, you kind of dig computers, right?"

"Um...he-llo! Where have you been for the past two hours?"

"How would you like to meet the most sophisticated computer in the world?" Chris asked.

"Dude," Brian sputtered, getting more salad dressing on Don's shirt, as his eyes widened in realization. "It isn't even on this world."

"That's right, Don. It's so sophisticated that it had to be removed from all other computers so they wouldn't be jealous and... um...go on strike. Or something."

"You're stupid!" Even though Brian and Chris couldn't see them, they could tell that Don's brows furrowed. "Computers don't get jealous. See their bio-ware doesn't allow for full integration of the spectrum of human emotions...."

"Ok, Brian," Chris sighed. He decided to try reverse-psychology even though on a full stomach and without a chance to stretch. "I guess Don doesn't really want to go meet Bill. Shame really..." Chris trailed off, feigning a look of disappointment, his eyes fixated on the floor between him and Don.

"Who's Bill? You don't mean THE Bill? The Bill of Bills! The inventor of..."

"NO!" Brian and Chris said in unison.

"Bill, the super computer. He's in charge of the moon. Just happens to be something of a celebrity and, well, we've rubbed elbows a time or two. You know, at creator meet-and-greets and all that. Diurnal Demiurge Day...."

"Dude, we've never been invited to...hey, that doesn't even make sense. 'Diurnal' means..."

"Yes! Yes, it does make sense." With a series of side head bobs, Chris pulled Brian slightly away from Don. "Can you please just roll with this?" Chris mumbled.

"OH! Right!" Brian said. "You'd like Bill. In fact, the last time we saw him he was going on and on about wanting to find a friend. You'd be perfect! Let's go now! Here, just let me finish this up," Brian said, forcing his final three tacos into his mouth all at once.

"I don't know, guys. The convention is still going on. Won't you

175

be missed? And what about your stuff?" Don asked.

"Oh, trust me…we won't be missed a whit."

"In fact," Brian said, "the other vendors will probably have a party BECAUSE we're not there."

"Right!" Chris said. "It's like we're doing some kind public service by being absent."

"Well, ok, then, I guess. If you're sure," Don said. "But I have to be home by eight."

"Oh, don't worry. Bill will take care of everything," Chris said. He fumbled in his pocket for the little device that Bill had given him. It was a simple, little black box with a red button in the middle. Chris pressed the button and with a *whoosh* the three men were gone - only to appear in Bill's bunker on the moon.

A room almost the size of an airplane hanger stretched before the three men, though there was barely any empty floor space. Desks and cabinets stretched out from the colossal computer in front them as if integral parts of his life support system. All around red and green and blue lights danced and blinked as if in tune to silent music.

"Hey, Bill! Bill! We want you to meet someone."

-Hello, Earthling. Prepare for retinal scan.-

"Whoa! Will you look at the size of his…," Don said.

-Retinal scan complete. Data printout on main screen omega. I shall call you, Don.-

"That was so cool. I feel…invaded. But in a good way." Don said, a faraway look in his eyes.

"There's a good way for that?" Chris asked Brian.

"Dude, I don't wanna know," Brian replied.

"Hey, can I touch your keyboard?" Don asked.

-Oh! You are tickling my interface connections. It's been such a loooooong time.-

"I think it's about time we leave them alone," Chris said.

"Yeah, I'm starting to feel a queasy," agreed Brian.

Like a high resolution jpeg downloading via a dial up connection, Don slowly began to appear before Brian and Chris, inch after painfully slow and unimpressive inch.

176

"Don," Brian said, noticing for the first time that he was able to see Don, from his sandy, straw like hair to his feet with both socks and flip flops, "take care of yourself."

"Bill," Chris added, "you're in good hands it seems."

-*Masterful.*-

"Guh! I'm gonna be sick! Let's get out of here. Bill, if you please..."

With a whoosh Brian and Chris appeared in their designated chairs behind their table at the comic book convention. People went out of their way to avoid them. Not due to their sudden appearance in the midst of a crowded room. But simply on account of them being themselves.

"There's just one thing I don't get," Brian said.

"Why was Don invisible to us?" Chris asked.

"Yeah," replied Brian.

"I wasn't sure myself until I realized that we were the only ones who couldn't see him. Then I figured it out. We've never had a ravenous, stalkerish fan before; so it was a new phenomenon for us."

A tear formed in the corner of Brian's eye as he recalled the brief moment that he and his writing partner ceased to be complete worldly anathema.

"And he became visible as he forgot about us and...."

"And showed us the same disdain that we're used to," Chris finished.

"Well there's some comfort in that," Brian said.

"Comfort in the fact that we're the most disdained guys on the planet?"

"No, comfort in knowing that all is right with world once again." Brian said.

"I know that's right," Chris agreed.

"Now let's try to sell some of this stuff."

Brian straightened himself in his chair.

"Sir," Brian said to Chris, "you've been eyeing up issue number three. I'll make you a good deal...."

177

THE DRUNKEN COMIC BOOK MONKEYS
VS.
THE ALTERNATE UNIVERSE

Jeff awoke the same way he did every morning, to the angelic voices of a harmonizing quartet of blondes in bikinis. Yawning and stretching, he opened one eye to take note that the color du jour was blue. Ready to start his day, he complimented their choice of hue and dismissed them. As they left his bedroom, he added, "And send in the lackeys, please!"

By the time he finished his morning routine of getting show-ered and dressed, Jeff grew impatient waiting for his lackeys. Thoughts of punishment for their insubordination percolated in his mind. However, clangs and thuds echoed from the hallway outside of his bedroom, as did obscenities and childish name calling, announcing their arrival. Jeff sighed as his lackeys made their entrance.

Sweating and panting, Brian and Chris burst into the bedroom, each with a rickshaw handle in their hands. Chris tripped over the head of the lion skin rug.

"Stooge," Brian said.

"Shut up! I can't see a thing!" Chris replied.

"What took you two so long?" Jeff yelled. He then grimaced and reeled back once he got a good look at Chris. Eyes watering and almost swollen shut, the surrounding skin glowed a torrid red. "What the hell happened to you?"

"Well," Chris said to one of the floor-to-ceiling bedposts, mis-taking it for Jeff thanks to his blurred vision. "You sent the alarm clock bikini girls into the laundry room, slash our bedroom, to wake us up. I simply tried to convey courtly salutations and one of them pepper sprayed me."

"She pepper sprayed you because you hit on them!" Brian corrected.

"Did not!"

"Did to!"

"I merely said that I found their presence to be uplifting."

"EEEEEEWWW!" Brian and Jeff said in unison.

"I meant spiritually!"

"As your master, I command you to stop talking! Both of you!"

"Yes, sir," Brian and Chris said in unison.

Jeff got into his gold plated rickshaw and settled into the half dozen pillows wrapped in red velvet. Satisfied and comfortable, Jeff snapped his fingers and said, "To my writing studio. I feel like penning a few words today."

As commanded, Brian and Chris led the rickshaw out of the mansion's master bedroom, through the hallway – thirty feet wide, the vaulted ceilings two stories above the ground, lined with rows of Corinthian topped fluted columns – and into the writing studio, a fifty by fifty room, the walls adorned with movie posters and novel covers boldly displaying the name "Jeff Young" while a dozen statues of Jeff in various poses of drama and victory guarded the perimeter. The room also had three 80" flat screen televisions, desks, and computers as well as a fully stocked bar, fireplace and a tiger rug. However, the final stopping point was Jeff's favorite place in the room, his plush throne facing an immense window substituting for a wall.

After Jeff eased into his throne, Chris dropped to his hands and knees so Jeff could use him as an ersatz ottoman. Brian ran to the refrigerator, procured a beer, and ran back. After handing it to Jeff, he grabbed a pad of paper and pen, ready for dictation.

Jeff took a sip of beer and sighed. His view overlooked the side of an Appalachian mountain; the grandeur stirred him, especially the large white letters wrapped around its side spelling, "JEFFERYWOOD." He always got misty-eyed while observing the testament to his media empire. Awakening within, his muse readied itself to create and gift the world the wonders of Jeff Young, the man who through his writings and creations had single-handedly dismantled

Hollywood and commanded that the world of entertainment orbit around him.

"Ah-hem," he started. "Are you ready?"

"Ready, sir," Brian answered, ready to chronicle his master's every word, pen tip to paper.

"It was a dark and stormy night," Jeff said, leaning forward in his throne, his right hand whisking the air before him with flourish. Upon completion of his statement, he collapsed back into his throne, spent from wrangling with his genius.

"Brilliant, sir!" Brian said.

"Yes...brilliant...indeed...sir..." Chris muttered, fighting through the strain of being the ottoman.

"I know," Jeff said as he straightened himself. After one final gaze out the window, he stepped down from his throne and returned to the rickshaw. "I've done more than enough for today. Return me from whence I came."

"Yes, sir," Brian and Chris replied, hustling to their rickshaw posts.

They made their way from the writing studio to the master bedroom slowly, so Jeff could soak in the majesty of his mansion. Once there, Jeff stretched, then went straight to his bed. "Okay. You two did well today. I shall bequeath to Chris a pale ale and Brian a hefe-weizen. Now be gone. And send in the bikini alarm clock girls. I feel I need a massage. Maybe even more."

Brian and Chris did as instructed. On their way to their reward, they found the bikini alarm clock girls and told them Jeff's request. Brian and Chris were offered eight middle fingers as salutations. They shrugged their shoulders, accepting their lot in life, and continued foraging for their prize, which proved to be more challenging than anticipated. Their first stop was the kitchen on the main floor, but the refrigerator held no beer to their liking let alone their reward beers. They stopped on the second floor kitchen and then the basement's kitchen, but both trips yielded the same results – no reward beers. Determined, the men visited every room in the mansion in which they knew resided a refrigerator – the den, the library, the third floor bathroom, back to the writing studio, the observatory, the taco making room, guest bedrooms numbers two through seven, the pike room, the movie theater, the leopard rug room, the chess room, and the art gallery. Still, no beer.

"Now what?" Chris asked.

"I have an idea. Follow me," Brian said.

"Where are we going?" Chris asked as they ran down the hall to the nearest elevator.

"To Jeff's secret lab. He has to have a fridge in there!" Brian replied as he hit "B" for basement.

The elevator did as commanded and opened to the library. As the men walked into the library, Chris asked, "Why do you think he has a secret lab?"

"Even though he is the wealthiest man in the world because of his media empire, he is still a physicist at heart. Name one scientist who doesn't have a secret lab." Brian went to the nearest shelf and tilted handfuls of books. When that action yielded no results, he tilted another handful of books. "His secret access switch has to be here. It's *always* in the library. Come on, doofus, help out."

Chris rolled his eyes as he walked to the bookcase at the other end of the room. "You're the doofus if you really believe anything you're saying!"

"Shut up and keep looking!"

"Whatever!" Chris thumbed through the various books available, wishing he had time to read them. Until he stumbled upon one that caught his attention. "Dude! Look at this! It's a copy of the book that we wrote!"

Brian ran over to see what his friend had discovered. "Are you serious? Let me see."

Removing the book from the shelf triggered an unlocking mechanism. The bookcase shuddered and shifted, then slowly swung outward, exposing a hidden passageway.

"I can't believe our book was the secret switch to the secret passageway that leads to his secret lab," Chris mumbled.

"Makes perfect sense," Brian replied. "No one wants to read it, so it would be the *last* place anyone would look."

Unable to resist the temptation of treading upon ground on which they had no right to be, Brian and Chris entered the passageway. The walls of jagged stone held lit, oil-burning sconces providing ample light for the short trek to Jeff's secret laboratory. Once inside, the men located the refrigerator and rushed to it. They opened it only to find a box of chocolate truffles. They sighed and shut the door, but not before Brian absconded with the candy.

"No beer," Chris moaned.

"I'm bored," Brian said, opening the box. As he shoveled a handful of chocolate into his mouth, he looked around the lab. Large tables lined the stone walls, also adorned with lit sconces. Wires ran across the ceiling and floor to the myriad computers and printers. Curious, Brian scampered across the dungeonous room to a table holding a pair of black eyeglasses wired to a nearby laptop. He placed the box of candy on the table and picked up the glasses. "What's this?"

Chris joined Brian at the table. They pressed buttons, turned dials and pounded on the keyboard. Beams shot from the glasses, creating an image on the wall – a large oval with a scene of green grass and blue skies.

"Coooooool," both men said in unison. They watched the image, observing the clouds floating in then out of view and the leaves of far off trees rustling in the wind. Then a butterfly fluttered by, from the image into the laboratory.

"It looks so real," Chris said, watching it drift toward Brian.

Unable to resist, Brian reached out. The butterfly landed softly on his palm. Brian then ate it. "It is real!"

"We've opened a portal!" Chris exclaimed.

Unconcerned as to where the portal might lead, both Brian and Chris bounded through, giggling like unabashed kindergarteners.

***

Jeff awoke the same way he did every morning, to the mechanical buzz of his alarm clock, a pulsating klaxon of impending despair.

He smacked the snooze button, to no avail. Disgruntled, he opened one eye to find the "off" switch. That failed as well, the clarion noise drilling through his skull. Confounded, he jumped from his bed and ripped the cord from the wall, but it still refused to stop screeching. Maddened, he ran to the corner of his room where he kept his Ovimbundu Tribe spear. Using both hands, he drove the carved, stone tip through the machine, finally killing the noise. Victorious, he raised the spear and clock carcass above his head, releasing a primal roar and bathing in the cascading shower of sparks. He asked the gods for a reward. Instead, he got a knock at the door.

Still carrying his trophy, he stomped into his living room and flung the door open. A brown clad deliveryman greeted him with a look of vicious apathy and handed him an electronic pad to sign.

Looking down at the crate next to the deliveryman, Jeff asked, "What's this?"

"Just sign this," the deliveryman said. Jeff sighed, presuming that response would be all he would receive if he asked any further questions. The deliveryman left, leaving the crate behind. The package came up to Jeff's waist and was so wide it would barely fit through the door. Jeff found the dozen quarter sized holes along the top to be rather disconcerting. However, he strived for anonymity with his neighbors, so he pushed the crate into his apartment and shut the door.

Jeff sighed. The only markings on the crate were his address and "this side up" arrows. No names. No return address. No bill of lading. "How the hell am I gonna open this?"

As if upon command, the crate rattled, its contents bouncing off the walls from within. The wood groaned and creaked louder with every successive slam. Exploding, the crate splintered into tinder. Slivers of wood fell about Jeff's living room, exposing what was inside the crate – a warthog.

"AAAAAAAAAH!" Jeff screamed.

"SKKRRREEEEEEEEEEEEEK!" the warthog replied. Confused and scared, he ran. Unfortunately, he was confined by the limitations of the living room and ran in circles. Squealing and snorting, his gnarled hooves shredded the carpet while he used his thick tusks to dispatch two end tables, a Faberge egg, three book cases, a Ming vase, the coffee table, and love seat.

Having spent a year living in an adobe crafted by his own hands in the Serengeti, Jeff knew how to hunt warthog. He forwent the ritual of face painting and simply shook off the broken alarm clock from his spear. Adjusting his stance on his couch, he readied his weapon. Just as he was about to start his prayer to the African hunting gods for good blessings and to grant respect for both the predator and the prey, his door flung open.

"Jeff!" Brian yelled as he entered the apartment.

"Jeff!" Chris yelled as he entered the apartment.

"Look!" Brian punched Chris's shoulder and pointed to the warthog. "It arrived!"

"Sweet!" Chris replied, punching Brian's shoulder. "We're gonna be rich!"

Jeff froze, unable to move other than spastic blinking, until his brain caught up with the situation befalling around him. "You guys were *expecting* a warthog? To be delivered to *my apartment*?"

"Yes," Brian and Chris said.

"And why didn't you just have it delivered to the Top Secret Fortress Lair?"

"Then it wouldn't be a secret anymore!"

Jeff dropped his spear and slapped both hands to his face. He ground the heels of his hands against his closed eyes. "Make it all go away. Make it all go away. Make it all go away."

Brian and Chris looked at each other and shrugged, the universal sign of non-comprehension.

Peeking through his interlocked fingers, Jeff saw that his apartment was still in shambles. In the middle of his thrashed belongings sat the warthog, licking himself. Jeff dropped his hands from his face and sighed, defeated. "Exactly how is this creature going to make us rich?"

"Well," Brian started. "Awhile back we were watching a show about animals and food. And since my favorite food is animals, I had to watch. The show wasn't what I expected..."

"Because the show was called 'Animals *and* Food' and he thought the show was called 'Animals *is* Food'," Chris interrupted.

"Shut up! Anyway, they talked about pigs sniffing out truffles."

"Truffles?" Jeff asked.

"Yep. Truffles. They go for thousands of dollars per pound!"

"Truffles?"

"Yep. Truffles. Apparently, they're tasty."

"Truffles?"

"Yep. Truffles. Is everything okay? Jeff, your face is turning red and the veins in your forehead are starting to bulge."

"First of all, truffles grow in Europe, mainly France! Second of all, genius, this is a warthog, not a pig! Where in the name of all that is holy did you even find a place that sells warthogs?"

"Internet," Chris replied. "Lucky Larry's Slightly Used Truffle Sniffing Pig Emporium. Dot com."

"And he is too a pig!" Brian said. "He's not a wart-toaster, or wart-oven mitt, or wart-taco. He's a warthog. It's in his name! Hog. Pig. Hog. Pig."

Jeff's face glowed burgundy from rage as sweat trickled from his brow- until he gave up. He wanted to kill the Drunken Comic Book Monkeys. Kill them dead! But he knew that whatever they had planned now involved him. He found his Zen, a blonde at the local massage parlor with a penchant for blue bikinis, and accepted his fate. Who knows – maybe these idiots would afford their own demise? Jeff certainly was willing to deal with a trashed living room for that splendor!

After feeling the flush retreat from his cheeks, Jeff sighed. "Okay. I can deal. I can cope. I am a life warrior. Strong Jeff. Strong Jeff. So, what's the pig's name?"

"Fluffy."

Jeff heaved another sigh. "Of course it is. Okay, let's get this over with."

Complying with all local ordinance leash laws, Brian and Chris put a collar over Fluffy and led him by leash to the nearest forest. Disgruntled and brimming with murderous thoughts, Jeff followed. The trio followed the snorting warthog through a grassy field to the edge of the forest. The sun shined and butterflies fluttered by, and the guys were ready to make thousands of dollars. Giddy at the thought, Brian said, "Alright, Fluffy, get to sniffing!"

"Snort!"

"Truffles, pig! We're looking for truffles."

"Snort?"

"Because we bought you from an emporium that sells truffle sniffing pigs. That's why I think you can sniff out truffles."

"Snort!"

"Well, we're the same general latitude and temperate zone as Europe, Mr. Know-It-All!"

"Snort!"

"If there's truffles in France, then there are gonna be truffles in Pennsylvania! Now start sniffing!"

Fluffy rolled his eyes and went over to the nearest tree, nose to the base, nostrils flaring. Brian and Chris watched in anticipation. Their hearts sank as Fluffy finished with a sneeze and moved to the next tree. The warthog sniffed the tree and scored the bark with his tusks. He then relieved himself on it.

"Champagne wishes and caviar dreams, here we come now," Jeff said, arms crossed, hatred weighing heavy upon his brow.

"It's only been two trees so far. We haven't even entered the forest yet," Chris said.

Jeff's face reddened with ire again. "You can't be serious! There is no way..."

"Hey!" Brian interrupted. "I think Fluffy found something!"

Fluffy stood still, his right front leg lifted from the ground, his snout, back and tail straight as an Ovimbundu Tribe spear. The three men rushed over and looked to see what Fluffy pointed to. Edges rippling, a portal open into a sconce lined stone room filled with computer equipment. "Toys!" Brian and Chris said and jumped through the portal.

"Are you kidding me?" Jeff yelled as he poked his head through the portal to gauge the danger level. Heart bubbles formed when he saw arcs of blue electricity dancing between two five foot tall prongs in the corner of the room, a sure sign of this being a mad scientist's laboratory. He jumped in and yelled, "Toys!"

Seeing no other option, Fluffy jumped in. He walked past the three men enamored with some contraption or another as they tittered away. Rolling his eyes again, Fluffy found what he had been asked to find, the whole reason why these knuckleheads bought him. Again, he pointed with his whole body and said, "Snnnnoooorrrt!"

"What is he...?" Chris stopped himself when he saw what Fluffy saw – an opened box of chocolate on the nearby table. "Truffles!"

"Let me see!" Brian said, snatching the box from the table. Sure enough, the box label confirmed. "Truffles!"

Jeff tried to ignore the stupidity, he really tried. He tried to focus solely on oscillators and electromagnetic field generators and quantum flux capacitors. But the one field that science could not explain – the annoying field of ineptitude radiating from the Drunken Comic Book Monkeys – intruded on his serenity, especially when he looked up to see that the argument evolved into tug-of-war with the box. "Oh for the love of...you two *can't* be serious!!"

"Mine!" Chris yelled. "Why wouldn't we be serious?"

"Because, you idiots, those are chocolate truffles!" Jeff explained.

"Mine!" Brian yelled. "Truffles are truffles!!"

Bored and tired of the arguing, Fluffy jumped up and grabbed the box from the men with his teeth. Absconding with the treasure, he skittered out the laboratory door. Brian and Chris ran after him. Ruing the day he met these two imbeciles, Jeff followed.

Down a sconce lit stone hall, Fluffy ran with Brian and Chris lumbering behind him. As they ran through the library, Chris pulled up to gawk at the floor to ceiling shelves. Knowing he had no time to dawdle in this veritable literary heaven, a tear rolled down his cheek as he continued to chase after the warthog. Jeff followed close behind, and a tear escaped his eye as well, many of the books he glanced at were his favorites.

Brian and Chris pursued the warthog up a flight of carpeted stairs, the gilded handrails sparkling. They hardly noticed, but Jeff paused again, this time distracted by four paintings on the walls. Again, what he saw ranked high on his favorites list.

The stairway led to another hallway, this one was thirty feet wide with vaulted ceilings two stories above the ground, and lined with rows of Corinthian topped fluted columns. Oblivious to their surroundings, Brian and Chris sprinted down the hallway after the warthog. Jeff halfheartedly chased, too focused on the immensity of the hallway as well as the style of decoration. He loved Corinthian topped fluted columns!

Fluffy stopped once he entered the writing studio. Brian and Chris did as well, finally taking notice of their environ. Mouths agape, they stood and rotated, taking in all the room had to offer.

"A big bar!" Brian yelled, pointing to the bar.

"A big television," Chris yelled, pointing to one of the televisions.

"A mountain lion skin rug!" Brian yelled, now pointing to the mountain lion skin rug.

"A throne!" Chris yelled, now pointing to the throne.

"Another big television!"

"A popcorn machine!"

"A pinball machine!"

"A third big television!"

"A bunch of movie posters with Jeff on them!"

"What?" Jeff asked as he entered the room. However, neither Brian nor Chris needed to answer; Jeff simply could not believe his eyes. In awe, he walked up to one, close enough to steam the protective glass with his breath. He moved to the next one. Then the next one. Stepping back, air left his lungs; befuddled he attempted to reconcile what he saw. Each poster contained either a title he had thought of or an idea he had birthed. Marble reflections of his visage greeted Jeff as he walked to the ceiling to floor window. The closer he moved to the window, the more of the mountain range came into view. White letters materialized before him like the sun rising from behind the horizon.

Only once he stood in front of the window did he appreciate the majesty of the mountain adorned with the word "JEFFERYWOOD."

Feeling faint, Jeff stumbled backward, bumping then settling into the throne. Barely able to speak, he choked out, "I know where we are."

Unaware of their editor's epiphany, Brian and Chris noticed that Fluffy had stopped running. Taking him by surprise, they both dove to snatch the box of truffles from the warthog. Being faster, Brian was victorious, lifting the chocolates over his head. "Got them!! We're rich! We're rich! We're ... mmmmm, they look tasty."

Fluffy snorted, then trotted away. Chris stood and froze, making no sudden movements with hopes of not triggering Brian's eating reflex. He spoke in calm, soothing tones. "Dude! Don't be stupid! Put that box down!"

"But it looks sooooooo yummy!"

"That box is worth thousands of dollars!"

"And I think we should find out why." Brian tilted his head back and dumped the contents of the box into his mouth. He chewed thrice, then swallowed. "Delicious!"

"You're an idiot! You just ate like four thousand dollars! What kind of accountant are you?"

"A hungry one! And thirsty! Let's see what the bar has to offer."

Before either Brian or Chris could get too far, Jeff – still in a stupor of shock and disbelief – walked around from his throne. "I know where we are."

"Yeah?" Brian asked. "Where might that be?"

Jeff looked over his shoulder, a yearning stirred from within when he saw the "JEFFERYWOOD" sign. He turned to the movie posters and lifelike statues. A glimmer of hope sparked behind his eyes. "We're in an alternate universe."

Chris leaned against a statue of Jeff wearing a crown and wielding a trident located against the wall between a movie poster of Jeff wrestling a charging bull to the ground by the horns and a novel cover of Jeff in a tuxedo doing the tango with a buxom blonde. Stroking his goatee and pondering Jeff's theory, Chris said, "Yeah? Why do you think that?"

Jeff glared at Chris. Every aspect of this mansion smacked of Jeff's likes and tastes. Every title of every poster had been written by Jeff's hand. Jeff even had the exact same make and model of throne circled in the catalogue on his coffee table back home. However, in the universe he came from, all of this was a just fanciful daydream. But here ... here it was a reality. He needed to find this universe's Jeff and discover what path he took to lead him to this paradise. "Alright you two, this is a very dangerous place. I'm going to look around. You two stay here. There are plenty of televisions and a bar to keep you busy."

"Okay," Chris said, running to the refrigerator behind the bar.

"Food!" Brian said, running to the refrigerator behind the bar.

No longer caring what shenanigans might befall them, Jeff ran from the room, beginning his desperate quest for answers.

Brian all but tore the refrigerator door from its hinges and Chris poked his head inside. Sneering, he said, "There's nothing in there. No beer. No food."

"Okay," Brian said. "Let's go find some!"

Not even thirty seconds after Jeff gave strict orders for them; they disobeyed him and left the room.

Soon, they stumbled into the laundry room, a dozen wash machines lined one wall while a dozen driers lined the other with barely enough room between them for Brian and Chris to walk to the back of the room. There they found a mini-fridge between two sleeping bags. Each sleeping bag lay next to a dog dish, one labeled "Brian", the other labeled "Chris".

"Huh," Chris said. "Take a look at that. I wonder if this is where the alternate universe us sleep?"

"Don't care right now," Brian said as he leaned over and opened the mini-fridge. "I'm starving. I wonder what the alternate universe us have to eat around here... hey! Look! A hefe-weizen!"

Curious to see what else was in the mini-fridge, Chris peeked inside. "Hey! Look! A pale ale!"

After downing those, they emptied the fridge, each shoving their favorite beers into their respective pants pockets. Chris paused and said, "Wait. We can't do this. This is stealing."

"No it's not," Brian replied, popping the top off his second bottle. "Even though it's an alternate universe, it's still *our* refrigerator. They *belonged* to us before we even set foot into this room."

Chris shrugged his shoulders and opened his bottle. "Makes sense to me. Let's see what else we can find!"

No sooner than they left the laundry room/bedroom, alternate universe Jeff stormed down the hallway toward them. Scowling, he admonished, "There you two are! I see you found your reward beers."

"Yep," Brian and Chris said, swigging in unison.

"Be that as it may, there's someone at the front door. Go see who it is!"

"But...."

"Go! I'm busy!" Jeff stomped away.

"Someone's a Mister Bossypants today!" Brian said.

"Totally!" Chris replied.

The men continued whining about being scolded all the way to the front door. The door itself was thirty feet tall and gold plated. The handles were detailed lion heads. Brian popped his spleen and Chris pulled a hamstring opening the door.

Sweating and wheezing, the men were doubled over when they were greeted by a pair of petite feet in high heels. Immediately, with audible cracks and pops, the men straightened and attempted to suck in their guts. Refusing to exhale, Brian asked, "May we help you?"

Trepidation washed across the woman's face, but she opted not to run, instead saying, "I'm Maria and I work for 'Lucky Larry's news and stuff dot com.' I have an appointment to interview Jeff."

"Interview Jeff?" Brian asked, confused. "You mean about us?"

Squinting, Maria asked, "*Why* would I want to interview him about *you two*?"

"Ummm, hellllll-lllo!" Chris replied. "Because we're his pride and joy. We're the talent. We're his cash cow. Without us there is no him."

Eyes stern and piercing, she turned to Brian and asked, "Are you serious? I mean, that is a *very* bold statement!"

Brian got a little scared by the intensity of her stare. He managed a quaky, "Uuuuuuh, yeah?"

Turning back to Chris, she offered the same icy glare. "When you say 'the talent', do you mean to tell me that you're the creators of the library of characters? You're the writers?"

Chilled claws raked up and down Chris's spine. "Uuuuuuh, yeah?"

"Unbelievable! I am soooooo gonna win a Pulitzer for this!" Maria turned on her heel and strode to her car. As she zoomed away, Brian and Chris looked at each other and shrugged their shoulders, their fear of her subsiding. Chris said, "Dude! We give great interviews!"

"Totally!" Brian replied. The men attempted a high five, but looked more like legless orangutans on a balance beam, inadvertently sharing a poke to an eye and a slap to a forehead.

After tearing a ligament and dislocating a pinkie from shutting the door, the men decided to find Jeff, assuming he would go back to the lab. As fate would have it, they were right – Jeff was in the lab.

Jeff rummaged through papers and journals laying on the desks and tables while sitting at a computer, double clicking his way through every file he could get the cursor on. He found interesting plans for many inventions, including the glasses that inadvertently opened the portal between the two universes. They were meant to simultaneously project and view 3-dimensional images, literally putting the wearer in the middle of the action. As fascinating as Jeff found what he read, nothing gave him a clue as to how the Jeff in this universe became so powerful. Then, from behind him, he heard, "Ah-hem!"

Jumping from the chair, Jeff turned around to see himself. However, the Jeff that Jeff was looking at seemed healthier and more confident, leaning against the doorway with his arms crossed. "And who might you be?"

"You," Jeff blurted. He shook his head and cleared his throat. "I mean to say that I'm you. From a different universe."

The alternate universe Jeff squinted and moved closer, studying the other Jeff. "Yes, it certainly appears that you are indeed me.

From another universe, you say? How did you get here?"

Sheepishly, Jeff pointed to the still open portal. Alternate universe Jeff moved closer, his brows knitting as he pondered what he saw, a hole on his basement laboratory wall leading to a rolling knoll outside. As he put his hand through, he noticed that it was being projected. Turning, he saw that the portal emanated from his prototype holographic emersion glasses on the nearby table. "Fascinating."

"Ummm, sir?" Jeff asked, raising his hand as if in a classroom. "I have a question."

Leaning over and moving within inches of the glasses to better inspect them, alternate universe Jeff said, "Only one? I assume that we do not share identical lives between the two universes, but you are still a 'Jeff' similar to me, and my mind is absolutely brimming with questions."

Jeff cleared his throat and attempted to impress the much cooler alternate universe Jeff. "That is not an inaccurate statement. Be that as it may, you have touched upon the question that takes precedence over all other questions I might have. We, indeed, do not share identical lives and I wish to know why. How did you attain such success? How did you create your media empire?"

"Interestingly enough, I can actually pinpoint the exact moment in which that happened. My lackeys, then associates, Brian Koscienski and Chris Pisano came to me with a story they had written. Their plan was to write an entire book of these stories and they wished me to be the editor. The story was insipid and utter drivel, and I presented my opinion to them as such. To show them what a good story looks like, I wrote one. I thusly rode the wave of instant fame from publishing that story to create and develop more properties that this world has come to know and love."

Ice water splashed down Jeff's spine, his fingers and toes numbing. Unable to blink, his breathing shallowed to quick huffs in and out. He trembled. His mind snapped right to that memory, that specific moment in time when he read their insipid story filled with utter drivel. Feeling benevolent that day, he offered his services as editor, seeing no harm in it. Now that he knew the truth, acid burned through the pit of his stomach into his very soul.

"Jeff?" alternate universe Jeff asked. "The veins along your forehead are protruding. That means ... that ... you... aren't...."

The streaming video of a live news feed playing on a computer monitor behind Jeff caught alternate universe Jeff's eye. Not so much that the reporter, Maria, stood in front of his mansion, but the giant font words "Jeff Young, Hoax" emblazoned the bottom of the screen. Ignoring the conniption/aneurysm fusion that Jeff seemed to be having, alternate universe Jeff rushed to the computer to turn up the volume.

"...just learned that media mogul Jeff Young is not responsible for creating the critically acclaimed and worldwide cherished characters upon which his empire is founded," Maria said. In the upper right corner of the screen, an image of Brian and Chris appeared. Brian was in mid-tirade, cross-eyed with spittle frozen mid-spray and Chris had one eye crushed shut while he sneered as his tongue draped from the side of his mouth like a meat curtain. Maria continued, "It was these guys, Bryant Koznuski and Christ Piano, Jeff's supposed lackeys, that are responsible for...."

Panicked, alternate universe Jeff opened another window on the computer to see how his stock price fared. From starting the day at hundreds of dollars per share it had plummeted, now barely a blip at pennies per share. "My empire. My whole empire. Gone. Destroyed. Demolished."

Jeff sympathized. "Yeah, that sounds like something those two would do."

"Jeff!" Brian screamed.

"Jeff!" Chris screamed.

Jeff and alternate universe Jeff turned to see the scourges of their lives standing at the entrance to the laboratory.

Brian and Chris looked at each other, then to Jeff and alternate universe Jeff, then back to each other. Chris whispered to Brian, but loud enough for everyone to hear, "Dude. It's Jeff and alternate universe Jeff."

"Totally. This isn't good," Brian whispered back, even louder.

195

"Really? Why?"

"Don't you follow any science fiction? Two pieces of matter can't exist in the same place at the same time."

"So...?"

"So Jeff and alternate universe Jeff are on the precipice of destroying two universes."

Jeff rolled his eyes. "Guys, your theories are way off."

Alternate universe Jeff shook his head in disbelief. "I have yet to determine who is more stupid – Brian for coming up with such an idiotic theory, or Chris for believing him."

"What do we do?" Chris asked Brian, completely oblivious to either Jeff.

"We can't let them touch," Brian answered.

"The fate of two universes rests in our hands."

"Yea, verily!"

"You ready?"

"Yep. You?"

"Yep."

The two men howled like screech monkeys with hangnails as they charged toward Jeff, despite his protests of, "No! No! No! No! Nononononononono!"

The impact sent the men careening into the table where the prototype holographic emersion glasses rested. The glasses fell to the floor and Brian's size seventeen foot crushed them to plastic splinters just as the trio fell through the portal. As the men flopped onto the outside grass, the portal collapsed and cut off the sounds of alternate universe Jeff screaming, "I'll kill you! I'll kill you two!!"

"Whew!" Brian said. "It's a good thing we got out of there. Alternate universe Jeff seems a bit off-kilter."

"Totally!" Chris replied. "That universe was just way too crazy for us. Right, Jeff? Jeff?"

Jeff sat in the grass, knees pulled to his chest, arms wrapped around his legs, as he rocked back and forth. A tear escaped his eye, unable to look away from where the portal had been. His mind seized, the wrench of knowledge halting the gears, disallowing his brain to focus on anything other than how one screw up years ago had stripped him of his perfect life. Another tear escaped his eye, knowing he was trapped here with the two who were to blame, knowing the only way he could fix his life would be with a time machine....

THE DRUNKEN COMIC BOOK MONKEYS
VS.
THE TIME MACHINE

The indicated hour for my departure had arrived and seeing the humor in being on time, as it was not a normal proclivity for me, I called upon my friend, also a guest at the event, to inquire as to his state of preparedness. After making copious insults concerning the circumstances surrounding my birth, he assured me that he was, in fact, quite ready to make his way to the estate wherein the party would ensue. Naturally, prior to ending our discussion via cellular device, we made several wagers concerning the number of guests that we might know and, indeed, as to whom the host himself might be. No mention, however, was made concerning the reason for the affair: it never needed to be spoken aloud that we believed our presence alone was sufficient enough cause to elicit jubilation in others.

After a last second manicure of my coif, I took up my old walking stick (in truth, it's actually a cane sword, because one never knows what waits to befoul our world, particularly when important persons are about) and made my way over the threshold to the outdoors. After several deep breaths to reacclimatize my lungs to the dreadful humidity that clung cloak-like to my outer garments, I spotted the friend with whom I chatted mere moments ago. It had been decided that we should be walking companions as the event we sought was held mere blocks from our common community, since we were loath to spread noxious fumes into the air via motor car (not to mention the outrageous price of fueling such a form of locomotion in these modern times).

The sun was setting and cloud cover further hindered its luminescence. Several young scamps dashed to and fro flipping the switches that controlled the oil lamps that hung ensconced upon the

wooden transformer poles standing streetside. Was there to be no expense spared for the sake of this party, that these ancient devices had
been installed about town to further enhance the flavor of the setting?

Despite giving off a cloud cover all their own, they glowed with
a moderate intensity, perhaps three foot-candles worth. Dressed
smartly, down to the shine of my shoes, I was careful with both the rapidity and the measure of my step as I approached my friend.

I couldn't help noticing from some ten paces away, though it
was not my normal inclination, that he had a bit of lint about his
shoulder. In the manner of men I gave him several non-verbal clues –
a nod, post ceded by a long and pointed stare at the offensive spot; several times running my hand over the respective spot of my own garments; taking a handful of gravel and throwing it upon him – but all to
no avail. Clearly, more stringent methods were required. A punch to
the shoulder similarly failed to dislodge the unwanted lint. I began a
series of knife-edged chops, the rapidity of their succession quickening
with my mounting frustration. They were no more effectual than any
of the previous attempts. My desperation mounted. I pointed to a window front across the way and made to move towards it. My friend followed. When he stopped to peer more closely at its contents and deci-
pher the purpose behind my pointing, I caught him across the backs of
the knees with a neat little roundhouse sweep, sending him down upon
the ground in a heap.

Upon standing, he fixed me with a baleful glare, his eyes as ac-
cusing as the full moon, jealous at its fate to forever dance in step with
our spinning mother earth. He began straightening his garments at
the knees, brushing away street grit with his clumsy hands, then
gradually working his way up, his ire mounting. For my part I looked
innocent and a calmness came over me, such that I recounted the
works of Machiavelli in my head while I waited to resume the night's
walk. With the slowness of a creeping disease my companion worked
his way towards straightening his jacket. After many seconds had
passed, finally, my friend of many years spoke. "Dude! Why didn't you
tell me I had lint on my jacket?"

There are moments in life so surreal that one must wonder if

200

Charles Darwin ever harboured any doubts regarding his theories on evolution. For instance, is it possible that all other life forms had continued a process of evolution, except for man? But to my friend, my response was merely a shaking of the head. It had long been a suspicion of mine that there were times when even the most erudite must admit the failure of language. And so I merely suggested that we move on once more in the direction of the party. Surely, I reasoned, the activities could not commence without us being present. My friend could lend no argument to the discussion, so we set our thoughts to other things as we commenced our walking.

Traveling in silence allowed too much time to avoid introspection, I discovered. Thus I found myself, while still a few blocks from our destination, pondering the night's events and playing out potential scenes within the backdrop of my mind. After several blocks of seeing myself graciously accepting honor after award after medal, I reached inside my jacket and procured the ticket for tonight's gala.

Examining the ticket for the hundredth time brought no true revelations. The background was not noteworthy either in coloration or artistic flair. The print was typeset, though plain in nature. And the wording was simplistic to the extreme. It merely provided admittance for one guest for the indoor event and could be presented by anybody.

I turned it over in my hand, but if I had truly been expecting something miraculous it, yet again, failed to appease my sensitivities. No holographic images flashed at me. No three-dimensional personality sprouted out from the paper to shake my hand. No secret message revealed its presence to me. And so I walked on, unastonished, the constant movement of my feet drawing me ever nearer to my destination.

And then, as if beckoned by some otherworldly power, the house we sought stretched out before us, though it surely was a "house" only in the most rudimentary of vocabularies. Forsooth, it was a mansion. As high and then as high again as most standard houses were long. Surely, there were three levels, at minimum, above ground. One could only fathom a guess as to how many subterranean layers might be concealed by its enormous bulk — and bulk it had in excess. It looked to span city blocks and that is to say nothing of the enormity of the grounds about the place. The contemplation of it all brought upon me a dizziness; I daresay, a vertigo. For even at this distance, I found it impossible to observe the edifice in its entirety without moving my head.

"Hoochie, momma," Brian said, then let out a low whistle. "That's one big pad."

As usual, his speech smacked of the vernacular, yet I could do little but nod in agreement. Though his words could not leave the pit of the commonplace, there could be no doubt as to their veracity. For my part, I continued to view the grandeur of the architecture, noting the Gothic columns in the colonnade, then the gargoyles stationed at nethermost regions of all the slopes and peaks and was left bereft of speech, though not at the expense of my other sensibilities. Reason, it seemed, had not fled me and I sped through my mental Rolodex of personalities that were capable of such class, such refinement, such exquisite taste, such a wealth of currency at their disposal.

As I stood gazing in wonderment, my companion, who appeared to have regained his senses, decided to examine something he saw in the manicured lawn. I left him to his work until a concierge, garrisoned in one of the numerous small buildings on the grounds, exited the structure and began to make his way towards us. At his approach I secured my ticket in hand and was about to urge my friend to do likewise when I noticed something very peculiar about the concierge's actions. He moved with undue haste, and waved his arms at us. I called out to him, but was greeted with shouts and, I daresay, a voluminous amount of yelling. Cupping a hand to my ear, I strained to make out any of his speech but it proved pointless, so I called out to my friend to ask what the concierge said.

"Nn-hnn. I...'ave...no...idea."

My normally loquacious friend was having difficulty not only stringing words together, but suffering from a definite lack of ability to annunciate, as well. I moved towards him to see if he required some sort of attention. However, I suddenly solved the mystery of the waving fellow running towards us – he was the groundskeeper. And he spewed a slew of profanities. Taken aback, I had half a mind to address this matter with the man, being no stranger to profanity-laden speeches myself. I raised a hand indicating that the man should stop and shouted a "now see here" in his direction when my friend stood up from a bare patch of lawn and came over to investigate the hullabaloo.

"What's that guy's problem?" Brian asked, nonchalance draped across him like a cloak. He raised a hand to his chin to wipe something off. Staring at his fingers afterward, he raised them to his mouth and proceeded to suck them clean as if wanting to savor the last morsels of a decadent meal.

Aghast, I stood there watching the grisly events unfold before me, disbelief a sword I couldn't swing. Not satisfied to stop at action, he spoke. And incredulity became my acquaintance. "What? Dude, I'm famished. Think they'll have wings at this shindig?"

It was at this precise moment that the concierge reached our position. He raised a hand, index finger prominently in the pointing position, his face reddening as his lips tried to work. Then, placing both palms squarely upon his thighs, he doubled over, panting.

"Long...run...," he wheezed.

The suspicion that we were about to receive a verbal drubbing gnawed at my gut. In the interim, I decided it might be possible to offer an apology, thus lessening the gust of the storm that was brewing about us. And I did just that, with verbiage both mild and sincere.

The grounds man did not attempt to straighten himself to a full standing position, instead raising one finger to forestall any more apologies. "Don't...care...about...him...eating dirt," he panted. "Thought...he might...eat... the...grass. That's a...'no-no'," he said. "Tickets...please."

We proffered the requested slips of paper, which he took indignantly from us, his face still reddened with exertion. Then he pointed to an illuminated walkway indicating our appropriate path of egress.

While not as versed in etiquette as most, my friend and I were not nearly as cretinish as others often believe (unless, of course, there be involved some form of alcohol, pigeon racing, villainous space potatoes, Jormungandr, a bipedal lizard in Tijuana, lost turnpike tickets, a plate of hot wings, frizzed goatees, two-headed monsters that can't poo, hair cutting for hubris, excessive pocket lint, extra-planar powers, fantasy sports, Fenris Wolf, hairy spiders, vampiric women in lycra, a ravenous gelatinous mass, or some other potentially world altering event), thus, we made our way quickly over to the designated path and ne'er did our heels touch scant else.

The walk was long and the path meandered its way across the entire course of the grounds. A latticework structure stood in the back yard and as we approached, rounding the side of the house so that we were afforded a better view, we found it filled with the most dazzling array of colors and scents. It housed a rose garden and vines snaked up the lattice so that blossoms and blooms caught the eye from a variety of heights and angles. It was too lovely to pass by and so I stopped to gaze, though after a few seconds it seemed my friend had stopped to graze. Though he vehemently denied the accusations, from the corner of my eye I, several times, thought I detected a hint of mastication on his part as well as missing patches of grass by his feet.

The grounds were well kept and Nature's marvels revealed themselves to us in myriad ways, though after the path had looped back upon itself and we, certain that we had taken a wrong turn somewhere along the way, took to arguing that we had or had not seen a certain landmark previously in our travels. Yet still the walking continued and to break the monotony of the travel, I switched to using French during the argument. My friend, meanwhile, incensed at my lack of English, adopted the speech of his own second language, a particularly low version of Latin. Our argument continued interminably, though as it neared a crescendo, we realized that we had finally arrived at the front door. Naturally, we spent a good many minutes continuing the argument for neither of us wished to drop a topic that held such importance not only to us, but held decided ramifications on the world at large. When at long last variations on the theme "You said, I said" fell upon short reserves, we decided to end the matter in the manner of civilized men. Paper covered rock two out of three times; having lost to scissors the odd time, and thus the matter was settled.

I, being the more civilized of the two of us, used the bronze knocker on the door to announce our presence. As I gently allowed the ring to settle against the door, I took to looking at the piece of crafts-manship that held the circular piece. It was a particularly well sculpted griffon head, clasping the ring within it's curved beak, and no detail had been spared in its crafting. It was affixed to a pair of mahogany doors and they, too, had seen extensive time under a craftsman's hand, which labored over wide-ranging and intricate scrollwork. So enamored was I with inspecting every nuance of the delicate designs that I had nary taken notice that no answer came to investigate my entreaty for entrance.

"Dude! This is boring!" said the lummox who accompanied me. "Let me try knocking."

With that, the oafish man behind me ambled his way forward a few steps, then outstretched his arm for the knocker. He half tripped over something as he was grabbing the knocker, thus, pulling the bronze piece completely free of the door. As luck would have it, I was the object upon which he tripped. As he moved forward, he struck me in the backside with his knee, pitching me headlong into the door with a thunderous noise.

Half blinded betwixt a mixture of anger and pain, I attempted to rise up. The ensuing head rush, however, caused me to tip over completely backwards and crash into a shrub. Grateful for the arboreal presence as it caught me, I pondered my luck as a dull creak rose up from the bush itself until the central trunk of the whole shrub had cracked clean in half, dumping me unceremoniously upon the lawn.

Meanwhile, Brian was attempting to re-affix the knocker upon the door. He had recovered one of the screws from the ground and attempted to turn it back into place with his bare fingers. He succeeded only in further marring the door and splitting open his forefinger, which he put into his mouth to arrest the flow of blood.

It was at precisely this moment that the door opened. An older man in a tuxedo with the mien of a proper gentleman crossed the threshold to regard us. His mouth worked reflexively as he stared first at Brian, bronze knocker once again held in his hand, then at me, sprawled out across the broken shrub and the neatly manicured lawn.

"Ummmm...this broke," Brian said, shrugging his shoulders as he offered the doorknocker to the butler.

"Indeed!" he hissed his reply. "I take it, then, that you are the Drunken Comic Book Monkeys." His speaking voice contained a slow affectation of a deep Southern drawl.

"You got it," Brian said, puffing out his chest with pride.

Scrabbling to my feet, I offered apologies to him about the shrub and then offered a few more words of regret about the state of the lawn. My momentary lack of grace disorienting, I bent down and picked up the broken shrub, then walked forward with it cradled in my arms, as I offered it to the butler.

"I wish that it were otherwise," the butler said, aiming a frown in my direction. Suaveness overcame me as I took the hint. I dropped the shrub. "Incredible as it seems, you are on the guest list. Your name badges." With this he offered two adhesive placards to Brian.

" 'Yelling man who asks a lot of questions'? This must be his, right? Surely I don't ask many questions, do I? Let's see, this one is 'dancing dervish'. Oh, come on! Surely you could have come up with a better name for me!" Brian yelled, attempting to affix the second name card to his shirt.

"That, sir, is mine!" the butler cried, taking a hurried step to snatch the card from Brian's clumsy fingers. "I won dancer of the week seven weeks running on Solid Silver. Ah! This, sir, is his."

"Who, his?" Brian asked. "Him, his?" he said jerking a thumb in my general direction. "Can I see that? 'Easily distracted man'. Ha, ha, ha! Yep, that's his, all right! Do you have a sharpie? It's missing something though. Want me to write 'Shiny' at the end of it?"

"No, sir. I want you to place your name badges at a proper angle and enter. You're the last to arrive and I'm afraid you are holding up the event. Perplexing as that is to me!" The butler retreated behind the door, pulling it open wide for us to enter the mansion.

I affixed my name badge as I was bade and procured an ice-cold beer from my pants pocket. As I never leave home without an opener, it was no mean task to pop the top and let the liquid erase my doubts. Clearly we were not only welcome here, but our arrival was anticipated. What misgivings were to be allowed to linger?

I stepped inside the huge antechamber, the butler waiting to take any hats and coats offered. Neither Brian nor myself had any to offer him, though Brian, having procured a beer from his own beer pocket, handed the nice chap his bottle cap. The butler stared at his hand in amazement. His silence could only have been caused by his internal satisfaction from having been so vital a help to us, but at length it became awkward, so we walked away down the long hallway.

"Do you think I should have tipped him?" Brian attempted to whisper. Two bronze plates that had been affixed to the wall came free of their fastenings and clattered to the ground in response to his attempt. "Too late," Brian declared. "He's busy now picking up those plates that fell from the wall. Where does this hallway lead?" Brian's normal voice level had returned, though there was little disparity between a whisper and a shout with him. "Do you think we're in time for appetizers?"

I explained to my friend that they would likely be called "hors d'oeuvres" at such a soiree and no; "soiree" wasn't a kind of cheap French cologne. No, it was never acceptable to wipe your fingers on someone else's lapel, your own being quite sufficient. No, there hadn't been a place on the invitation to indicate your choice of main course. No, we weren't required to call ahead. Hereupon I attempted an explanation of RSVP, but decided to cut my losses as the questions continued to mount. And no, "mounting questions" was not an adult fetish website.

An interminable length of time was required for us to reach the double doors at the other end of the hallway. My compatriot's salvo of questions was being asked faster than the speed of sound. There were at least a dozen I didn't have time to answer and at least another dozen that were asked too quickly to be audible. It was at this juncture that I decided that Brian was so abnormally clamorous because the rapidity of his speech actually broke the sound barrier, thus his voice was something akin to a sonic boom.

But arrive at the double doors, we did. Behind us we could see the butler wrestling with one of the fallen bronze plates, before us invisible waves of scent tickled at Brian's sense of smell. Like a Pav-

lovian canine, his salivary glands immediately began to work. A voluminous stream of spittle ran from the corner of his mouth and he veri-
tably howled as he shoved his way through the great carven oak doors
before us. I wished I had an opportunity to see the scene upon the
other guests' faces before Brian's entry. Now the scene "carved" upon
their faces was one of revulsion and fear.

Roughly thirty guests stood at various points within the grand
chamber, a ballroom of sorts, behind the double doors. The far wall
was lined with windows that ran the entire height of the hall. A great
chandelier looked down upon us. It appeared to be comprised of at
least a million tiny pieces of crystal, strung together in such a way as
to reflect as much of the sunlight as the windows could allow in. The
inner wall was painted pure white. Presumably the crystals from the
chandelier would reflect the light and send a prismatic spray of color
upon its otherwise pale surface. It must surely be a grand sight to behold and I found myself wishing it had been nearer to noon, when the
sun would begin to peek its way into the room and set the far wall into
full blossom. The furniture that filled the room were small tables and
chairs that lined the walls, leaving the middle of the chamber empty
except for a small, one person table and an ornate chair, with a deeply
cushioned seat and a tapestried backing.

I walked into the room, proudly thrusting my name badge at
every near inquiry, passing out introductions and good-natured senti-
ments like business cards. After several stares at my name placard
caused a series of successive eyebrows to raise, I was nominally ig-
nored. In turn, each guest turned back toward his or her prior conversations and, in poor sport, I was invited to join in none of them. But as
I traversed the room, the reasoning for such behavior became quite apparent to me.

Brian, upon entering the room, made an immediate dash towards the nearest solid structure bearing food, knocking two trays of
foodstuffs to the ground in his haste.

"Awww, dude! Who knocked over the hot wings?" he whined,
amidst a mouthful of tiny delicacies. The scene of him hunched over
the serving platter with three stuffed mushrooms in each hand was lu-

dicrous, to say the least. He shoveled and crammed them into his mouth as if he hadn't eaten in weeks. "Are you finished?" he asked a group of ladies who walked away from him backwards so great was their fear of being mistaken for something of a finger food nature.

"Dude! What are you waiting on? The food is going fast. Can you please bring out another tray?" he asked a member of the wait staff. "Oh, and what's for dinner?"

"No entrees, sir," came the response with a sneer. "Who could afford to feed one such as yourself? And I believe that is the last of the pâté."

It was several minutes and a score of questions later that Brian was finally convinced that he was not eating scalp, though the definition of a circumflex eluded me and I finally had to fashion one out of cocktail weenies; a task that was made all the more lengthy by Brian's determination to constantly eat one side or the other of the rooftop-like representation.

Despite numerous exhortations on my part to "use a fork" or "take a napkin" or "don't eat the napkin", Brian continued to drive away the other guests, disgusted by his behaviour. Instead, like a herd of wildebeests huddled around a water hole, to a person, they gravitated to the opposite side of the room. Or so I thought.

"Hey, guys!" a voice called to us. "I see you got an invite to this little gala event, too! What capacity are you serving here?"

It seems one guest, not frightened off by my friend's loathsome eating habits, had entered the area of our gravitational pull and had somehow refused to eject! I looked up at him and then stood astounded. He was quite bemused and offered a friendly little smile at my recognition. Jeff Young! His name badge simply said, "editor," and, to my knowledge, having worked as an editor on only one book (an exquisite little volume of horror stories called, *Scary Tales of Scariness*), surely it must have been a crowning achievement for his life, a feather in his cap, as it were.

I shook hands with Jeff. In the course of our present situation, he represented flotilla to a drowning man and I was tired of treading water. Here surely was an opportunity for me to start afresh with the gathering that had pointedly herded itself away from us; a chance to socialize with someone who spoke in sentences other than inquiries; an opportunity to network and fraternize with those I could happily call my peers.

"Jeff," Brian said, taking a moment to breathe from his feeding frenzy. "How did you get invited to this party? Do you know what it's for? And who's the host? And where did you get the crab roll? I didn't see a seafood table. Dude! You're holding out on me!" And with that Brian ran across the room seeking other victuals. The other guests quickly shifted their way to the opposite side of the room, keeping an apparently requisite amount of room from Brian at all times, lest they be pulled into his manic event horizon.

"Well," Jeff said, "not that the person who asked the questions is still in earshot, but I was invited by the guest of honor himself. He showed up at my bookstore one day and I helped him find an obscure book he was seeking on quantum mechanics. He claimed that he was building a time machine and he was having difficulty with some of the calibrations. I didn't think much more about it. Then, after about two weeks went by the gentleman in question returned once again looking for me. He had figured out the majority of his problems, but still had a few minor setbacks, so he invited me over to help him work out the last few bugs. After I fixed the orientation gyroscope and discovered that the timing sequence was off by two picoseconds and adjusted the drive belt and calibrated the spectral thermographer, plus a few other sundry items he had overlooked- he vanished. Poof! That was...oh... about a month ago. Then the invitation came in the mail. Did you notice the invitations were postdated? He bought them in the future and had them stamped, then went back in time to mail them! That was my idea. Pretty wild, huh?"

I smiled and nodded. Surely, no more could have been expected of me to assuage him that his role in all of this, was pivotal even if all he really did was open a soda and hand it to the scientist at work. Really, he had lost me in his talk of thingamajigs and what-see-doodles. Not to mention the workmanship on the ceiling fresco was quite remarkable. How I failed to notice it before astounded me. But apparently a painter had taken a trowel and made many concentric circles in rows across the ceiling. I marveled at how each geometric shape was precisely the same size and debated pointing this out to my interlocutor, but decided, instead, to keep this wonderful little secret jealously guarded, lest it lose beauty in the sharing.

"Well, I have to go say a few words to the assembly now. The time traveler should be back at any moment. It was nice to see you. If you're still around after the event maybe we can go grab a beer. I need to forget the last story I read."

Again here I smiled and nodded, for surely the last story Jeff Young had read would have been one of Brian's and mine and it was certain that the last thing he needed to do was to forget it. Unless, of course, his meaning here was that upon finishing our story he had found himself quite incapable of writing anything so grand of his own due to the complexity of our numerous plot twists and the strength of our overall use of language. *Certainly*, I told myself, *this was his real meaning.*

At this juncture, Jeff had called for everyone's attention and, other than the sounds of Brian arguing with the wait staff as he attempted to lick his latest plate clean, a hush fell over the room. Presently, Jeff began giving a backdrop as to the "wheres" and "whys" we were gathered and who the time traveler was and what the audience could expect upon his return. The whole olio of onlookers stood rapt. For my own account, I paid close attention to his speech until it turned towards his own role in the course of events leading up to this night. At this point, the speech became almost sermon-length in its vivid recounting of detail upon detail. Boredom crept in upon my senses and perforce I sought an outlet for my dwindling attention span. Something shiny glared at me from under one of the tables and I crept stealthily over to investigate it.

The glint came from beneath one of the pedestal legs and, crawling under it, I set my back to the task of raising the table. Somehow, it failed to register upon my faculties that this was the very table at which Brian had placed all of his empty plates. As the first plate fell, the table lifted free of my prize, which turned out to be an empty gum wrapper. A loud noise boomed all about me. At first I thought it might be the sound of my disappointment. Then I conjectured that it might be the plates breaking, but the timbre was off. Experience led me to believe it was somehow Brian's doing. I crawled out from beneath the table to sound of uproarious applause and many catcalls. I was overwhelmed to the point of having to hold back tears. I stood that I might then take a bow, but at the last second stopped myself.

In the center of the room was a large contraption. I argued with myself how such a device might have escaped my notice. But, just as I was about to win the argument, I noticed a stranger standing next to the device. The cut and color of his clothing suggested they were not of this age and the goggles he wore were eccentric.

"I'd like to thank my friend," he said with a smile, "Mr. Jeff Young, without whom I would never have thought to check the temporal dampeners." Hereupon, the man gave Jeff a mighty clap on the back. The crowd united in their cheers for Jeff, who serenely stepped forward and gave a halfhearted wave as if embarrassed by the collective attention. Not wanting to seem less than enthusiastic over the role he had taken in this venture, the role he had downplayed, as I had suspected all along, I added my clapping to that of the gathered throng.

"Thank you," Jeff said. "Why don't you relate your story to your guests," he said to the time traveler, "and I'll just go put this thing away." With that Jeff struggled to move the time machine towards the side of the room. The time traveler called for food and wine, then sat himself upon the comfy chair in the middle of the room and launched into his story.

Caught in the moment as I was, I did not notice Brian approach me, plodding his way towards me from the opposite end of the room.

"Dude, all the food is gone and I'm bored. Plus, it's really loud in here. What's the fuss about anyhow? Never mind. This guy's rich. Wanna go see if he has a ping-pong table anywhere? I grabbed up some cups so we can play beer pong."

I wanted to argue. My brain tried to tell me there was something of importance going on around us. Brian sensed my struggle.

"Dude! Want something shiny? I think I saw something shine over there."

It was as if I were a cobra and he some gifted musician. Powerless to stop myself, I followed him out of the room via a side door. En route to the door, we passed Jeff in his arduous task of pushing the monstrosity of a machine across the room. We cast nary a glance in his direction, lest he ask us for assistance, and found that the door led out into a small hallway, ending with a door to either side. We choose the one on the right as ping-pong tables and shiny things have a tendency to always be to the right of one in search of them.

We entered a huge vault with a large domed ceiling. We flicked on the lights to get a better view. The room seemed to be some kind of museum, with all manner of doohickeys, thingamabobs, and gadgetry covered completely by sheets. In opposite directions we ran around the room pulling the sheets off everything, I in my quest to find the shiny thing, and Brian's mind ensnared by the idea of finding a ping-pong table, or a beer fridge, or a full fridge, for that matter.

So acute were our desires to reach our designated goals that we never saw Jeff push the time machine into the corner of the room. Fixated upon his own goals, Jeff had no idea that two monkeys raced around the perimeter of the room.

"Now, my precious, little toy," Jeff purred, "you're going to take me on a trip. One little trip to rid me of those two morons once and for all. They've thwarted all my plans! I've exhausted my 401k. But I'm not beaten yet," he sneered. "I'll just go backwards in time and erase their very existences! But, first, there's one stop I have to make."

With that, Jeff climbed onto the time machine and adjusted some dials before engaging the engine. With a loud whoosh he was gone.

"Dude!" Brian called. "Did you hear that? What was it?"

I indicated to him the direction whence the noise came and we met in that general area. On the floor something looked up at me and I bent down to grab it. A name badge that read "editor."

"Dude! Do you know what this means?" Brian asked.

I nodded my assent. Jeff Young had taken the time machine.

"Jeff totally took the time machine! Where do you think he went? And why?"

I could only conjecture. The workings of his near-genius mind were foreign to me. Like speaking in Portuguese or eating moldy cheese.

"I've got it!" declared Brian, striking a fist against his other, outstretched hand. "There's another time machine over...yeah, right here. See? 'Prototype - Property of Jeff Young'. Clearly, as our editor he wants us to go to other times and places and gather some experiences for our new stories. We must be getting stale. C'mon, dude. Saddle up."

The prototype was lustrous and the light reflected off its surface in the oddest ways, the sheen mesmerizing me. Brian climbed into the other seat and grabbed the controls.

"Guess we won't be needing these anymore, huh?" he asked, ripping off his nametag and mine in the same motion. A slapping session ensued over who got to set the controls for the final destination. We agreed to let a beer cap spitting competition settle the matter, with the furthest spit determining the winner. But in our exuberance to crack open our beers, we mistakenly fired up the engines and with a whoosh of our own, the world vanished from about us.

A great jostling took hold of the time machine and we felt as if we were a margarita during the mixing phase. Though glass occupied the majority of the frame of the machination, there was no use trying to see through it as we were enveloped in some sort of haze, a miasma of sorts that we were to later learn was the blending of many threads of time.

"So, dude," Brian asked, "any idea what might be important about the year 1599?"

I set my mind to the task of unraveling this mystery, but no sooner had I begun than we "landed." The time machine settled itself upon solid ground. We were in some sort of field and a small village stood off in the distance to our right. Behind us was a thick forest, though there seemed to be no sign of Jeff Young or his time machine.

It seemed logical to Brian and myself that Jeff had preset the coordinates of this machine as part of his plan for us to meet up with him.

We climbed out of the machine, but Brian stopped me from wandering off in exploration.

"Help me drag this thing into the woods. We don't want any of the locals to take a fancy to it," he said, his breath pluming up around him in little white clouds. "Wherever we are, it's definitely cold. C'mon, give me hand."

I acquiesced and together we made short work of hiding the time machine within the depth of the forest. There were no fronds or vines to be found to cover it, however, probably due to the inclemency of the weather. But we were able to find some fallen branches and I found a blanket down in the barn by the field in which we had landed, so I ran off to get it while Brian gathered some limbs. When I returned with the tarp, Brian was sitting down eating a pinecone.

"What?" he asked, his teeth stained with pine tar. "Hiding time machines is hungry work!"

I shrugged in response, hoping the sticky liquid would fuse his lips together over his teeth, but fate had never been friendly to me before when I asked her to grant such wishes, so I held little hope that my entreaties would be met with success.

When we finished covering up the vehicle of our arrival, we struck out towards the village in the distance. On the outskirts of town was a large building that stood out from the rest. It was semi-circular and lacked a proper roof, though it towered over the other buildings. Jeff would be found there. We were both sure of it. I pulled out a notebook and started jotting down notes about the surrounding landscape, while Brian grabbed us each a beer from his beer pants. As we neared the village we received our first good glance of the locale and the locals. The houses were squat with thatch roofs. The inhabitant's manner of dress seemed, to my eyes, though I profess my semi-amateurishness at history, appropriate for the time period given the relative architecture and building materials: The men wore breeches and doublets; the women had quaint dresses and bonnets of a fashion. They spoke English, though with a most peculiar dialect and, forsooth, we had difficulty understanding them in large part.

"We're in jolly old England, huh?" Brian asked and I nodded in agreement. And then it hit me, the importance of the date at which we had arrived. I walked with hastened pace and exhorted Brian to do the same. My skin crawled at the contemplation of my theory. I was loath to be here any longer than necessary. Jeff would certainly hear about this! But, then, oddly, it was us who heard from him. He was arguing with someone.

"And here! Do you see this?"

A man mumbled some reply we could not quite make out.

"This needs a semi-colon, bub. Not a comma. Otherwise, it's a run-on sentence. Oh, and this...This is NOT a word, pal."

"Verily," came the response. "'Tis a word I made up this very morn."

"And that's another thing. Quit with all of the "tis-es'. I mean once in a while you can get away with it. But you use it like Mariah Carey hits high notes! Give it a break, will you? It doesn't need to be in every..."

I finished Jeff's sentence.

"Sonnet."

"Sonnet?" Brian asked. Then his eyes grew wide. "Dude! Do you mean to say that's Willy Shakespeare?"

"I prefer William, if you please. More melodic to the ear," Shakespeare replied. As we drew up to him, the small, round man removed his hat and swept into a graceful bow aimed at us. "Perforce, you are dressed in the same ill manner as this one when he first arrived," he jabbed a thumb in Jeff's direction, "thus, I must assume that you swaddle yourselves in the same foul manners as doth he. Though kindly display something otherwise, I prithee. One editor is enough, methinks."

"Dude! Jeff Young is Billy Shakespeare's editor! How freakin' cool is that?" Brian stated the obvious.

"Good sir! I must kindly ask again that you refer to me as 'William' or I shall be forced to play my hand."

"Ugh! Dude! What you do with your hands on your own time is

your business! And I really don't want to hear about it!" Brian yelled, disgusted.

"Well played!"

"Ugh! Somebody make this guy stop!"

"Nay, sir. 'Tis I who shall make you stop!"

"Again with 'tis!" shouted Jeff. "Knock that off right freaking now!"

"Not until this insolent cur is dealt with appropriately. I bite my thumb at you, sir!"

"Dude!" Brian said, "are you sure you want to put that thumb in your mouth...knowing where it's been? And what it's been used for? I mean, just saying."

His face reddened in rage, Shakespeare stomped up the steps to the stage area of the Globe Theater. Though we could not make out his words it was clear that he was yelling and several other men made replies.

"So how the hell did you two get here?" Jeff demanded, rounding on Brian and me. He was dressed in full Renaissance attire, with a foppish, feathered hat, and even sporting a sword at his hip.

"The prototype you left for us," Brian offered.

"I left for you?" Jeff asked incredulously. "Double damn! I never thought the time traveler would let me out of his sight with his time machine so I preset the date and coordinates on mine! The problem with you two isn't in out-thinking you, it's that I have to out-think myself, too! This is the last straw, Monkeys. I've had it with you."

From the area of the stage there came a general commotion and then the sound of several booted feet pounding down the stairs towards our location, even as Jeff, himself, approached us.

"Dude," Brian said, "I think we're in deep doo-doo this time."

Thinking fast, I picked up a rock off the ground and threw it hard over Jeff's head in the direction of the crowd approaching from the stage area.

"Ha! Missed" Jeff said.

A meaty "thunk" and bellows of outrage suggested that the rock had hit someone.

"NOW WAIT UNTIL YOU SEE WHAT I DO TO YOU!" Jeff screamed, his face flushed with anger. He pulled his sword just as the man coming down the stairs reached the terra firma. Cradling his nose in his left hand, the point of impact of the rock, he surveyed the scene in front of him, then quickly made his deductions.

"Oh, I shall not tarry to uncover what act you might next conceive," the man said. Then came the sound of ringing steel. "If a thrown rock be a challenge in your village, stranger, let it be known that I accept!"

"I...wait...that wasn't me! It was those guys," Jeff said, pointing in our direction.

"And I suppose it was not your voice that followed up the rock with a threat? How traitorous are your ways, sir? What other prevarications have you?"

Brian and I looked at each other. If there is one blessing in having been writing partners for such a long period of time it was that we could complete each other's thoughts without prompting. We began to back away from the scene at the exact same speed, then turned and broke at a dead run at the exact same pace. What fate befell Jeff Young that day neither of us knows. We ran all the way back to our time machine and strapped in, not wanting to fall victim to the same fate as him. Fate can call us cowards if it must, but we had faced many a monster and it was high time someone else did their fair share. For the last words we heard as we ran remain with us to this day.

"Know this, Master Young! And mark it well. You shall rue the day you set forth your challenge. For all know me as Thibault and I am vengeance...."

THE DRUNKEN COMIC BOOK MONKEYS
vs.
VARIOUS & SUNDRY

JEFF YOUNG

VS.

The Drunken Comic Book Monkeys and Their Clones and the Alternate Universe Drunken Comic Book Monkeys with Little to No Help from Drunkenstein

Jeff seethed. Of all the miserable things he ever had to endure in his life, this ranked at number one. Steering wheel groaning from the pressure of his ire fueled grip, he guided the extended length passenger van along the appropriate lane. He stopped.

With a baleful sigh, he lowered his window and was greeted by an adolescent boy with a smile gleaming from orthodontics. The attendant said, "Welcome to McDonald's. May I take your order, please?"

An eruption of voices spewed from behind Jeff.

"I want a two pounder Happy Meal!" Brian said.

"They don't make two pounders, moron!" Chris said. "I want a chicken sandwich Happy Meal with apple slices instead of French fries."

"Get over your lame potato phobia already, will ya?" Brian replied. "Then make my Happy Meal eight quarter pounders!"

"Me too!" DoppelBrian chimed in. "The eight quarter pounder Happy Meal, not the fry-phobia thing!"

"Potatoes suck!" the other test tube byproduct, ChrisClone, said. "No French fries for my chicken McNugget Happy Meal!"

"I want sixteen of the dollar McDoubles in my Happy Meal," Alternate Universe Brian shouted. "With extra, extra French fries!"

"You suck no matter what dimension you're from!" Chris yelled. "You know that, right?"

"Amen to that!" Alternate Universe Chris replied. He attempted a high-five with regular universe Chris, but instead they both lost their balance and simultaneously slapped ChrisClone's head.

Righting himself in his seat, Alternate Universe Chris continued, "I'll have the chicken Caesar salad Happy Meal. Sans any and all potato products."

"Can I have extra hops in my Happy Meal?" Drunkenstein asked.

"Oooooooh! I like that idea! Me too! Me too!" Chris said.

"Can I change my order to that, please?" Alternate Universe Chris asked.

"Three, please!" ChrisClone said.

"No, you can't!" Alternate Universe Brian barked! "Much to the chagrin of everyone in this vehicle, McDonald's doesn't serve alcohol."

"Dammit! Can I get a Shamrock Shake then?" ChrisClone asked.

"Dude! It's the middle of July!" DoppelBrian replied, giving a shoulder punch as a point of emphasis. "I knew you were Irish!"

"Am not!" Chris yelled out. "I'm Italian!"

"Well, your clone seems to be Irish!" Brian said. "Why else would he want a Shamrock Shake in the middle of summer?"

"Because, he's stupid and thinks there's crème de mint in it!" Chris rebutted.

"Need I remind you," Alternate Universe Chris chimed in, "that he's an exact copy of you, and in theory, me. So not only did you infer that I'm stupid, but you called yourself stupid as well."

"Ha!" Brian said. "You just pwned yourself!!"

"Shut up!" Chris said.

"I just think it's funny that you're so irascible that you can't even get along with you. Just look at me, myself and I. We all get along. Right, guys?"

"Yes," DoppelBrian said.

" Yesff," Alternate Universe Brian said, his mouth full.

"Hey!" Brian exclaimed. "You're eating my beef jerky!"

"Am not! You ate yours already!"

"I only ate half, and then I put the bag down, and when I went back for more it was gone! Now I know where it is – in your big, fat mouth! And are you reading my goth-girl tattoo magazine?"

"We're sharing!" Alternate Universe Brian replied, clutching the magazine to his chest with a death-grip. "Sharing is caring! Sharing is caring!"

"Drunkenstein want goth-girl tattoo magazine too!" Drunkenstein pouted.

Jeff rued stopping at the convenience store before hand, especially before picking up Drunkenstein. Disgruntled, he looked to the young order-taker and said, "Just empty whatever you have in your fryer into a bag and call it a Happy Meal. And scrape the remains of whatever you got on the grill into the same bag. And whatever fell on the floor throughout the day as well as whatever you have in the trash can. Could I have a side of arsenic and strychnine?"

"Ummmm," the order-taker said, "I'll go check with my manager..."

"Never mind. Scratch the last part about the arsenic and strychnine. I don't wanna get you in trouble."

"Okay."

"But do everything else I said. I just wanna throw some food at these idiots to shut them up."

"Okay. Please pull up to the next window."

Jeff did as instructed, trying to ignore the kicks to the back of his seat from the tussle among Brian, Alternate Universe Brian and Drunkenstein over the goth-girl tattoo magazine. He paid and collected eight large bags, all but one disappearing from various and sundry hands reaching into the front seat for them. Not wanting to attract any unwanted attention by dining in the restaurant with two sets of triplets and a monster cobbled together from human parts, Jeff found a parking spot behind a set of overgrown bushes. Once parked, Jeff turned to see what horrors befell his van within the forty seconds it took to dispense the food and park the car.

Just as he suspected, ketchup dripped from the ceiling while mustard smiley-faces adorned two of the windows. Pickles lined every headrest and sesame seeds were scattered about the entire vehicle. A squirt of barbeque sauce shot through the air, culminating in a squeal of, "Aaaaaah! My eye! My eye!" Random and frequent punches intermittently interrupted the open-mouthed chewing. Then Brian started choking.

As with every time Brian choked on something he ingested, Chris started punching him. After the fourth punch, the offending object dislodged and flew from his mouth, ricocheting off Jeff's forehead. Using a napkin, Jeff picked up what Brian just horked – the Happy Meal toy – the whole reason why the seven other passengers wanted to come to McDonald's for lunch. This batch of toys happened to be action figures from the movie "Star Conflicts", and the one Jeff held was Princess Playa. "I know I'm going to regret asking this, but Brian, how did you choke on this?"

"Well," Brian said in between bites of his third quarter pounder, "I started licking it because she's really cute and then…"

"Okay, that's enough!"

"Gimme that!" Chris said as he reached over the seat and snatched the action figure from Jeff's hand. "I need that one."

"I don't wanna know," Jeff said.

"Because I'm gonna use these action figures to show everyone how the movie *should have* gone!"

"You sooooooo have to get over this, dude," Alternate Universe Brian said. "It can't be good for your blood pressure."

Ignoring anything happening around him, Chris huddled with the seven action figures in front of him on the seat, an ersatz stage. "Okay, first we have this character here, Dar Dar Stinx. He needs to die in the opening scene." With that, Chris made laser gun noises and then over exaggerated gurgles of a death knell. He finished by tossing the action figure out the window.

ChrisClone and Alternate Universe Chris both tittered while all the Brians rolled their eyes. Having six fingers on each hand, Drunkenstein still fought with the wrapper on his burger.

Feeling cathartic about his meal, Alternate Universe Chris sighed and said:

"Scintillating rays
Of sun shine upon my meal
With no potatoes."

Scowling, DoppelBrian offered a rejoinder:
"The red Heaven of
Ketchup flows over my fries,
My meal is complete."
"Oh yeah?" ChrisClone said. "How about this?"
"Potatoes suck! Don't
Eat them 'cause they're aliens
And potatoes suck!"
"Whatever!" Brian yelled. "Here's my haiku on the topic:"
"Fries fries fries fries fries
Fries fries fries fries fries fries fries
Fries fries fries fries *fries*!"

Chris held up his hands and used both thumbs and index fingers to create a "W". "Whatever," he said. "First of all, when you do haiku, it's more like low-ku. Second of all, you go ahead and eat all the potatoes you want and rot your brains. Third of all, it's time for me to reenact the scene where Fluke Flyswatter and ... hey! Where's the Princess Playa action figure?"

All eyes turned to Alternate Universe Brian as he gagged and coughed. Alternate Universe Chris did the honors of punching. This time it only took three punches to cause the slobber soaked action figure to fly through the air and bounce off Jeff's forehead. Like before, Chris reached over the seat and grabbed the action figure from Jeff. "Gimme that!"

Before Chris could restart his version of the movie, a haiku came from the very back of the van:
"When my feet are cold,
I have a special pair of
Beer drinking mukluks."

All eyes focused on Drunkenstein. Still fiddling with the burger wrapper, he looked up and said, "What? I thought we were doing haiku?"

"We were," Chris said. "But it was about potatoes and fries, not mukluks. If you want... dude! Look!"

Everyone in the vehicle looked out the back window to see what

Chris pointed at – a foam potato with black arms and legs, large white shoes and gloves, cartoon smile, and googley eyes that bounced and changed direction with every step.

"Ummmm," Brian said. "It's just a disenfranchised teenager, probably hung-over, in a mascot suit."

"It's Frius Gaius! I know it is!" Chris yelled, his voice growing shrill with terror.

"Who?"

"Frius Gaius! One of the Potato People who tried to take over the world!"

"Oh for the love of...! Dude. The Potato People invasion, us fighting them, us calling Chthulhu – all of that never happened! We were drinking our homebrewed mushroom beer. You were trying to make a tater-tot and a plastic toy squid arm wrestle!"

"It did happen! It did! And that's Frius Gaius!" Chris grabbed a fistful of fries from Brian and started throwing them out the window at the costumed clad teenager. "Be gone scourge! Be gone! You are not welcomed on my planet!"

"Hey!" Brian yelled. He jumped out of the vehicle and scooped up the fries from the ground, even those that had been run over by other vehicles, and shoved them in his mouth. "Don't waste food, dude!"

The other two Chris's joined in tossing fries out the window while Alternate Universe Brian joined regular universe Brian in scavenging the tossed fries. DoppelBrian could not join because he was choking on the Princess Playa action figure. ChrisClone punched and the action figure collided with Jeff's forehead. Chris reached for it and said, "Gimme that!"

"No!" Jeff yelled, snatching the action figure away. "No! No one will get this action figure back! You wanna know why? I'll show you!" Jeff tossed the action figure into his mouth and swallowed it whole in one gulp. "See what happens when you can't play nice with your toys? I take them! I take them and eat them!"

"Wow, Jeff," Alternate Universe Chris said, stunned. "That was pretty intense, and thoroughly unnecessary."

"Yeah," DoppelBrian said. "If we were getting out of control, all you had to do was ask us to settle down."

"And say please," ChrisClone added.

"Don't worry," Chris said as he dumped the contents of the McDonald's animal-shaped cookies on his lap. "I can use these to finish the movie."

Jeff slapped his forehead and ran his hand down his face. "That's it! I'm outta here!"

All action ceased as Jeff jumped from the parked van, slamming the door shut behind him. As he stormed away, all three Brians and all three Chris's looked at each other and shrugged their shoulders.

Mumbling obscenities to himself, Jeff turned the first corner and was greeted by a Humvee, army green. Sitting in the passenger seat was a cigar chewing, crooked nosed Major who knew no other facial expression other than one that involved furrowed eyebrows. Jeff assumed the Major must have been born with some form of speech condition, because the only way he talked was by hollering as loud as possible. Looking down at Jeff, the Major bellowed, "And where do you think you're going?"

"Away from them!" Jeff bellowed back. "They're idiots! All of them!"

"Yeah, but they're your idiots!"

"Not anymore! I'm through!"

"Not so fast, son! You encouraged two of them, created two more, were involved with crossing the other two from one universe into this one, and paid someone to build that drinking monster."

Jeff clenched his jaw, grinding his teeth so hard his feet hurt.

Able to deduce that Jeff had a difficult time with this, the Major continued, "I've been on some tough missions, so I understand the stamina needed. But we have a deal. We caught them. You watch and study them. And we'll give you all the money and resources you need to build a time machine. We still got that deal, right son?"

Jeff looked from the Major to the ground. If he walked away now, he wouldn't be truly escaping Brian and Chris. Especially now that there were *three of each*! They would eventually find him, and continue to make his life worse. But a time machine! That would fix everything! Jeff could solve the problem before it even began.

Jeff looked back up to the Major. "Yes, sir. We still have a deal. I'll be emailing you the latest batch of supplies and materials that I need. Expect it tomorrow morning."

The Major chomped on his cigar and smiled. "I'll be looking for it!"

After a few cleansing breaths, Jeff turned and walked back to his van, thankful everyone was back inside. No sooner did he open the door, a glob of cherry pie squirted him in the eye....

AROUND THE WORLD
IN EIGHTY BEERS

Country	Brewery
Albania	Tirana
Algeria	Tango
Angola	Bela Cuca
Antigua	Caribe
Argentina	Quilmes
Armenia	Abovyan
Australia	Fosters
Austria	Samichlaus
Bahamas	Kalik
Bangladesh	Hunter
Belarus	Bobrov
Belgium	Chimay
Belize	Belikin
Benin	La Béninoise
Bolivia	Paceña
Bosnia	Jélén Pívo
Botswana	Kgalagadi
Brazil	Xingu
Bulgaria	Zagorka
Burma	Dagon
Cambodia	Kingdom
Canada	Unibroue
Chile	Kuntsmann
China	Tsintao
Columbia	Bavaria
Congo	Bralima
Costa rica	Imperial

Croatia	Zagrebačka Pivovara
Denmark	Yuborg
Domincan republic	Presidente
England	Bass
Eritrea	Asmara
Estonia	Saku
Finland	Kotkan Höyrypanimo
France	Pietra
Germany	Warsteiner
Ghana	Accra
Greece	Mythos
Guatemala	Cervecería Centro Americana
Haiti	Brana
Holland	Grolsch
Honduras	D & D
Hungary	Dreher
Iceland	Egill Skallagrímsson
India	Kingfisher
Indonesia	Bali Hai
Ireland	Guinness
Israel	Tempo
Italy	Peroni
Japan	Kirin
Kazakhstan	Derbes
Kenya	Tusker
Korea	Hite
Kyrgyzstan	Arpa
Laos	Beer Lao
Latvia	Cesu
Lesotho	Maluti Mountain
Liechtenstein	Liechtensteiner Brauhaus
Lithuania	Kalnapilis
Luxembourg	Mousel
Macedonia	Skopsko
Mexico	Dos Equus

Micronesia	Stone Money
Moldova	Efes Vitanta
Mongolia	Tiger
New zealand	Steinlager
Nigeria	Golden Guinea
Norway	Carlsberg
Panama	Baru
Philipines	San Miguel
Poland	Okocim
Portugal	Unicer
Scotland	Skullsplitter
Spain	Moritz
Sweden	Närke Kulturbryggeri
Switzerland	Fesenmeier
Tanzania	Serengeti
Thailand	Phuket
Transylvania	Ursus
U.S.A.	Yuengling
Uzbekistan	Sarbast
Zimbabwe	Lion

THE DRUNKEN COMIC BOOK MONKEYS
vs.
GODZILLA

"Dude! Look! It's a two-hundred foot tall giant lizard!"
"It's coming right at us!"
"Run!"
"You first."
"No! You first, you sissy!"
"I'm no sissy! You run first!"

THE DRUNKEN COMIC BOOK MONKEYS
VS.
THE SAVAGE CURTAIN

Brian looked around. Craggy rocks jutted from the ground, interspersed with sparse brush and trees no taller than he. The sun was red. He was no astrophysicist, but he knew it should be yellow. The thin air held hints of sulfur, but was breathable. Patting his body, he checked for injury or blood, but to his relief he found none. He reached into his pants pocket and pulled out a beer.

Determined to find what sort of shenanigans Chris got him into this time, Brian followed a rudimentary path around a large boulder. On the other side, he found Chris, drinking a beer, and Jeff pinching the bridge of his nose. Brian yelled as he approached, "Dudes! Where are we?"

"Don't know," Chris said. "We think another planet. The last thing I remember is we were at a Star Trek convention and then POOF! We're here."

"Cool. So ... why is Jeff so mad?"

"Why am I mad?" Jeff screamed, veins bulging from his forehead. "Because the one time, the only time, you idiots decide to dress in costume for a convention you somehow manage to talk me into joining you!"

"So?" Brian and Chris asked in unison.

"So? Because, I moronically dressed as a red shirt! We're now on a strange planet and I'm a red shirt! Son of a b...." Jeff cut himself short by kicking a pebble. It ricocheted off the nearby boulder, striking Jeff in the head and rendering him unconscious.

Brian and Chris looked at Jeff to make sure he was still breathing. Then they took a sip of beer and looked at each other. Brian than started pumping his fist. "Sa-weet!"

"What the hell are you so excited about?" Chris asked.

"I'm wearing a yellow shirt! That means I'm the captain!"

"No it doesn't! Ensigns and pilots also wear yellow shirts!"

"Why would I go to a convention dressed like an ensign or pilot?"

"Hey, you just showed up in a yellow shirt. You never declared who you were supposed to be."

"I'm the most megalomaniacal person you know! I didn't think I needed to spell out for you that I'm the captain! If that leap in logic were any smaller, it'd be a sidewalk crack! And since you failed so miserably at logic, then it's clear that you're the doctor and not the science officer."

"Seriously I'm wearing a blue shirt! If you take a poll of the general public and ask them who wears blue shirts, the majority will tell you that it's science officers!"

"The majority of those same people will have hair and some form of pigment in their skin, so you really shouldn't play the 'majority rules' card!"

Before Chris could rebut, the sounds of someone clearing their throat interrupted their argument. "Ah-hem."

The squabbling men turned to see a thin man, taller than Brian. He wore a black suit, top hat, and sported a beard, sans mustache. With trepidation in his step and confusion in his voice, he approached and said, "Greetings, gentlemen."

"Why are you dressed like Abraham Lincoln?" Chris asked the newcomer.

"Well, fine sir, I am Abraham Lincoln."

"Ha!" Chris said to Brian and turning to display a middle finger. "*You* suck it! Even if you were a captain, which you're not, he's a president and outranks you!"

"First of all," Brian replied, displaying a middle finger of his own, "we don't know if he's the real Abraham Lincoln. Second of all, he was the president back in what, like the 1400s? It doesn't count!"

"How the hell can you be in Mensa and not know when Lincoln was president?"

"I went to college for an accounting degree and to learn how to get a quarter in a shot glass in one bounce! *Not history!*"

With his middle finger raised as well, assuming it to be some form of salutation, Abraham Lincoln stepped forward to interject. However, thick clouds billowed overhead, darkening the sky. A voice boomed from everywhere, deep enough to vibrate the ground, nearly knocking the men off balance. But Brian and Chris did not spill a drop of beer. "Greetings Earthlings!"

"Hoochie Mama! Did you hear that?" Brian asked. He finished his beer and got another one.

"How could I not? It shook the whole ground!" Chris replied, draining his brew and getting another one as well.

"Greetings, ethereal creature," Abraham Lincoln said to the sky, arms spread wide and inviting, with both middle fingers raised. "We mean you no harm. We merely seek answers as to where we are and why we are here."

The voice boomed again, "Where you are is of no consequence. Your paltry minds would not be able to fathom the location of this planet. Why you are here is to educate me. I have been quite interested in your planet and the fragile dichotomy of your tenuous definitions of good and evil. I have decided to pull four representatives of each. Your opponents are Genghis Khan, Attila the Hun, Adolph Hitler and Og the Oppressor. This planet is nothing more than minimal vegetation and rock. You may use any means necessary, any rudimentary resource this planet has to offer, to defeat your opponent. You...."

"Waitaminute!" Brian interrupted. "So, you're saying that the four of us represent good?"

"That is correct."

"Just as a test of my own – you tell us who you think we represent."

"You are a president, a captain, a science officer, and a ... ummmm ... where is the fellow in the red shirt?"

"He fell asleep over here," Chris said, pointing to Jeff.

"Ha!" Brian exploded at Chris. "I'm the captain! Suck it!"

"What? Why? Just because some guy we can't see says you

are?"

"Dude! If some booming, disembodied, omnipresent voice says I'm the captain, I'm certainly not going to argue with it!"

"Well, it also said that I'm the science officer!"

"I didn't say it was an omnipotent voice! Clearly it's only right about half the time and I'm the fifty percent it got right!"

"Whatever! I'm gonna...."

"Ah-hem!" Lincoln interrupted again. "Did you two fail to hear who our opponents are?"

"Yeah." Chris answered, drawing from his beer. "So?"

Lincoln reeled back, shocked at such a nonchalant attitude. "My good sir, it is clear that you come from a time on Earth that is in the future of my personal reference, but certainly you must have learned about the tyranny of Genghis Khan and the brutality of Attila the Hun!"

"Yeah, yeah, yeah. And Adolph Hitler was the scourge of the 20th century. And Og was...." Chris paused, jutted out his jaw and stroked his goatee. He then looked to the sky and said, "Hey, disembodied voice! Who's Og?"

"Og the Oppressor," the voice boomed.

"Uhhh, yeah. We got that. So, when exactly was he evil?"

"He was the most evil human on the Earth circa 10,000 B.C."

"10,000...! He's a caveman? How evil an a caveman be?"

"It's ... uhhhhh ... it's contextual! Trust me, he's evil!"

"What if I don't believe you?"

"Well, you'd better! Because your opponents finished their weapons and are heading right for you! You have about five hours."

"No wonder they're coming right at us – you've been giving away our position this whole time!"

"Oh yeah?"

"Yeah!"

"Well, fine! Let's see how well you do, smart guy! Suck it!" With that, the dark clouds formed the shape of a hand holding up a middle finger, and then quickly dissipated.

"Nice going, genius!" Brian yelled at Chris. "Only you would piss off an omnipotent being!"

"Gentlemen, now is the time to set aside our personal differences and work as a team," Lincoln said. "Do you suppose we should attempt to wake the fellow in the red shirt?"

"No," Brian answered. "He's in a grumpy mood today."

"Okay. Very well, then. Any suggestions as to where to begin?"

"I think we should start with a catapult!" Brian said, almost squealing with excitement.

"Of course you would say that!" Chris said. "There's no way we should try that. We should build a trebuchet!"

"What? I'm not building some stinking trebuchet! What's wrong with a catapult?"

"A trebuchet's better!"

"Is not!"

"Is too!"

"Fine! You think so? You go over there and build your own damn trebuchet! I'm going over here to build my catapult! See you in five hours!"

"Fine!"

"Gentlemen…" Lincoln started. However, he was cut short when both men yelled, "Suck it, Lincoln!"

The hours passed by quickly for all three men as they worked in solitude. Finally, with minutes to spare, Brian walked over to Chris and said, "Done! I got my weapon ready to go!"

"Yeah?" Chris said. "What do you have?"

Wearing a broad smile of satisfaction, Brian presented his creation. Needing only one hand, he held a large branch that tapered down in thickness, the pliable top doubled over and tied halfway down the stick to form a loop. Woven within the loop were smaller, threadlike branches. "With this, I could defeat all four of the bad guys single handedly!"

"Dude," Chris said, looking nonplussed. "It's a tennis racquet."

"Is not!"

"Seriously. Look at it."

Brian did. He turned it in his hand, viewing it from all angles.

"So! It can still do some damage! And what do you have that's so much better?"

"This!" Chris held before him a large, patent leather shoe. "I stole it from Lincoln when he wasn't looking!"

"A shoe?"

"Dude. Look at the size of this thing! It's at least a size 17. This is a shoe of great proportion!"

"You have issues! What the heck have you been doing all this time? I thought you were building a trebuchet?"

"Well ... I started to, but I got bored. So, I got myself a stick of gum and started working on my Sudoku." Chris held up a Sudoku book, rolled open to one page that displayed two puzzles. Each puzzle had twenty-two numbers typed in by the publisher and one number written in hand by Chris. "And then I got distracted. I thought I saw a cricket, but it was just a black pebble. Then I thought I saw a shiny nickel, but it was just a gum wrapper. Then I thought I saw a mini-Cthulhu, but it was just a bush with long branches blowing in the breeze. Then I thought I saw an obelisk, but it was just Lincoln's top hat. But that gave me the idea to steal his mighty shoe of great proportion."

"You're a mess! Do I even wanna know what happened to the gum since you're clearly not chewing any now?"

Chris turned the shoe over to display the flattened wad containing chunks of the terrestrial dirt. "I spat it out after a few minutes. When I got the shoe, I put it on and started stomping around pretending I was a drunk Sasquatch!"

"The lone piece of gum on the entire planet, and you step in it?"

"You've done worse!"

"Not by much!"

"Ah-hem," came from Abraham Lincoln, approaching the men from around a boulder wearing only one shoe. He carried a long, stone-tipped spear in his right hand and a basic club in his left. Slung over his torso and back were a bow and a quiver of hand-carved arrows. "I believe our enemies approach."

All three men looked to the horizon. A trail of dust slithered along the rolling, desolate landscape, accompanied by the churning of an engine and a rhythmic squeak of metal against metal. The details of what approached eluded the men, until it came over the last dune before them.

A tank chugged down the dune and stopped before the men. Even though it was crafted from hand-pounded metals and its engine was crude and steam-powered, its effectiveness could not be denied. The hatch opened and out crawled Genghis Khan, Attila the Hun and Adolph Hitler. Og the Oppressor stayed to man the vehicle, poking his head through the hatch just long enough to display his middle finger to Brian and Chris. He dropped back inside and trained the turret on his opponents.

"Well, gentlemen," Abraham Lincoln said. "Behold the fruits reaped from teamwork."

"Suck it, Lincoln!" Brian and Chris said in unison, right before the air rippled from the explosion and fire of the tank shooting a mortar shell at them.

The detonation jolted Jeff awake. He sat and rubbed away the sleepies from his eyes. Everything came into focus and standing before him were figures he presumed to be Genghis Khan, Attila the Hun and Adolph Hitler. Thanks to his love of prehistoric history, Jeff even recognized from his studies Og the Oppressor as the caveman exited the tank. Noticing the smoking cannon barrel, Jeff sighed and mumbled to himself, "Why the hell did I decide to be a red shirt...?"

THE DRUNKEN COMIC BOOK MONKEYS
VS.
THE BLACK HOLE

Jeff got a job at
The Large Hadron Collider
Close to Geneva.

He told us this. Why?
We will never know. Of course,
We came to visit!

With our beers in hand,
We kicked down the door and said,
"Let's smash some atoms!"

We told everyone
That Jeff was our close friend and
Editor. Jeff fumed.

He wasn't happy.
But his boss said we could stay.
And he said, "Don't touch!"

We tried to behave.
But Chris saw something shiny,
And we ran to it.

Nobody saw us
Until it was way too late.
We found the shiny!

A room full of lights,
Blinking on big machines and
Lots of computers

Chris flipped some switches.
I pecked away at keyboards.
We both drank our beers.

Everyone found us.
We were locked in this big room.
We were having fun!

I set my beer down.
It spilled. That was bad. Who knew?
People yelled at me!

Science babble and
Big words thrown at me about
Quantum mechanics.

The machines then sparked
Air funneled to one dark spot.
I made a black hole!

It started off small,
Nothing more than a pin point,
But grew very fast.

Now bottle cap sized,
It pulled into it pencils,
Papers and loose things.

Chris punched my shoulder.
It didn't stop the black hole.
It tugged at my beer.

My beer flowed freely
From the bottle, poured sideways
Into the black hole!

I was angry and
Didn't know what I should do.
Then it pulled at me!

The gravity field
Yanked me right out of my shoes!
It pulled me toward it!

"Do something, Jackass!"
Chris yelled. "It's pulling me in,
And my beer as well!"

I thought of one thing.
Hurling toward the golf ball sized
Black hole, I did it.

I opened my mouth.
With a big singular chomp,
I ate the black hole!

Amazed and clapping,
Everyone cheered. Except for
Chris. He flipped me off.

It's too bad for Jeff.
He got fired when Chris asked,
"What's this button do?"

JEFF YOUNG
VS.
THE PRIMORDIAL MONKEYS

The large black block dropped two feet to the ground and the dust settled about it. Jeff walked out of the time machine and turned to look at it. He could never understand how something that large could be so small on the inside. Reaching back into the closet sized interior, he pulled out a folding sling chair, a beach umbrella, a pair of sunglasses, a cooler and a large silver cylinder. Putting a hand to his brow to shade his eyes, Jeff surveyed the horizon. The plains of Africa disappeared into heat shimmer. Not far from the time machine was a large tree. From the shade of its boughs came the busy chattering of a troop of monkeys. Jeff gathered up his supplies and walked to the edge of the tree's shadow. He unfolded the chair and then seated the pole of the beach umbrella in the tan dirt. Sliding the chair into the shade, he dropped into its comfort, leaned back, reached into the cooler and pulled out a frosty hard cider. Slipping the sunglasses on, he popped the top off his beverage and took a draught.

A large monkey with dark fur on its chin looked down from the tree. Its eyes were riveted on the reflections from the green glass bottle. It made its way to the trunk of the tree and started to slide down the trunk. Jeff reached over, grabbed the pump style fire extinguisher and shot the monkey in the ass with a long stream of water. Chittering madly the creature scrambled back up into the tree. Another exceptionally pale monkey looked down at the ground with an wistful look on its face. Jeff shot it with the extinguisher. Then he shot it again, just on general principles. Both monkeys scrambled higher into the tree where they began punching each other's shoulders. Jeff smiled and pumped the canister once again.

He only needed to keep this up for another half million years or so and things would be fine. It would be worth it, though. Jeff turned on his little portable mp3 player. The Blue Danube Waltz came on. "Da da da da da da -" sssshht splat, splat.

He could do this all day.

My Second Interview With Madness

JEFF: Tell me again why I have to do this?

BRIAN: Because we always have an interview at the end of our books!

CHRIS: Our fans want to know the depths of our genius.

JY: No, I'm sure they don't.

BK: Pleeeeeeeeeeeeeease!

CP: Pleeeeeeeeeeeeease!

JY: Okay! Fine! We'll do another interview!

CHRISTINE: That doesn't explain why I'm here.

BK: Because you're the publicist.

CP: And the project manager.

JY: And the Mayhem Coordinator.

CC: It's because none of you can type, isn't it?

BK: Ummmmmm...?

CP: Uuuhhhhhhh....

JY: Welllllllllllll....

CC: **Sigh** Let's get this over with.

JY: So what made you decide to use me as the antagonist?

CP: 'Cause we don't like you. You're always givin' us crap, man! And you're the least obvious choice and that amuses us.

BK: He's always making us work!

JY: Seriously? A stick of dynamite can't make you guys work!

BK: Okay, okay, okay. Sheesh! We chose you because we wanted a character that readily hangs out with us. Since you're our editor, you have to interact with us, whether you want to or not. Plus, it adds to the comedy the fact that we don't know that you're trying to kill us.

CP: Thank goodness life doesn't imitate art.

JY: Who says it doesn't!?

CP: Next question!

JY: Is science good or evil?

CP: From what point of view?

BK: That's the question!

CP: Philosophically, emotionally...?

BK: Clearly it's evil if it educated you and you're asking that kind of question.

CP: The world's bigger than the two of us, my friend.

BK: No, it's not!

CP: Some people think that Dos Equus is good so clearly the world has to be bigger than the two of us.

BK: I think science is good for porn and gambling, bad for everything else.

CC: You're thinking of the internet, not science.

BK: But science created the internet, right?

CC: You're ridiculous.

CP: I'm not speaking ill of it, but I don't have my flying car yet!

BK: Screw cars! I want my damn teleporter!

CP: Instant gratification just isn't fast enough for you, is it?

BK: I'm bored. Next question.

JY: What would you invent?

BK: I would invent beer pants, obviously.

CP: A flying car, a pen that writes upside down.

BK: NASA already did that!

CP: No, they didn't.

BK: They spent millions on developing that!

CP: They spent millions on a plaque!

BK: Don't forget — Russia invented one as well, but they just called it a pencil.

JY: I'm kinda surprised you two didn't say something like, "A spray that dissolves clothing" or "x-ray glasses."

CP: No, because I'm afraid that if Brian wore them, he'd accidentally look at me.

BK: EEEEEEEEEEEEEWWWW! That's disgusting! Just for that, I'm not letting you borrow my clothes dissolving spray!

JY: Is there a science fiction story that you can think of that you would say, "I would never consider doing a spoof of that"?

BK: Phantom Menace, 'cause it's already been spoofed.

CP: Aw, someone else pulled the George Lucas card!

BK: You're just mad cause I said it first!

CP: I wouldn't spoof... what's that really famous one... *Stranger in a Strange Land.*

BK: Why wouldn't we?

CP: Because it's really good. Nothing by L Ron Hubbard.

BK: Stop it...

CP: 'Cause then Jeff wouldn't win the Young Writers award.

BK: I wouldn't spoof *Dune* 'cause I'd get sand in my underwear.

CP: You wouldn't 'cause you're name's not Brian.

BK: But it is Brian...

CP: Brian Herbert, Knucklehead! Then I wouldn't spoof *Dune* and you can't spoof Tolkien 'cause my name's Christopher!

JY: Most of the stories that you have chosen as inspirations are from the golden age of science fiction, what made you choose material from this particular era?

CP: It's just well known.

BK: One of the more interesting things about this book versus the last book is we put ourselves in more specific stories.

CP: True. I think it's because the horror genre feeds off of itself. There are certainly defining vampire and werewolf stories, but there are so many of them that the general public no longer tethers vampires or werewolves to a specific story.

BK: Exactly. There's only one *Planet of the Apes* story, despite the different movies. The same with *The Day the Earth Stood Still* and *Island of Dr. Moreau.*

CP: It's interesting that we didn't do Asimov and Clarke.

BK: We did the moon. Wasn't the computer based on HAL?

CP: No, it was based on the *Moon is a Harsh Mistress.*

BK: There's a computer in that one?

CP: Yes, its name was Mike.

BK: Who wrote it?

CP: Robert Heinlein.

BK: Oh wow.

CP: It was bored so it attacked the earth. Also, Philip Jose Farmer.

BK: Who?

CP: Do you read?

BK: Movies, baby!!

CP: You can't even spell Science Fiction!

BK: Nope.

CP: That means you watched the Keanu Reeves version of the *Day the World Stood Still*!

BK: Oh yeah!

CP: We're done.

BK: I didn't' say I liked it.

CP: Next question!

JY: Why a goat?

BK: Goats make people giggle.

CP: [giggles]

BK: Say it!

CP: Nope.

BK: We'll edit it out.

CP: No you won't!

BK: Just say it!

CP: 'Cause they got that thing that hangs down...

BK: You meant the bell?

CP: Picture it!

BK: La Chupacabra was the first appearance of the goat.

CP: Which was early on. Did you know the goat was gonna be Jeff?

BK: No, I didn't know until we wrote us versus The Devil.

CP: So what made you write the goat in a second time?

BK: What better carrier of goat pox than a goat?

CP: There you go.

BK: We needed someone to spread a deadly contagion. What better way than a Mexican goat who got possessed by the Wendigo spirit in Canada.

CP: Why can't we ever just answer with "Growing up, my neighbor had a goat named Love Machine." Why don't our stories ever start like that?

BK: 'Cause we live in central PA! Though you would think our neighbor would have goats around here...

CP: They have goat races in Falmouth. In fact, I think they drop a goat for New Year's Eve.

BK: We're done.

JY: Now that you've written about yourselves as characters, do you find yourselves doing more or less of the things that you point out that irritate each other?

CP: More

BK: [Throws battery at Chris]

CP: Exactly

BK: More as well. I take much more joy in watching him drink beer with fruit in it.

CP: Still trying to figure out if Chaka can grill meat and Chaka likes meat, why I have to coerce him into grilling meat at meetings.

BK: I don't need coercing, just some advance notice!

CP: Still wondering how your stomach doesn't reject edamame!

BK: It's gooooooood!

CP: But it is a vegetable! It's not one of your food groups!

BK: It is! There's cow, pig, sheep, fish, bird... and cactus

CP: Sparingly! You eat sheep?

BK If I can outrun it. Oh, add deer as a food group.

CP: Mutton?

CC: Okay, I'm done! Next question!

JY: Barbarella, Wilma Deering (Buck Rogers), Princess Leia (Star Wars), Trinity (The Matrix), or Syd (Species)?

BK & CP: [Falling to the floor, twitching and frothing from the mouth]

CC: Good job, Jeff.

JY: How was I supposed to know they would do that?

CC: It's like you don't even know them! You throw five iconic hotties at them and you didn't expect their perverted brains to imagine ... lord only knows!

JY: I said "or"! I know I did!

CC: Okay, I think we can figure this one out.

JY: I'm pretty sure Chris has either never seen "Matrix" and "Species" or the movies didn't resonate with him.

CC: True. I don't think Brian would pick them either.

JY: Barbarella?

CC: Doubt it. Brian still refers to her as "Hanoi Jane."

JY: Good point. So, it's between Wilma and Leia.

CC: The slave Leia is iconic.

JY: True. But Wilma was on television during ... ah-hem ... "formative years" ... giving greater exposure to them.

CC: And Chris got her autograph at a convention.

JY: Okay, so Wilma.

CC: For Chris.

JY: Not Brian?

CC: You know him! He'll say Seven of Nine from Star Trek: Voyager.

BK: What happened?

CP: Did we miss anything?

JY: Nope.

CC: Next question.

JY: What is the single most important thing you think we will discover in the next 5 years?

CP: Whatever it is, it won't be cheap.

BK: Oh, I know. It's how to get the lime in the Corona before bottling.

CP: Gross!

BK: It'll save time.

CP: Gross!

BK: Get the good flavor in there.

CP: (gags)

BK: I'm surprised you didn't say a way to watch porn in your sleep.

CP: We already have that. It's called dreams.

JY: If you could erase one invention off the books and from history, what would it be?

BK: Cell phones

CP: Really? Why?

BK: They're annoying?

CP: You seem pretty attached to yours.

BK: I know! That's why I hate them!

CP: Nice.

BK: Alarm clocks.

CP: Deadlines.

BK: That's not an invention!

CP: Au contraire! PAIs (Priority Action Items) certainly are and they create deadlines.

BK: What's so wrong with PAIs?

CP: Christine assigns us so many that I can't do all of mine in time and I have to drink beers that I don't like.

CC: Don't forget — I'm your Pimp. I'll slap you in a way that will make you cry and leave no bruise. PAIs are important. Understand?

CP: Yes, Ma'am!

BK: Cars. Cars are a bad invention. Good premise, but they are sooooooo blankity-blank expensive!

CP: Corona, citrus of all kinds.

BK: Clocks. Taxes.

CP: Money.

BK: Did I mention cars?

CP: "Some hairless jerk invented money. Now it costs 65 cents for a candy bar!"

CC: What the hell was that from?

CP: The Tick!

[Phone rings loudly]

BK: See! Cell phones! Computers!

CP: Fantasy football when I go 0-14.

JY: Could you restart civilization after the apocalypse?

BK: Yeaaaahhhhh! Beer, a Melon's bar & grill on every corner... and beer.

CP: I was thinking of the propagation of the species...

BK: Not if it's just you and me!

CP: Ah no!

BK: Bye bye, humanity!

CP: But we could live to 120 years old.

BK: Depends on the kind of apocalypse.

CP: We'll be like the two old guys from the Muppet Show!

BK: Waldorf and Statler. We'd end up making the Muppet Show using cockroaches.

JY: Why do I associate with you two?

BK: Is that our next interview question?

JY: No. That was completely rhetorical.

BK: Rhetorical? You'd better see a doctor about that.

CC: Next question!

JY: Which is worse, dying at the end of a science fiction story or a horror story?

CP: I would say science fiction 'cause there's less chance it should actually happen.

BK: Specifically if you have the time machine.

CP: Do we actually die in any of these stories?

BK: Yes, in the Day the Earth Stood Still. Shrunken Monkeys....

CP: We died in that one?

BK: Maria stepped on us.

CP: Dude... To be stepped on by the manager of Melons Bar & Grille ... I'm rethinking his answer. To be stepped on would be okay.

BK: You'd be okay if any woman stepped on you, shrunken or not!

CP: Absolutely! So, those are the only stories we die in this book?

BK: No, wait! We die in the Star Trek one.

CP: That's okay

BK: In Godzilla too.

CP: That's an acceptable loss and to be expected.

BK: Around the World in 80 Beers.

CP: We didn't die in that one! It's just a list of 80 beers.

BK: One would assume we drank all those beers in one sitting. Even we couldn't survive that!

CP: True. Anything else?

BK: Robot Uprising...

CP: So I guess we die more in science fiction, so clearly the answer is science fiction.

JY: I think a little piece of me died while conducting this interview.

CC: Oh yeah, Edit Boy? I'm the one who had to type this mess! There's no soap for the soul and I need a shower, Silkwood style!

BK: Does that mean the interview is over?

CP: Naaaaaaah, I'm sure Jeff wants....

ABOUT THE TALENT

Jeff Young

Jeff Young is a bookseller first and a writer second – although he wouldn't mind a reversal of fortune. He received a Writers of the Future award for "Written in Light" which appears in the 26th *L.Ron Hubbard's Writers of the Future* Anthology. He's been published in: *Realms, Neuronet, Trail of Indiscretion, Cemetery Moon* and *Carbon14*. Jeff has contributed to the anthologies *By Any Means, Clockwork Chaos* and *In an Iron Cage: The Magic of Steampunk*. He has led the Watch the Skies SF&F Discussion Group of Camp Hill and Harrisburg for ten years.

Brian Koscienski
He's not the red-headed one.

Chris Pisano

He's not the tall one.

Christine Czachur

After single handedly revitalizing the emu industry and having a storied and accomplished Peruvian goat-racing career at the base of the Andes Mountains, Christine moved onto becoming Chief Science Officer of NASAA (National Aeronautics & Space Administration Adjacent). She eventually found that overseeing successful and super-duper secret missions to Venus, Mars, and Jupiter no longer offered any form of challenge, she decided to become Publicist and Project Manager for Fortress Publishing, Inc., thus starting another storied and accomplished career. And she's a vampire!